The Legen...

History's most powerful heroes!

Robert of Penrith and his illegitimate half brother, Piers, were raised as differently as possible, but they've become reluctant allies since a deadly raid on their father's land left them exiled. Now, along with their friend Brian, they are determined to rise up, to reclaim their birthright and become fierce warriors of legend that the world will remember forever!

But their journeys won't just be shaped by revenge and redemption. Because these warriors haven't considered the power of romance...

Read Robert's story in:
The Iron Warrior Returns

Read Piers's story in:
The Untamed Warrior's Bride

Now read Brian's story in:
Her Warrior's Redemption

Her Warrior's Redemption is a crossover story, connecting The Legendary Warriors series with The MacEgan Brothers series!

Meet the MacEgan Brothers, beginning with *Her Irish Warrior*

And you can discover more about Honora MacEgan, who appears in this story, in *Taming Her Irish Warrior*

All available now!

Author Note

Her Warrior's Redemption was inspired by gladiators. After researching the aftermath of the Fourth Crusade, I saw an opportunity to create a fictional fighting arena in Constantinople. Brian of Penrith left to go on crusade as an adolescent, but in *Her Warrior's Redemption*, he is enslaved along with an Englishwoman, Velaria of Ardennes. They become friends and allies, fighting for their survival as they fall in love.

Velaria of Ardennes is a character descended from my MacEgan Brothers series. Her parents were the main characters of "The Warrior's Forbidden Virgin," and her aunt is Honora MacEgan, the heroine of *Taming Her Irish Warrior*. I wanted to revisit some favorite characters, so if you've followed the MacEgan series, this gave me a chance for a crossover book. If you missed previous books in The Legendary Warriors series, these include *The Iron Warrior Returns* (Robert and Morwenna) and *The Untamed Warrior's Bride* (Piers and Gwendoline).

If you'd like me to email you when my new books come out, you may subscribe to my author newsletter at www.michellewillingham.com/contact. I always love hearing from my readers.

HER WARRIOR'S REDEMPTION

MICHELLE WILLINGHAM

Harlequin

HISTORICAL

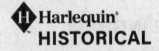

Harlequin®
HISTORICAL

ISBN-13: 978-1-335-53978-6

Her Warrior's Redemption

Recycling programs for this product may not exist in your area.

Harlequin Enterprises ULC
22 Adelaide St. West, 41st Floor
Toronto, Ontario M5H 4E3, Canada
www.Harlequin.com

Printed in U.S.A.

RITA® Award finalist and Kindle bestselling author **Michelle Willingham** has written over forty historical romances, novellas and short stories. Currently she lives in southeastern Virginia with her family and her beloved pets. When she's not writing, Michelle enjoys reading, baking and avoiding exercise at all costs. Visit her website at michellewillingham.com.

To Catherine N. for being amazing,
and to Atossa for your friendship and for sharing
your wonderful horses, especially Ripple.

Prologue

Byzantium, 1208

Brian of Penrith walked alongside the men of his travelling party while the sun blazed against his face. The ground seemed to sway beneath his feet after sailing for the past few weeks. His shoes were cracked and worn, his skin burned from the relentless heat. He'd travelled for nearly a year, all the way to Byzantium. Or what had once been Byzantium before the sacking of Constantinople, he supposed. He'd heard rumours about the land being divided up since the Crusade had ended, but it meant nothing to him any more. He hadn't joined this caravan to fight for God.

No, this was his penance, to atone for his sins. His best friend Robert was dead—all because Brian had lost control of his temper, acting recklessly without thinking. He couldn't bear to stay and witness the grief on his sister's face, for she had loved Robert more than life itself.

It was your fault. You deserve this suffering.

And so, he'd willingly accepted the endless days of exhaustion and hunger. He didn't really know what he was searching for beyond absolution.

He'd traded one group of travellers for another until he'd found another caravan returning to Constantinople. Some were mercenaries while others were merchants seeking their fortune. But he'd joined them on their journey, hoping to find a new purpose. Or, at the very least, an escape.

The hills of the city were like nothing he'd ever seen before. Massive domes and towers guarded the city being rebuilt after the Crusade. The scent of wood and ashes permeated the air, but some of the surviving buildings were gilded, revealing the owners' wealth. Despite the ruins, it surprised him to see baskets and containers of bright flowers. Nearby, a group of men unloaded clay containers of wine from another ship at port.

One of the merchants came to walk alongside him, and he passed Brian a skin of water. 'We'll arrive in Constantinople by nightfall. I know a man who can give you a place to stay.'

'I've no coins,' Brian started to say, but the merchant raised a hand.

'You'll work for him and earn your place.' With a sly smile, he added, 'You want to learn to fight, don't you? This man knows how to train the strongest fighters in the kingdom.' He reached out and pinched Brian's arm. 'He can turn you from the weak insect you are into one of the greatest warriors in the world.'

Brian jerked away from the man, embarrassed by his lack of strength. He already knew how to fight, though he'd grown too thin on the journey. Robert and his half brother, Piers, had trained him as a boy, teaching him some of their techniques, though he'd never had the chance to master them. But he remembered.

No one knew of his fighting abilities, for the long journey and the meagre food had taken their toll. The merchant was right. He *was* weak, for he hadn't fought in over a year.

Yet the man's words resonated within him. What if *this*

could be his new purpose—to become a fighter and defend those weaker than himself? The idea was appealing, for he'd always admired warriors who could protect others.

'Well?' the merchant prompted. 'Do you want to learn to fight?'

Brian met his gaze. 'Yes.'

'Good.' The merchant nodded his approval. 'You'll come with me tonight and join the others. We'll get a meal in your belly before you begin.'

He would stay for a time, Brian decided. Long enough to get stronger and fill out the muscles he lacked. And perhaps the fighting would grant him the skills he needed to become someone else—a man of honour.

Hours later, Brian met the owner of the arena where the fighters trained. The man, Kadir al-Kumar, was large and ungainly with a long black beard and dark eyes. He spoke no English, but the merchant conversed with him easily in the Byzantine tongue. Brian didn't understand what they said, but Kadir passed a stack of coins to the merchant.

They were continuing to argue when he suddenly felt a hand on his shoulder. A female voice whispered at his ear. 'You need to leave. Now.'

He turned and saw a servant girl holding a pitcher. She appeared to be the same age as himself, and her light brown hair was bound back in a braid, revealing sun-kissed streaks of gold. Blue eyes stared into his with a warning, and her mouth tightened in unspoken fear.

It startled him to see someone from his homeland here, especially a maiden who spoke his language. He kept his voice low and averted his gaze so as not to draw attention. 'How did you come to be here?'

'I've no time to tell that tale. Just…heed my warning

and leave, as soon as you can.' Her voice was tinged with desperation, and he wondered why.

'They told me I could come here to train,' he insisted. 'I want to learn.'

'Not here, you don't.' She pretended to fill his cup, keeping her voice low. 'They're not who you think they are. Kadir is buying you. You're to become his slave.'

Brian narrowed his gaze on the men. They were laughing, and the merchant pulled out a set of dice for gambling. Though he didn't want to believe such a thing was possible, he couldn't ignore her warning. 'Why would he want to buy me?'

'For his fighting pits,' she said dully. 'You're English, like me. Many citizens would pay good coins to watch us fight and die.'

He stole another look at the men, wondering if she was right. The merchant had warned him that the Byzantine people still hated the crusaders who had sacked the city.

'I have nowhere else to go,' he admitted. 'And no silver.'

'You have your freedom,' she said. 'That's worth more than any coins.'

Though he didn't want to believe her, she had no reason to lie to him. She reached for his cup and pretended again to fill it. 'Find the house with three crosses above the door. A Norman lord lives there, Alexander Berys, Baron Staunton. If you see him, ask him to help free me.'

'Where can I find the house?' he asked.

'Look for the Hagia Sophia church. It's the largest in the city. He lives not far from there, west of the church, so he says.'

He guessed she'd never been there. Likely she'd been unable to leave this house. 'Are you a slave in this household?' When she nodded, he asked, 'What is your name?'

'I am Velaria of Ardennes.'

'My name is Brian. I was raised in Penrith.' When the men glanced over at them, Velaria lowered her head and moved to the next guest, filling his cup.

Brian took a sip of the wine, his mind spinning. This young woman needed help, and if he disappeared tonight, he might be able to get her out. Though it was dangerous, and he understood none of the Byzantine language, he wanted to help her.

She turned back and met his gaze. In her expression, he saw the loss and hopelessness. He didn't know if he could find a way to buy her freedom. But perhaps this was Fate's way of granting him a second chance. He had failed to save Robert.

But maybe he could save her.

Brian waited until the men were sleeping, their bodies passed out from gluttony and drunkenness. In the darkness, he kept his footsteps light while he searched for the girl. Velaria wasn't anywhere in the stone kitchen, but he found a set of steps leading below ground.

She'd asked him to leave and find the Norman lord within the city. He was torn between trying to bring her with him or seeking help.

He decided to go down below to see if she was among the servants. Slowly, he crept down the stairs. An acrid stench assailed his nostrils, and he blinked into the darkness where only a single oil lamp was set into a stone crevice to offer light. Was this where Kadir kept his slaves?

Brian waited a moment for his eyes to adjust and saw rows of swords, maces, and daggers gleaming in the yellow light. He stepped closer and heard the clinking of chains.

Never would he forget that sound. The four of them—

Piers, Robert, and his sister, Morwenna, and himself—had been captured by English soldiers after a raid at Penrith, years ago. They'd fought for their freedom…but Brian knew what it was to be kept in chains. Velaria was probably telling the truth. This was a place of captivity, not a place where they trained men to fight.

Brian crept back up the stairs, not daring to go any farther. He didn't know where Velaria was being held, but he would try to find the Norman lord within the city.

He slipped outside the house into the darkness. The night air had grown cooler, and he stopped to look for the Hagia Sophia. The church stood atop a hill, and he tried to remember the direction of the setting sun. Velaria had said to look for the door with three crosses. But the city was an endless maze of wooden houses, half of which had already burned down. He started walking towards the hill, hoping he would find the house from there.

The moon rose golden above Constantinople, illuminating the shadows of a nearby mosque. As Brian began to wander the streets, he saw dozens of beggars sleeping along the road while the scent of ruin and fire lingered.

Brian found a discarded torch and lit it from one of the dying fires in the city. As he continued to search for the lord's house, the voices of doubt intruded on him.

You've travelled nearly a thousand miles. And for what? To fail again?

There were many people in this city who needed help, not just the girl. But as he continued walking, he couldn't stop thinking of Velaria. Despite her status as a slave, he'd sensed her bravery. Though she had tried to conceal her features by keeping her head lowered, she was quite pretty. Her blue eyes had captivated him, and he'd never met anyone like her.

Velaria had tried to warn him, and he was grateful for it. Had her family travelled on Crusade? How had she come to be so far from England? And had her parents died? She seemed to be alone, like himself—but he wanted to help her.

His feet ached in the worn shoes, but he continued searching, house by house. He had been walking for nearly an hour when he suddenly heard dogs barking. At first, Brian didn't know what was happening, and he ducked into the shadows to stay out of their way. Then, he realised they were coming closer. He quickened his pace, moving down a narrow passageway—but the dogs seemed to follow.

They were tracking *him*, as if he were an escaped slave. Which seemed impossible for why would anyone go to such lengths to find him? He was a serf, not worth anything at all.

But the snarling grew louder, and he had to find somewhere to seek shelter. Brian hurried down another passageway, turning towards the outskirts of the city. By sheer luck, he found a doorway with three crosses marked upon it.

He took a deep breath and knocked on the door. The barking intensified, as if the dogs were coming closer. Brian pounded the door harder, hoping someone would answer. When no one did, he tried the door handle and it opened easily.

He moved inside and bolted it shut behind him. His heart raced while his lungs burned with fear. There was no one in the house—at least not that he could see. With his back against the door, he wondered whether Lord Staunton was here. And what could he say to the man?

An oil lamp flared, and a man staggered forward, the scent of wine permeating his skin and clothing. He spoke in the unfamiliar language, but Brian answered in English.

'Velaria sent me to you. She said you could help. You are Lord Alexander of Staunton, are you not?'

At that, the man eyed him in disbelief. 'I am, yes. But you've gone half-witted if you think I could help you.' He shook his head. 'Foolish boy. They despise us here.' He came closer until he stared into Brian's eyes. 'They want all crusaders dead after what our men did to the city.'

A knock sounded at the door, and Brian begged, 'Please. I will work for you. She is being held as a slave by Kadir al-Kumar. She needs your help.'

At that, the Norman lord shook his head. 'I can help no one, boy,' he muttered beneath his breath. 'They only allow me to live because of the bribes I've paid. The Byzantine fighters took my wife prisoner when we were trying to escape.' After a long pause, he added, 'She's gone now. But I will not rest until I've found her.'

In his eyes, Brian saw the face of a man who was barely hanging on to his own survival. Baron Staunton had clearly loved his wife, and the resignation in his eyes didn't bode well. Brian didn't think there was anything he could say except, 'I'm sorry.' He lowered his voice and pleaded, 'Will you let me hide here for the night? I'll leave at dawn, I promise.'

Lord Staunton studied him for a moment. His expression turned bleak, and he shook his head. 'I must answer the door, or they will break it down. There's nothing I can do for you, boy. But there's another door in the back. You can leave through there.'

Disappointment and frustration shadowed Brian, but he had to seize his only chance at freedom. He hurried to the back of the house and found the narrow passageway, slipping outside just as the Norman lord opened the front door to answer. Brian didn't hear what the man said, but he kept his head down and hurried down the street.

As soon as he reached the end, two men were waiting. They seized him by his arms, and raw panic flooded through him. Brian reacted out of pure instinct, hardly aware of anything at all. Before they had a firm grasp, he twisted free, reaching for the blade at the first man's waist.

The world seemed to blur, and he remembered the training Robert had taught him.

'Keep your balance. Be aware of your surroundings.'

He would not let them take him into slavery. Brian kept his eyes firmly on his enemies, remaining in a defensive stance while he glimpsed another street that could be an escape. Though he lacked a shield, the blade would be enough.

'So. You *do* know how to fight,' came the voice of Kadir as he spoke English. The man stepped forward and regarded him. 'That will be useful.'

'I am leaving,' Brian told him.

Kadir laughed. 'You might escape for a time, boy. But every person in this city knows who I am. They won't hesitate to turn you in.'

'I won't be your slave.' He hadn't travelled all this way to lose his freedom.

When one of the men darted forward, Brian spun and slashed his arm. The man let out a foul curse, but Brian had his gaze locked upon his second opponent. He held steady for a moment before he bolted towards the other street. An invisible snare seemed to tighten around him, for he had no idea where he was going.

Just as he reached the edge of the city, a sharp pain blasted through his shoulder. An arrow had pierced him, and blood ran down his side.

His lungs burned as he struggled to keep running. But a small crowd gathered before him, closing in. They stared at him with hatred, and from behind, the dogs continued to track him.

Brian tried to turn in a different direction, but all around him, the beggars cut off his escape.

'You see?' Kadir's voice cut through the stillness. 'They work for me. All the people of Constantinople know that I am generous to those who are loyal. And I punish any who disobey me.'

The man moved in close, and when Brian tried to wield his blade, Kadir tore the arrow free. A cry broke forth, and Brian dropped to his knees from the brutal pain.

'I like your spirit, boy. You are fortunate that I do, for I will allow you to heal before I put you in my fighting pits.'

Brian was hardly aware of Kadir's words as he was dragged to his feet, blood spilling from his shoulder.

'That spirit may be the only thing that keeps you alive, boy.' He laughed again. 'I hope you enjoyed your last night of freedom.'

As they took him away, Brian glanced up at the moon, the bleakness settling into his bones.

He would never see his sister again. But after everything he'd done, this was what he deserved.

Chapter One

One year later

Velaria sat in the darkness, her heart pounding. All around her, she heard the crowd screaming for the next match. It didn't matter that each week, new competitors were brought in. One would die in every fight.

She was glad Brian of Penrith had not been one of them. After he'd healed from his shoulder wound, he'd spent the first few months building up his strength in secret. Thankfully, he already knew how to fight, just as she did. And now, he had become Kadir's greatest fighter.

Savaş, the crowd had nicknamed him. War.

Savaş or Brian—it didn't matter what they called him any more. He'd become their champion whose victories were forged in blood. But to her, he was the only friend she had in this pit of hell.

A deafening roar resounded from above, and she wondered whether they were cheering for his victory—or his death. She'd tried to remain indifferent to his fighting matches. But even now, her nerves tightened with fear. If Savaş didn't return, she would be alone once again. And the thought was a gnawing shadow of emptiness that threatened to bury her.

It wasn't wise to let herself feel anything for anyone. But he had made the prison bearable, giving her someone to talk to. Someone to pray for. And for now, it was all they had.

Their prison was below ground in a large chamber with only one narrow entrance and a single locked gate. Each day, they wore manacles, their wrists chained together in front while they awaited their turn to fight. Velaria never knew when her name would be called, and it only added to the anxiety of wondering whether this would be her last day alive.

She'd fought here every three days during the past year, ever since Kadir had sent her to the pits as punishment. She'd gone from serving girl to fighter after defending herself from men who believed she would offer them more than drinks. She'd survived those early fights, and like Savaş, she'd battled for her life.

But at the cost to her immortal soul.

Six heavily armed guards patrolled the entrance leading to the fighting arena. Last spring, one man had tried to escape after he'd won his match. He had wielded his sword against the guards—only to be slaughtered in front of everyone, his body displayed for days as an example.

No, there was no means of escaping this prison. At least, not yet.

The noise of the crowd died down, and footsteps approached through the dark passageway. Velaria held her breath and only exhaled when Savaş emerged into the prison. He gave his sword over to the guards, who kept their own weapons trained upon him until his manacles were locked upon his wrists once again. He walked inside their prison and sat down beside her. She didn't have to ask if he'd won—he was alive.

His dark hair was damp with sweat, his beard ragged.

They never gave Savaş a blade for shaving, but she'd seen him shear off his beard just before a fight so his opponent could not use it against him. It was the same reason why she kept her own hair in tight braids during a match. Most women cut off their hair, but Velaria had found a way to bind it up. It was her one vanity, the reminder of the lady she'd once been.

'Are you hurt?' She didn't see any visible wounds, but she couldn't tell for certain in the darkness.

'No.' But his voice held the weight of guilt that he'd been forced to take another man's life. He picked up the sharp stone and carved a mark into the wall behind them. She couldn't even count the marks any more, there were so many. Yet, he somehow knew.

They never spoke of it, but it was only a matter of time before one of them didn't come back from a fight. An ache caught her deep inside, but she forced the fear away.

He reached for her hand and squeezed tightly. 'Are you ready for your match? They're calling for you.'

No, she wasn't ready. Not at all. But there wasn't a choice, was there? She squeezed Savaş's palm in return, stealing comfort from his touch.

He touched his forehead to hers. In a low voice he said, 'Walk with God, Velaria. And win.'

She kept his hand in hers, as if she could somehow take strength from it. And when they called out to her, she forced herself to let go of him.

Velaria stood and walked through the narrow opening of the prison until the guards opened the door. Their weapons remained pointed at her back while she continued towards the row of swords. She chose a thin, lightweight blade and steadied herself.

Her aunt Honora had trained her to fight with a sword,

years ago, believing that every woman should know how to defend herself. At the time, Velaria had enjoyed sparring with her brother, never imagining that the skill would become her means of survival.

For a moment, she breathed in and out, making her peace with what was to come. At first, they'd only given her other women as opponents—those who had been imprisoned, like herself.

During her first fight, she'd merely wounded the young woman, not wanting to kill her. But after they'd dragged the girl away, after they'd raised Velaria's hand in the air as the champion, they had slit the girl's throat.

With one stroke of a blade, her own hope had died. There would be no mercy in these fighting pits. They were here to die, God help them.

Ever since Constantinople had fallen, the people of Byzantium loathed the crusaders and any other foreigners. Kadir had found a way to build his own wealth by feeding that hatred. Like the ancient Roman coliseum, he'd built his own smaller arena with enslaved gladiators. It didn't matter that the fighting tradition had been outlawed centuries ago. Whether Kadir bribed officials to look the other way or whether no one cared, it didn't seem to matter any more. The people flocked to the matches, eager to see crusaders suffering at the hands of their own fighting champions.

From the moment she had first met Savaş, there had been an innocence about him, of someone who had never experienced fighting like this. She still found him handsome, even after they'd both endured this prison. His dark hair was cut short with his own dagger, and his blue eyes were solemn. In them, she saw a man who wanted to become someone better. And she knew why Kadir had wanted him.

He'd planned to make Savaş fight a seasoned warrior in

front of the crowd to entertain them. She'd seen it happen, time and again. Crusaders or travellers...young or old, it was all the same. They were all brought here for the same reason—to fight and die.

But Savaş had won his match.

The crowd had been furious, bloodthirsty for his death. Kadir had brought him back a second time, then a third. And after Savaş continued to win and grow stronger, something had shifted. Now, he'd become a hardened warrior with no emotions at all.

Velaria had learned to do the same. It was the only way to survive.

But sometimes, in the darkness, she would rest her head against his shoulder and imagine being home again. His quiet strength brought her comfort during the endless nights. Sometimes she wondered what it would be like if she allowed herself to love him.

It was a foolish thought, and Velaria shut it off when she made her way through the tunnel to the fighting arena. She hated killing opponents who were fighting for survival, and sometimes she wondered if she ought to simply surrender. She had given up on her family ever finding her. There would come a day when she would lose, and that would be the end.

But then, she thought of Savaş and steeled herself to fight again. They had an unspoken vow to survive, to be there for each other.

The gate opened before her, the sunlight blinding. Velaria took slow steps, giving her vision time to adapt. Then she held the sword in her right hand and accepted the shield another guard handed to her.

Time to fight. Time to empty herself of all regrets and every part of her that was human.

She shielded off all emotions, tightening them off until nothing else remained. Slowly, she walked towards the arena amid the noise of the crowd. She wore a short tunic that hung to her mid-thigh and trews, and she had braided back her hair.

When her vision adjusted and she saw her challenger, she realised that Kadir was losing patience with her. This time, she wasn't facing a woman—it was a man. And from the look of his lean arms, he knew how to fight.

A shuddering breath of nervous energy caught her. She would have to play a role if she meant to survive. Velaria bent her shoulders, lowering her blade to touch the sand. She averted her gaze, feigning fear. And from the uncertain expression on his face, her opponent wasn't eager to kill a woman.

She didn't want to take his life either. But there was no choice, was there? The only thing she could grant this man was a quick, merciful death.

She wore the mask of a terrified woman, one that was slightly real. If she made a single wrong move, today might be the day she finally died.

Savaş would be waiting for her, back in the prison. She would see him again if she fought for it. And that was something to live for.

Velaria started to lift the sword but lowered it again, as if the weapon was too heavy for her. The man appeared filled with regret. He was a new slave, one who had been kept apart from all of them. Another crusader.

'I do not wish to kill you,' he said in English. This time, it was no effort at all to show her regret. But this was what Kadir wanted—for her to slay one of her own countrymen.

Or, more likely, he meant for her to die.

As the man drew closer, Velaria continued to keep the

tip of her blade in the dirt, waiting for him to make the first move. She hated the woman they'd made her become. Someone who fought to win, all pretence of honour gone.

She'd never been taught to fight like this, not by her father or her aunt. But now she had no choice at all—not if she wanted to survive.

Now, every time she faced an opponent, there was only one way to push back the horror—to remember the man who had seduced and abandoned her. Because of him, she'd been found by a group of merchants who had sold her into slavery.

As she fought, she imagined the face of the knight who had ruined her life. She pictured Sir Drogan's mocking smile and released her fury and grief, letting it fill her up until she saw only the face of her most hated enemy.

When the Englishman's blade slashed towards her, she dove to the ground, lifting her own sword. There was a moment of shock before her opponent realised what had happened and dropped to his knees.

A hollow ache caught in her heart, and tears burned her eyes. God above, she hated the monster she'd become.

The crowd erupted in fury that the fight had ended so soon. But she didn't care whether they were entertained. Instead, she strode towards the first row to where Lord Staunton sat. The drunken baron stared back at her, and she said the same words she always said to him. Little good that it did.

'Send word to my father. Sir Ademar of Dolwyth. Tell him where I am.'

As always, Lord Staunton ignored her plea.

No sooner had she spoken when a fist struck her ear. Her cheek stung from the blow, and she turned and saw the guard who intended to bring her back to her prison cell.

In one motion, Velaria grabbed his arm and flipped him on his back. She rested her foot against his throat with her sword in her hand. Then she stared up at Kadir—as if asking whether to kill the guard.

The crowd cheered their approval, and Kadir raised his arms as if he were a benevolent emperor, allowing his subject to live.

Velaria knew better than to rebel against him. And so, she lifted her foot, stepping back from the guard. She met the baron's gaze once more before she walked back into the darkness of their prison.

She returned her weapon while the other guards held their swords to her back. Then they chained her hands and forced her back into the enclosure. Savaş was waiting for her in the shadows. Though he said nothing, she sensed his thankfulness that she'd survived. Velaria sat beside him, leaning her head against the cool stone wall.

'That was a quick fight,' he said quietly.

'It was a crusader.' She closed her eyes, saying a silent prayer for his soul. 'He…didn't know what I could do.'

Savaş didn't ask questions, for neither of them wanted to talk after a match. Sitting beside him, with his body pressed against hers, brought her a comfort she couldn't name. She took one deep breath after another, trying to hold back her emotions. He seemed to sense it, and put his arm around her shoulders, bringing her close. 'Did you speak to him?'

She knew he meant the baron. 'He won't help us.' After a year, Lord Staunton had become even more distant. He'd given up on everything after he'd failed to find his wife.

'Why doesn't he return to England?'

She shrugged. 'I don't know. He may not have the funds for the journey.' And yet, he continued to pay coins to see their matches each week. It made no sense at all.

In the darkness, Savaş continued to hold her close, resting his head against hers. She savoured the touch, for no one else understood what she endured each day or the person she had to become in the arena. But she was grateful for his presence. Without him, she couldn't stand the loneliness or the imminent threat of dying.

'We'll find a way out,' he said quietly. 'I promise.'

'I hope so.' But she already knew the futility of hope. Their fortune and skill would end one day. She breathed slowly and rested her hands upon his heart. It was a forbidden embrace, but she knew better than to imagine more between them. Death was the only certainty here, and unless they somehow escaped, they could never be more than friends.

From the gate, she heard the clatter of a sword dropping, and the guards chained the wrists of another fighter. Eligor had been among the Italian crusaders months ago when he'd been sold into slavery. He strode inside and smirked at the sight of them. 'You look comfortable with Velaria, Savaş. Why don't you share?'

She stiffened the moment she heard his voice. She'd never liked Eligor, and his arrogance irritated her. Slowly, she eased out of the embrace to sit against the wall.

'Leave her alone, Eligor,' Savaş warned. His voice held the edge of a warning. Even so, Velaria wasn't about to stand aside and let Eligor speak to her like that.

'You don't interest me.' She raised her chin in defiance.

Eligor smiled slowly. He took a single step closer, and Savaş cut him off. 'Don't.' He could easily kill Eligor, and the man knew it.

Velaria sensed the tension, and Savaş stood in silent protection. Though she could defend herself well enough, his reputation as a fighter was far greater. He remained in front of her in an unspoken threat, and she moved to stand by his side.

Resentment brewed in Eligor's face, but thankfully, he backed off and returned to the opposite side of the cell.

The next fighter didn't return. Neither did the one after him. Kadir deliberately kept the Byzantine and crusader opponents apart. If they had been imprisoned together, at least half would have been dead by morning.

Here in the darkness, the stillness unnerved her, of men waiting to die. The next fighting match was in three days. She could only pray that she and Savaş would both survive.

His reassurance, that they would find a way out, meant nothing. She'd been in Constantinople for two years now, and they had outlasted the other prisoners. Despite her pleas to Lord Staunton, it seemed hopeless to imagine she would ever return home to England.

The last fight ended, and three more prisoners were dead. The guards extinguished the torches, and she remained beside Savaş. Neither of them could sleep.

The first few hours after a fight were the worst. Even on the days when he wasn't fighting, Savaş trained. His discipline was unmatched, and she admired that, so she often trained alongside him.

But after a match, her muscles ached. And she knew Savaş felt the same way. She had found a way to ease the pain, but they always waited until after sundown. In the darkness, no one would see them.

Velaria knelt beside him and waited in silence. Savaş took her chained hands and brought them to his shoulder as he turned his back to her. She was careful not to let her chains touch his skin as she massaged the knots from his shoulders and neck, pressing against the tension. There were a few scars, but most of his skin was ridged and taut with muscles. During the past year, the fighting had transformed his body from a lean strength into that of a fierce warrior.

Savaş inhaled when she reached a sensitive place, and she softened her touch, gently working out the pain. She continued down his back, finding the places that hurt. But she couldn't deny that she enjoyed moving her hands over his bare skin. Then she began massaging his arms.

She was grateful for the darkness that hid them from view. Aside from the sound of their chains, she could almost imagine they were alone, somewhere far from Constantinople. She knew this was wrong, to touch a man so intimately. But it was more than a means of easing his pain. The touch helped ground her once again and made her feel human. In the darkness, no one could see her weariness or the guilt she bore. When she stopped, she rested her forehead against his back, taking comfort from the warmth of his skin.

'Your turn,' Savaş murmured.

He moved her braid to the side, but his chains brushed against her spine as he did. His hands moved to her nape and slowly, he began to massage her neck. The sensation was so good, her skin prickled with goose bumps. She revelled in his touch, nearly moaning in thanks. Instead, she closed her eyes and bit back any sound. As he continued to stroke her shoulders, the heaviness of emotion slid over her.

There had been a time when she'd given her heart and had known another man's touch. But it was nothing like this. Drogan had used her—whereas Savaş had only treated her with gentleness. If they were living a different life, one not shadowed in death, she might have wanted more from this man. She might have…wanted him to touch her elsewhere. She might have reached up to his face and brought his mouth to hers. Or perhaps brought his hands to her bare skin.

Instead, she simply accepted what it was—the only comfort they had in this place of captivity.

When he'd finished, Savaş turned her to face him. He rested his forehead against hers, and she could feel the warm breath against her cheek. It was this moment she savoured, one where she imagined something more between them.

Then at last, he pulled back and moved to the far end of their prison cell, leaving her to sleep alone with her nightmares.

Sleep was fitful, caught in fleeting moments. His body ached, but his mind grew even more restless. Brian tried to blot out the memory of what he'd done this day and the man who had died at his hands. This wasn't the person he wanted to be.

But if he gave up, Velaria would suffer. He had sworn a year ago that he would find a way to get her out—a way for them to go home to England. She was one of the bravest women he'd ever known. Her courage made him want to be a better man, to somehow get her out of this prison. In a way, she offered him a chance at redemption after he'd failed to save Robert.

Brian tried to return to sleep, but memories pulled him back to the night when his sister, Morwenna, had been imprisoned. The Earl of Penrith had punished her for stealing a golden pendant, but it wasn't theft—it had been a gift from their mother.

Robert had come up with a plan to rescue Morwenna. Brian had hidden food for their journey while his friend had disguised himself among the guards. At first, the escape plan had seemed plausible. They had arranged a pathway through the underground tunnels that led outside the castle walls. Brian had mistakenly believed that they could get her out before anyone found them.

But that night, he'd heard his sister's screams.

Lord Penrith had sentenced her to be whipped, and the moment Brian had heard her cry out, he'd lost sight of everything except rescuing her. He'd been ready to break down the door to fight off the men who held her captive.

Robert had tried to stop him.

'Wait,' he'd warned. *'We have to have a plan.'*

But Brian had had no intention of waiting—not when he'd been able to hear his sister suffering.

'We don't have time for a plan. He's killing her while you're standing there trying to think of what to do.'

He'd been raging with impatience, frustrated that Robert was trying to hold him back.

Yet his friend had not been deterred.

'If you go in there right now, the soldiers will kill you, and it won't stop her flogging. We're outnumbered. We need more men to help us.'

'There are two of us, and we can fight,' Brian had pleaded. *'We're strong enough.'*

Instead, Robert had told him to go and fetch help. He'd warned him.

'If you open that door now, they'll kill us both.'

Brian opened his eyes, staring back into the darkness. The familiar shame of his mistake cloaked him, for he'd ignored Robert. His impulsive attempt to save Morwenna had resulted in disaster.

Robert had sacrificed his own life to save theirs. Brian had never forgotten the look of resignation in his friend's eyes—the look of a man facing death. All because of him.

The heaviness of regret pushed against his conscience.

Even now, he was haunted by the mistakes of his past. Never again would he act without thinking.

And yet...during the past year, he'd failed in his quest to find an escape. They had already witnessed the deadly punishment for those who attempted to raise a weapon against the guards. But although he was no closer to finding a way out, he tried to keep faith for Velaria's sake.

They needed an ironclad plan, one where he had the answers for any potential problem. And Eligor was definitely one of those problems.

Late last night, Brian had overheard the fighter talking to one of the guards in a low voice. He didn't trust the man, and his instincts had gone on alert. Eligor was plotting something, likely to raise himself up in Kadir's eyes or to seek his own escape. But Brian didn't know what it was.

Velaria lay curled up on her side, sleeping quietly. A faint light emanated from a torch at the far end of the cell, and he could barely see more than her shadow. A tightness caught in his chest, though he tried to shut it out. She was in danger, even more than last eventide.

Although she had been paired with a male fighter, she'd won the fight too quickly. Kadir wanted his crowd to be entertained—and that meant drawing out the fight, feigning injuries, and playing to the people. He would punish her for her opponent's swift death, even if it had been merciful.

Brian's gut twisted at the thought of her coming to harm, though he tried to suppress the fear. One of them would die, sooner or later. For that reason, it wasn't wise to become her friend. And yet...the emptiness inside him and the need for human touch and comfort were too strong to overcome. The isolation in this place was so vast, he'd seen men succumb to the darkness, yearning for death.

Velaria understood his torment, for it mirrored her own.

She knew what it was to lose hope with every passing day. But she gave him a reason to keep going, if for no other reason than his promise to get her out. He savoured the moments at night when she massaged his shoulders, and he did the same for her. He couldn't deny that he was attracted to her still. Despite her thin frame, she captivated him.

Sometimes when she wasn't watching, he studied her features. He'd memorised the beautiful curve of her cheek, the blue eyes that held courage beyond that of any woman he'd known. Even her braids framed a face that haunted him.

Yet despite their companionship, it was unwise to ever seek more. They were prisoners, friends, and he had to keep a slight distance from her. For if he dared to lower that boundary, it would kill him every time she stepped into the arena.

She turned to her side and was just waking up when the guards arrived. 'Velaria!' one called out. 'Kadir has summoned you.'

Brian tensed but made no move towards her. She glanced at him, and he kept his face expressionless except to give her a nod of support.

She walked towards the narrow entrance where the guards were waiting. Four had their weapons trained on her, and they kept her wrists chained as they escorted her out. Brian waited until they were gone before he turned to Eligor.

The man wasn't asleep, and when Brian glanced at him, Eligor's face curled in a sneer.

'Worried about your woman, are you?'

'What did you do?' Brian stared back, his hands clenched into fists. Though it was a mistake to confront the man and demand answers, he couldn't stop himself. Velaria was out of his reach, and he couldn't protect her. His mind imagined the worst, and he wanted to take out his anger on Eligor.

'Kadir will give her to his men,' Eligor taunted. 'She should be entertaining them instead of fighting. She's nothing more than a wh—'

Brian struck him hard before he could finish the insult. Eligor leapt to his feet and wiped the blood from his mouth. 'So you *do* want her. Interesting.'

'Leave her be. We're all dead anyway.' Brian kept his voice cold and detached.

'She should have been dead months ago,' Eligor spat. 'But if she doesn't please Kadir's men well enough, no doubt she'll die during the next match.'

Fury ripped through Brian at the man's words. He struck out again, and this time Eligor blocked the blow, following up with his own punch. Brian welcomed the pain, for it made him focus. He heard the guards ordering them to stop, but like Eligor, he ignored them.

He avoided the next blow and swung his fist into the man's gut, cutting off Eligor's breath. Then he followed it up with another strike to his ear—and as he'd hoped, Eligor dropped to the dirt, unconscious.

Brian flexed his fingers and glanced over at the guards. They spoke among themselves quietly but seemed unconcerned. Eligor lay motionless for a while, but as time dragged onward, he regained consciousness. Then he leaned back with his hands chained.

In the darkness, Brian could feel the man's silent hatred brewing. And yet, he didn't care, for Velaria still had not returned. As time passed, his worry heightened, transforming into frustration. He began his training exercises, falling into the familiar pattern of exertion. He needed the physical imaginary battle to take his mind off what was happening to her.

'Savaş!' a voice called.

He walked towards the entrance, and the guard stepped aside, revealing Alexander Berys, Baron Staunton. It was the last person he'd expected to see.

'My lord,' he said quietly.

For a moment, the Norman stared at him. 'Your next fight is in two days.'

'It is.' He wasn't certain why the man was reminding him of what he already knew. But when he studied Lord Staunton's face, he saw the spark of...something. 'Will you be there?'

The man shrugged. 'Possibly. But I need to return home to England. I've been here long enough.'

The slight shift in his tone brought a flare of hope Brian hadn't felt in years. This was it, then. Their one and only chance to escape.

The Norman lord stared at him once more. 'You need to win, Savaş. Don't fail.'

He bowed his head, hiding the emotions that threatened. 'I will.' But before the man turned away, he asked, 'What about Velaria?'

Lord Staunton met his gaze in silence, promising nothing. All he said was, 'The ship leaves the morning after your fight.'

Then he turned his back and departed. Brian understood what he hadn't said—there was a chance both of them could leave, if he could find a way to help her escape.

This time, he would not be reckless or impulsive. He needed a strong plan, one that accounted for every possibility. Her life depended on it.

He returned to the far end of the cell to make his plans. He was so caught up in considering the arena and how to get her out that he lost track of time, until the guard finally returned with Velaria.

She stumbled inside, and when she started to lose her balance, he moved to her side and caught her. In the dim light of the torches, bruises swelled against her face. She looked as if she'd been beaten and tormented for hours. Some of her braids had come undone, the wild strands falling against her shoulders.

He held her for a moment, fully aware that she was trembling.

'Let go of me,' she whispered.

Brian obeyed immediately while a coldness poured through him. 'What did they do to you?' Part of him didn't want to know. And she didn't answer, either.

Only yestereve, Velaria would have returned the embrace. Her aversion to touch could only mean one thing. And it made him want to tear Kadir apart.

'Here.' He removed his tunic and rolled it up, making a slight pillow. 'Lie down and try to rest. I'll get you some water.'

She curled up on her side, pulling her knees to her chest. This wasn't the same woman who had fought and killed a crusader only a day ago. They had done something to break her spirit, and if she couldn't find the inner strength to keep going, she would die.

Brian refused to consider it. Somehow, he would find a way to convince her to fight. She couldn't give up so soon— not when they were so close to winning their freedom.

He went to the bucket and dipped out a wooden cup of water, but she didn't take it. Instead, she remained huddled on her side, her knees drawn up.

His gut tightened, and he tried a different tack. 'Lord Staunton came to see me,' he told her. 'He's returning to England, so he said.' Velaria didn't look at him, though she'd heard him. 'He told us we have to win our fighting matches in two days.'

Again, her silence stretched out. Within it, he sensed her hopelessness and surrender. And he couldn't stand by and watch her fade away.

'You cannot give up. Not now.' He pulled her hair away from her cheek and poured a little water on it to cool her skin. 'Lord Staunton can take us back with him. You'll see your family again.'

She didn't react, didn't flinch. Her lips were bruised, and he washed her face gently.

'Rest now. In the morning, we train again.'

Her shoulders trembled, and he realised then that she was crying softly. He tried to find words of comfort, something he could say that would make things right. But there was nothing that would take away the pain she'd suffered.

He didn't truly know why her punishment had lasted so long. It seemed overly harsh, but he supposed she was fortunate to still be alive. At last, he leaned in close and murmured, 'Don't give up, Velaria. Fight and win this battle so you can have your vengeance on Kadir.' His forehead touched hers and he said, 'Walk with God.'

Chapter Two

Velaria's entire body ached. Every part of her hurt, but she still had to fight again. After she'd been summoned, Kadir had killed every hope she'd had. He'd taught her a lesson in the truth she'd never wanted to face. She was only here to die. There would be no future for her except death.

He'd been toying with her, using her. Byzantine nobles had placed bids on her to become their concubine. She'd fought back viciously when they'd tried to touch her, and Kadir had ordered her beaten in front of them. She was fairly certain her ribs were bruised or broken.

This next fight would be her last. Kadir would pit her against someone physically stronger, someone brutal. And that would be the end.

It didn't matter what Savaş had told her about Lord Staunton's plans to help them escape. She'd given up on every thought of freedom. It wasn't going to happen. Not any more.

She'd returned to the prison, her spirit broken. A part of her had desperately wanted to believe that someday they would get out. Now she knew the truth—it was over. She would die in two days.

'Get up, Velaria.'

Savaş's words were quiet but firm. She didn't want to move, not now. And so, she ignored his command.

'I'm not letting you give up,' he said. 'Not when we're so close.'

Once again, she acted as if she hadn't heard him. But this time, he reached down and lifted her to her feet. 'You're training with me this day. I won't let you lie there and surrender.'

When she lifted her gaze, she saw fury in his eyes. Never before had he looked at her that way, but she flashed him her own defiance. 'There's no reason to fight. Not any more.'

This time, he took her arm gently and led her away from the others to the corner of the prison. 'Tell me what happened to you.'

'No.' She had no intention of reliving that day. It was locked away deep inside her, a memory she would never think of again.

'Why are you giving up?' he demanded. 'Why, when we're so close?'

'*You* are close to escaping,' she corrected. 'Not me. I'm going to die in that arena.'

'You won't die if you continue fighting.'

But she didn't believe him. Her body was bruised and swollen from the beatings she'd endured. She couldn't imagine one more fight.

'I can't,' she confessed. 'And it doesn't matter anyway. Even if I win the fight, he'll have me killed.'

'Lord Staunton has made plans,' he said. 'If you want to go home again to see your family, then fight for it. Stop feeling sorry for yourself.'

At that, her anger blazed. 'I'm not feeling sorry for myself.' He didn't understand her fate, for he was a man. Even if she somehow survived this last battle, Kadir would sell her to one of the Byzantine lords, who would use her whenever he wanted. She'd rather die than face such a fate.

He circled her. 'You're better than this, Velaria.' She didn't like his tone, and he pressed further. 'Your family is wealthy, aren't they? They have noble blood.'

'Why does that matter?' Her father and brother hadn't come for her. Likely, they were ashamed that she'd run away with the knight.

But there was a sudden shift in Savaş's demeanour, something barely perceptible—as if her nobility bothered him. 'Is your father a baron, like Lord Staunton?'

She shook her head, watching him as he circled. 'He's a knight. My grandfather was an earl.' She still didn't understand why he'd asked.

'Then you are a woman of worth,' he said softly. 'Act like it.' His hand moved towards her face, and out of instinct, she blocked it. 'Good.'

Part of her recognised that Savaş wasn't going hard on her—he'd never planned to strike her. But he continued staring, and she forced herself to focus. He moved his leg towards hers, and she leapt out of the way to prevent him from bringing her down.

There was look of approval in his eyes. 'Again.' He took her through the series of training exercises they had practised together, but she was aware that the other fighters were watching. Grudgingly, she admitted to herself that Savaş was right. She needed the training to pull herself out of the darkness threatening to drag her under. The physical exertion—even though it hurt—was necessary.

When they both stopped to catch their breath, she realised what he was trying to make her understand. Anger could be her weapon against the man Kadir chose as her opponent. She could pour her rage into the fight and even if she died, she would go down swinging.

Savaş gave her a drink of water, and she took it. His fingers brushed against hers, and in that moment, a pang of regret struck hard. He was a good man, one who deserved a better life than this. Despite the endless days of suffering, he had remained at her side.

And if fighting one more day would help him escape, she would gladly enter the arena. She didn't know what Lord Staunton planned or how he intended to get Savaş out, but she would play her role.

Even if she died in the attempt.

The day of the fight, Velaria picked up her ration of food, and Eligor's hate-filled gaze slid over her.

'I told Kadir about you and Savaş,' he said. 'He was quite interested to hear it.'

Though he was trying to spark her temper, she refused to respond. Though she wondered what lies Eligor had spread, she refused to show any fear in front of him.

'Save your breath for your last fight,' she said. 'Perhaps you'll lose today.'

He only smiled. 'I told Kadir you were giving yourself to Savaş each night. That's why he offered you to those noblemen.' He stood up, stepping close. 'Did you enjoy it, Velaria?'

Nausea rushed through her, and she stood up. Without thinking, she struck his ear hard. A moment later, Eligor swung back, and she ducked to avoid the punch.

Savaş moved to her side then, and he caught Eligor's wrist. 'Leave her alone.' His voice was cool and controlled, but she heard the fury beneath it. 'Unless you want me to break your wrist before your fight today.'

Eligor stared back. 'It doesn't matter what you do. Both of you will lose.'

His words were weighted with confidence, and Velaria

demanded, 'What do you mean?' It sounded as if their fights would not be fair, as a penalty for their friendship.

He lifted his hands and tried to step back. 'You'll see.'

Savaş released his wrist, and Velaria walked back with him to the opposite side of the prison. 'I don't like this,' he said. 'Something's different.'

She agreed, but there was little point in arguing with Eligor. Not when he was right—she would probably lose today.

In Savaş's eyes, she saw his worry—which was a mistake since there was nothing he could do. Kadir wanted her to die. He wanted her death to be public, and he wanted her to be humiliated. Even if she won the match, it would be the end for her.

For a moment, she drank in the sight of this man. She memorised Savaş's lean face, darkened by the sun…the beard stubble that covered his cheeks and jaw, and the blue eyes that were darker than her own. Her heart ached at the knowledge that she would not see him again. But she would do what she could to save him.

'We should probably remain apart for a little while to appease Kadir,' she said softly.

'I don't give a damn what Kadir wants,' he shot back. 'Aye, he's angry at both of us.' He lowered his mouth to her ear and murmured, 'But today, we make our escape.'

She didn't believe it was possible. 'How?'

'We entertain the crowd. We win their approval so he cannot kill us. As his champions, the people pay good coins to watch us fight, Velaria. If we give the crowd what it wants, we can both survive.'

She didn't believe that, but she had no desire to dim his hopes. Instead, she answered, 'I will try.'

The door to the fighting arena opened, and the light burned her eyes. It seemed that Kadir was starting the first match early, for normally it would be a few hours before the fighting began.

'Velaria,' a guard called out.

It was too soon. She was usually one of the last to fight. A sudden chill rushed through her, and she wondered if Kadir intended to have her executed in front of everyone. Fear pulsed within, and Savaş caught her hand.

'Make them pay for what they did to you,' he reminded her. 'And walk with God.'

For a moment, his face was so close to hers, she wondered if he would kiss her. Was it so terrible that she wanted that comfort before she went off to die? But if that was what he'd wanted, he would have done so already.

Velaria squeezed his palm before she took the long walk towards the narrow opening. Four guards awaited her, their weapons poised to strike. They let her out, but this time, they didn't unfasten her manacles. And she was given no weapon at all.

Inwardly, she cursed, for she knew what was about to happen—her own execution. She cast one last look back at Savaş. For it was now about to end.

Velaria didn't return after her match.

A bleakness filled him up inside for Brian knew what that meant. But he hadn't been prepared for the grief that sliced through him. Once again, he'd been unable to save someone he cared about.

Despite his best efforts to restore her confidence, they had shattered her.

Damn them. She hadn't deserved this.

Inside, his emotions were raw and out of control. He needed to gather himself, to pour his rage and grief into the fight that lay ahead. But there was an empty place beside him where Velaria should have been. She wasn't here to lean up against him and put her hand in his. And the ache caught him like a physical blow.

Stop thinking of her.

He had his own match to face, another battle to fight and win. Lord Staunton had hinted that he could help them escape, but Brian didn't know when or how. Now it was time to stop waiting. He knew the arena well enough— which areas were well guarded and which had weaker defences. He imagined fighting his way out, and the plan took shape within his mind as he considered all the ways it could go wrong.

Eligor returned from his fight, bleeding and bruised. The man slumped on the opposite side of the prison, his chained hands resting on his knees.

Brian despised the man for what he'd done to Velaria, but he forced himself not to provoke Eligor and draw more attention to himself. It wouldn't bring her back and it would only waste his strength for the next fight. Eligor would die alone one day soon, and it wasn't worth the effort.

The fights continued, and Brian was surprised they hadn't called him yet. He guessed Kadir was saving him for last. Half the men returned, and the other half were dead. The same as always. But the endless waiting drew out the anticipation, making him wonder what lay ahead. It was nearly nightfall, and the fighting would cease soon enough.

Then, at last, a guard called out, 'Savaş!'

He tamped down the emotions, pushing back the grief and rage until there was only silent indifference. He needed the control to get through this match so he wouldn't think about his opponent's impending death. Slowly, he took deep breaths until he felt nothing at all.

Brian walked towards the entrance and chose his sword

while the guards surrounded him. After he left them behind, he went outside and saw that the sun was beginning to set while the air remained dry and hot. He gripped his sword, finding the cool stillness within him. The crowd roared its approval, and he waited for his opponent. It would probably be a large man, an experienced, skilled fighter. He stared at the other entrance, waiting for his enemy to emerge.

Slowly, a figure appeared amid the dust, the sunlight casting its shadow as Brian stared at the opponent he had to kill.

A blend of joy and dread coursed through his veins when he saw the face of Velaria. Joy that she was still alive—and dread when he realised she was now his opponent. This was their punishment, then, to fight each other until one of them died.

The horror on her face mirrored his own feelings. She didn't want to kill him any more than he wanted her to be hurt. But if they refused to fight, both of them would die. Their only hope of survival was to escape together.

'Savaş,' she murmured. The anguish in her tone and the expression on her face told him that she expected to lose.

But he would never raise his weapon against her, not in a thousand years. He circled her slowly, his weapon lowered. He kept his voice quiet. 'We're going to escape this day, Velaria. But before we do, we're going to entertain the crowd in a way they've never seen before. So if the worst happens, they won't kill us.'

'I won't fight you,' she insisted.

His expression tightened, and he stared at the crowd. 'Oh, yes, you will. We're going to show them our training.'

They moved to the centre of the arena, and the crowd of onlookers was already cheering and placing wagers.

'Is Lord Staunton here?' he asked.

She glanced behind him. 'In the first row.'

'I don't know what plans he's made, but our only way out is through the crowd,' he said. 'The entrance on the opposite side of Kadir's platform isn't guarded heavily. We could make it.'

Her eyes still held the intense sadness, but he wasn't going to give up on her. She raised her weapon, and he repeated, 'It's training, Velaria. Nothing more.'

She took a deep breath, but he saw the shadows in her eyes, the weariness in her posture.

Kadir spoke to the people in their native tongue, explaining how his two greatest fighters had rebelled against him and deserved to be punished.

Brian understood only a little of his speech, but if they could gain the sympathy of the crowd, the people might help Velaria and him escape. The guards would not harm the bystanders, and if enough of them cleared a path, they could get free.

When Kadir gave the command to fight, Brian raised his weapon and met her gaze. 'Are you ready?'

She gave a slight nod, which encouraged him. With her own sword raised, they began to circle one another. He kept his voice barely more than a whisper, 'You first.'

She swung her blade, and he defended himself, blocking the strike. A sudden energy rose within him, the anticipation of freedom. If they played this game correctly, there was a chance of victory. He recognised her pattern and footwork and responded, remaining in a defensive stance.

'Now you,' she murmured.

He spun and began the next pattern, lunging towards her while she blocked him. It was familiar training, and he saw the moment she began to hope. Brian intensified his pace, knowing that it would heighten the crowd's enjoyment, and she knew how to respond. Over and over, they fought, using the sparring motions they regularly practised.

Brian drank in the sunlight and the air, tasting the freedom that was to come. He would do whatever was necessary to get them both out. And if anyone tried to stop them, he wouldn't hesitate to defend her.

Velaria responded to his blows with her own swordplay, and she added a twist of interest to the fight when she spun away and brought her blade low, forcing him to jump.

He couldn't deny that he was enjoying this. Her eyes flashed with intensity, but behind her, he could see Kadir's impatience. The man had expected a quick death for Velaria, not this.

Brian didn't care. This was about the crowd more than anything else.

'Move towards Lord Staunton,' he said. She didn't reveal that she'd heard him, but as he attacked, she backed up, getting closer to the Norman baron.

Abruptly, she switched positions and pressed her weapon close to Brian's throat. He blocked it and held her back. When he spied the baron nearby, he demanded, 'How?' He needed to know what plans Lord Staunton had made, if any.

'After the fight, go through the crowd,' the man answered. 'The guards won't stop you. Then find your way to the port.'

Though Brian hadn't left the city in years, the port lay east of Constantinople. They could keep the setting sun to their backs and find it.

He quickened his pace, though Velaria's breathing was hitched, and she was clutching her broken rib. They would have to find another way of pleasing the crowd. He brought his blade up close, and their weapons held steady a moment while he pretended to push her back. 'Disarm me,' he commanded. 'Then I'll dive and catch their interest while I get the sword back.'

She lifted her blade high, and he loosened the grip on his hilt. When she slashed hard, his weapon went spinning away. He dove into the dirt and rolled, seizing his weapon as he leapt into a fighting stance. The crowd responded in a cheer, and she faced off against him with her sword in one hand, her legs in a balanced stance.

It was time to make their move and escape. 'Are you ready?' he asked again.

A faint smile rested at her mouth, and she gave a nod. But before he could guide her to bolt towards Lord Staunton, the gate to the prison slowly rose up. And God help them, four more prisoners entered the fighting pit.

Eligor was one of them.

Velaria's heart sank. They had put on a good demonstration for the crowd, but Kadir's thirst for blood had put it to an end.

There were so many fighters. All were skilled, and Kadir intended for only one to be left standing. It was a reckless move, one she'd never guessed he would make.

When she saw more coins being exchanged, she realised this was about wagers. Kadir had likely gambled a good deal of his money. But he would lose most of his strongest fighters—and for what? She didn't understand it.

'Stand at my back,' Savaş ordered. 'Take a moment to breathe. And don't move from my side.'

It was their best hope of survival, to fight together. His back was sweaty from exertion, as was hers. But she held her sword, waiting for someone to make a move. Instead, the men gathered around Eligor, as if planning a strategy.

'Savaş, they're going to attack all at once,' she predicted.

His back tensed against hers as he scanned the threat ahead. 'We need more weapons.' But there was only one way to get another sword—by killing one of their opponents swiftly.

For a moment, Velaria's emotions faltered. Ever since they'd taken her from the prison, she'd prepared herself for death. Kadir was furious with her, but although he could easily have had her executed, he'd wanted to earn money for her death.

Velaria was prepared to die—but if she did, Savaş would be surrounded. She had to stay at his back and guard him, just as he guarded her. She owed him that.

Self-pity had no place for her now. She had to lock away her feelings, shutting out anything that made her vulnerable. She couldn't think of the men who would die or what would happen next. This was about protecting him. She studied the four men on the opposite side of the arena, who were still making their plans.

But Savaş shocked her when he turned and kissed her lightly. The crowd rose to their feet and cheered.

The touch of his mouth upon hers was so fleeting, she almost wondered if it had truly happened. Colour rose to her cheeks, and she hardly knew what to say or do. 'Why did you do that?'

'Because now the crowd is on our side, not theirs.'

Of course. It had nothing to do with their friendship. Yet, the warmth of the sudden kiss had brought a deep ache within her heart, a yearning she didn't dare acknowledge. Once again, she bundled up her feelings and pushed them back. Velaria took her position at his back, hardening her heart to what lay ahead.

All four men charged forward, and three attacked Savaş

at once. Velaria swung her sword at her opponent's wrist before he could block the move. In one blow, she removed his hand. A scream tore from the man, and he dropped to his knees, clutching his wrist as he bled out swiftly. She picked up his fallen weapon and used the second sword to block a blow aimed at Savaş's neck.

Her arm reverberated from the force, but she faced Eligor down with cool annoyance.

'You aren't playing fair, Velaria,' he chided.

'Neither are you.' But she gave the second sword to Savaş while she parried Eligor's next strike. He fought with vicious strength, whereas she had only her defensive skills. It seemed as if he was trying to separate her from Savaş, and she kept her back pressed to his.

Eligor swung at her legs, and it forced her to leap out of the way. But a moment later, she deflected another blow aimed at Savaş. Her heart raced with fear—not for herself, but for him.

She lacked the strength to defeat Eligor—not when she'd already been fighting for most of an hour. Her arm ached with exertion, and it hurt to continue fighting. Her enemy seemed to sense it. No doubt he intended to wear down her endurance.

'You don't have to do this,' she said to Eligor. 'Kadir cannot make you fight us.'

'I don't intend to die today,' he shot back.

'You could escape instead,' she suggested. 'If you leave now, no one would stop you.'

'Kadir promised me my freedom if I defeat all of you,' Eligor countered as he struck again.

'And you believe the man who enslaved us? I thought you were smarter than that.' She pressed her weapon against his. 'Take your weapon and go.'

His expression seemed to flicker, as if he'd not considered whether their master was lying.

'We have a better chance of getting out if we stand together against the guards,' she insisted. 'There's no need to fight each other.'

Savaş held his swords against his opponents. 'She's right. We should leave together while we still can.'

One of the fighters considered it, and a moment later, he ran towards the crowd. He leapt into the arena stands with his sword drawn. But he made it no more than three rows before two men attacked him, stabbing him in the back.

Eligor's expression never changed. 'Not much of an escape, was it?'

'He shouldn't have gone alone.' But even so, her hopes died down. Now it seemed that making their way through the crowd was a sure path towards death. Their only hope was to be the last two standing. And then what?

'If we stay together—'

Eligor cut off her words when he lunged with his blade. Velaria barely managed to block it. He pressed his advantage, and she was barely aware that Savaş had defeated one of his opponents. Now there were only two. But she could only defend each blow while her arms cried out with exhaustion. Her bruised ribs made it impossible to breathe, and Velaria lost track of the endless attack—until Eligor's sword slipped past her defences. She couldn't move, for fear that he would skewer Savaş.

Time seemed to hold still when she saw the blade coming for her. In that instant, she had a choice—step aside and live…or watch Savaş die. There was no choice at all. She accepted her fate, even as she tried to divert the last blow.

But before the blade could slice through her, Savaş's

sword stopped it. His last opponent fell to the ground, and there were only three of them left.

Eligor recognised his fate the moment she did. She and Savaş could easily kill him, and he was outnumbered and outmatched.

She tried one last time to get through to him. 'Join us, and we'll fight our way out, Eligor.'

But his face remained sullen and unmoving. He didn't believe her—and truthfully, she didn't trust him not to turn against them.

He lifted his weapon and paused, waiting for one of them to strike. But she and Savaş held steady, their swords poised. She'd done all she could to stop the fight, but it was over now. Eligor couldn't win.

And yet, after they defeated him, their own escape plan seemed impossible. She glanced over at Lord Staunton, who was gripping the edge of the stands, his face locked upon the fight.

'Kadir won't let either of you live,' Eligor said. 'Even if you win.'

'I know.' Velaria didn't move, and the noise of the crowd grew louder as they demanded a fight. 'But I also know he won't grant your freedom.'

Eligor glanced from her to Savaş. Then he made his move, slashing his sword towards Savaş. Just as Savaş was about to block it, Eligor pivoted and his blade sliced towards her. Velaria leapt out of the way to avoid him.

Eligor attacked again, his speed impossibly fast as he struck. She barely held on to her sword, and her heart beat wildly. But just as she was regaining her balance, Eligor turned to Savaş, caught between them with his back exposed.

This was her moment to save him. She hesitated, for there was no honour in killing Eligor from behind.

Yet she had no choice. Her honour had long ago disappeared, replaced by the need to survive.

Velaria lifted her blade and brought it down with all her strength at Eligor's back. But at the last moment, he threw himself to the ground, and she tried in horror to stop her blade from striking Savaş.

A scream tore from her as her sword sliced through his flesh, cutting him down. Savaş sank to the ground, blood pouring from the wound she'd inflicted across his shoulder.

Oh, God. What had she done? Only instinct kept her from going to him as Eligor moved in for the kill. He'd done this on purpose, to distract her enough to kill them both and win.

Her heart was bleeding, as surely as Savaş was dying at her feet.

It's my fault.

She was sobbing, even as she poured herself into winning this last fight. Rage erupted within her, and she dove to the ground, spinning out of the way as her left hand curled into the sand. When she sprang to her feet, she waited for the right moment and cast sand into Eligor's eyes. He flinched, and she struck hard, her sword tearing through his flesh until he stared at her in shock as she pulled the sword from his body.

The crowd was thunderous, but she could only kneel beside Savaş, the tears pouring down her face. He was still alive, but barely.

'Go,' he ordered, his voice low. 'This is your chance for freedom. Take it.'

'I can't.'

Not without you.

But she was fully aware that he was dying before her eyes. She tore off a piece of Eligor's tunic and tried to stanch the blood flow.

'You must.'

But she was frozen with anguish, unable to move. To her horror, his eyes closed, and he grew still. Velaria was dimly aware of someone speaking to her, but she wasn't conscious of the words. Raw pain caught in her throat at what she'd done. Two guards came to take Savaş away, and she released her own cry of anguish, screaming at what she'd done.

The crowd fell silent, almost as if they knew not what to do.

But as she passed by Eligor's fallen body, the numbness mingled with grim satisfaction that she'd won the fight.

The price had been far too high. A surge of grief flooded through her, and it was only instinct that kept her walking.

She was dimly aware that the crowd was applauding, but Velaria's focus was on finding Lord Staunton in the stands. He was her only hope for survival now. If she returned to the prison, she was as good as dead. They would slice her throat the moment the door closed behind her. But the baron was nowhere to be found.

The guards were already coming for her. Once they reached her, she would only be captured again. Or worse.

Velaria kept her sword in hand as she quietly walked towards the crowd. She didn't bother to hide her tears but let them flow freely as she met their gazes. Slowly, the people parted to let her through. And when she looked back at the guards, the crowd closed the space, preventing the men from reaching her. She reached the doorway and turned back to the crowd, touching her hand to her heart in silent thanks.

When she reached the open streets, no one tried to stop her.

Chapter Three

Inwardly, Velaria felt as if she were dying, as surely as Savaş had. Her entire body and mind had gone numb with anguish and self-loathing. If Savaş hadn't ordered her to go, she never would have left his side. His last act had been the unselfish choice to save her life.

You don't deserve to live.

The words echoed in her mind as Velaria trudged east towards the port. She wished with all her heart that she could have saved him. All of this was her fault. Yet, despite everything she'd done, she had to keep her promise to escape. Otherwise, his death was for nothing.

Velaria kept the sword at her waist and traded her shoes for a *keffiyeh* to cover her hair and face. It was better if she disguised herself as a man.

When she finally reached the water's edge, she stared out at the ships. It was impossible to tell where Lord Staunton was. He might have already sailed away.

She waited by the pier until well after the sun went down. No one approached her, but eventually, she saw Lord Staunton approaching on horseback. He carried a torch in one hand and stopped a moment when he saw her waiting. For a moment, Velaria hesitated before she lowered her *keffiyeh* and exposed her face.

'Follow me,' he said.

She covered her face once more before he led her away from the pier and towards another small boat. It was barely large enough for both of them. But Lord Staunton helped her inside and began to row.

'Stay low,' he warned. 'I've taken enough risks today. We cannot be caught.'

Despite the rescue he offered, she was still grieving for Savaş. Her heart felt as if it had been torn from her chest, and it seemed impossible that he was gone. Even now, none of it seemed real.

'It should have been me,' she whispered. 'I should have died in that arena.'

The Norman said nothing except, 'Kadir broke our agreement. After the bribes I paid him, you were never supposed to fight.'

Velaria crouched low in the boat as he rowed them out. Though she tried to shield herself from the grief and concentrate on her escape, all she could feel was emptiness. Savaş was dead, and it was her fault. She would never sit beside him again or hold his hand in the prison. All because she'd been too swift with her weapon and couldn't stop her motion fast enough.

She'd had no time to say farewell to him, either. Even now, it felt selfish, and she wished she'd stayed behind, even if it had meant her own death.

'Where are we going?' she asked quietly.

'I have a friend who will give you a place to sleep tonight. And then we'll sail back to England,' Lord Staunton said. 'My wife, Clare, awaits me at Staunton, near Cornwall. I'll arrange for you to return home.'

'She's alive?' Velaria hadn't known of this. 'I thought she was gone.'

'I thought so, too.' He leaned in closer and said, 'In a way, I have you to thank for that.'

She stared back at him, not understanding. 'What do you mean?'

'My wife was taken from me two years ago,' he answered. 'I thought she was still in Constantinople, which is why I stayed to search for her. But she was taken with other slaves to Italy.'

'What does that have to do with me?'

'Your brother travelled to search for you,' the baron answered. 'He never reached Constantinople because he thought you were in Italy among the other slaves.'

Tears welled up in Velaria's eyes at the realisation that her family hadn't forgotten her.

'Your brother tracked the merchants there, and he kept searching,' Lord Staunton continued. 'By the time my missive arrived at your home, your brother had already freed the slaves and returned to Ardennes. He brought my wife, Clare, back to England with him, along with a few others.'

'You sent my family a missive?' she asked in disbelief. 'When?'

'A year ago,' he answered. 'The first time you asked. I never knew if it arrived.'

It felt as if all the air had left her lungs. Her brother had been so close, and yet, he'd never found her. This time, her tears did break free.

'One of the merchants told me about your brother's rescue,' the baron added. 'That was how I learned Clare was alive. In return, I swore I would save you.'

'You should have saved Savaş.' Her voice held the bleakness that lingered in her heart.

'I meant to save both of you.' For a moment, Lord Staunton seemed to hesitate, as if he wanted to say something. Then he finished with, 'You'll stay here tonight, and then I'll come for you at dawn.'

He brought the boat towards a private pier in front of a large house. A man and a woman awaited them, and she heard Lord Staunton speaking to the man quietly. The woman's face held sympathy, and she held out her hand.

'Come,' she murmured.

Velaria followed the woman inside, fully aware of the blood and dirt all over her. The house was immaculate, with mosaic tile floors and high ceilings. The windows were open, and a breeze passed through them. But Velaria could hardly enjoy it, for she was still numb at losing Savaş. He should have been here with her. It seemed impossible to imagine that he was dead.

The woman led her into a private bathing chamber where the floor of the room descended into a bath. Marble stairs led directly into the pool of water, and Velaria removed her bloodstained garments. The woman brought out lengths of linen as drying cloths, and she set aside another gown for her to wear afterwards. After she was naked, Velaria stepped into the water and walked until the water reached her waist. Then she sat upon one of the submerged benches with her knees drawn up. Although the water felt wonderful, she couldn't stop herself from trembling.

Savaş was gone. She was alone now, and at any moment, Kadir's men might find her. A tremor gripped her heart, becoming a physical shiver as shock claimed her. But before she could descend into despair, the woman stepped into the bath to help her.

She spoke soothing words in the Byzantine tongue, as if she somehow understood what had happened. Then, she helped Velaria untangle her braids and wash her hair. The simple gesture broke through the anguish, helping her push it back and regain control.

For a moment, it felt as if she were standing outside herself. It had been years since she'd had the luxury of a full bath instead of a bucket of water. The woman helped her dry off with the linen cloth before combing out her damp hair.

Last, the woman gave her a soft robe that covered her from neck to ankles. Velaria couldn't remember the last time she'd worn something so finely made, and it evoked memories of being home.

Her family hadn't abandoned her. They had tried to find her. The thought should have reassured her, but it only made the shadow of emotion well up within her heart.

The woman led her to another room with a small bed against the wall, and a tray of olives, rice, and lamb awaited her at a low table with cushions on the floor. Velaria forced herself to eat, though she barely tasted the meal. Her guilt weighed upon her so heavily, she could hardly breathe.

After she sank into the bed, she drew her knees up, and memories of the arena came flooding back. If only she could have stopped her sword. She gripped her coverlet hard, trying to keep her emotions from falling apart.

Savaş had been the greatest friend she'd ever known. He should have lived. But now he was gone.

And as night descended over the city, she could only weep for what might have been.

Lord Staunton returned before dawn, and Velaria followed him back into the small boat. The Byzantine woman gave her provisions and a gown, along with a veil to cover her hair and shield her face from the sun. Velaria thanked her, but it felt strange to wear her hair down. Even though she now appeared more like a woman than a warrior, she'd kept a blade strapped to her thigh as protection.

The Norman lord rowed them towards a larger vessel and helped her climb aboard. Half a dozen men were preparing the boat to leave, and she didn't know where to go. Lord Staunton answered her unspoken question. 'You can remain on deck while we sail or go below, as you choose. The ship is small,' he apologised, 'so you'll have to share your cabin at night.'

A tightness slid under her skin, and she moved her hand to her blade. The last thing she wanted was to be sharing a space with strange men. But then again, she was grateful for her freedom. Lord Staunton had protected her last night from those who would have found her on the streets and brought her back into slavery.

'Thank you,' she said to him at last. So many things could go wrong, but she wanted to believe that there was a chance at seeing her family again, even though she feared she would not make it back.

She stared back at the towers of Constantinople, watching the city that had held her captive for nearly two years. And her heart bled at the knowledge that she wouldn't see Savaş again. He should have been here with her after all the days of their captivity. Another thorn of grief pricked her heart.

Lord Staunton walked towards the bow and stared out at the water. Within the hour, they were sailing southwest. The boat swayed on the water, and only after the city was in the distance did the Norman lord beckon to her. 'Come. There's something I want to show you below deck.'

He led her down the narrow stairs, and it was dark with only a lantern or two for light. She saw several hammocks for the crew members and two doors at the opposite end.

Lord Staunton opened one of them, and a lantern illuminated the space. But instead of more hammocks, she spied a figure lying upon a pallet on the floor.

For a moment, her heart began to pound. Another man knelt beside the body, but she could not see who it was. A cold chill slid over her, and she followed Lord Staunton inside.

When she moved closer, a gasp caught in her throat. 'Savaş,' she murmured, falling to her knees. Although his eyes remained closed and he didn't move, at least he was still breathing. She turned to Lord Staunton. 'You went back for him?'

He nodded. 'I paid Kadir for both of you. He won't follow us.' After a slight pause, he added, 'I would have bought your freedom sooner, but I had to wait until my share of the profits came in. I spent a good deal on bribes over the years, and I needed the funds to buy passage for all of us on this ship.'

To the other man, he asked, 'How is he?'

'Alive, for now.' The man's voice was heavily accented, as if he were from Italy. Then he stood. 'Is she here to help?'

She realised then that the older man was a healer from the way he was examining Savaş's wounds. 'Will he recover?' she questioned, hardly daring to hope.

'It is too soon to tell,' the healer answered. 'I cannot say whether the blade that cut him will bring a fever.'

Her heart sank at that, and Velaria voiced a silent prayer for his life. 'What can I do to help?' she asked the healer. 'Do you need water or bandages?' She would do anything if it meant saving Savaş's life. Her emotions were caught up in fear, joy, and worry.

'You know him then?' the old man asked.

'He was my best friend,' Velaria answered. She moved

closer and took his hand in hers. His skin was so cold, it terrified her. 'Savaş, can you hear me?'

But his eyes remained closed, his face rigid with pain. She didn't know what that meant and couldn't bear the thought of losing him again.

'Please heal him,' she begged. The sight of the blood-soaked bandages terrified her for fear that he'd been rescued only to die.

The healer mashed herbs together and created a new poultice. He brought the herbs and laid them upon Savaş's wounds, wrapping them against the stitched flesh before he sat back. 'I have done all I can. His life is in God's hands now.'

Velaria thanked him as he departed, and she sat beside Savaş's unconscious form. It seemed that her prayers had been answered, but he lay so still, she didn't know what to think. She took a blanket and covered him with it. Her emotions were holding on by a thread and when she held his hand again, the tears fell freely.

'We're going home, just as you promised,' she said. 'Savaş, I'm so sorry about what I did. I never meant to hurt you. Please forgive me.'

But he didn't squeeze her hand or respond in any way. Velaria lay down beside him, trying to warm his skin with her own. Her heart ached at his suffering, but she was so grateful for every breath he took. For a moment, she simply kept his hand in hers, still in disbelief that he was here, and they were both free from captivity.

The hard floor pressed against her spine, but she wasn't aware of anything except each breath Savaş took. She clung to hope and held his hand, trying to will the strength back into him. He had done the same for her on the night she'd been attacked by Kadir's men. And he had taken care of her, trying to build back her courage.

She could do no less for him.

It felt as if he were a thousand miles away from the world. Somehow, the young man he'd been, Brian of Penrith, no longer seemed to exist. Instead, he'd become the man they'd forged in blood and battle—Savaş. It seemed right to claim the name as his own, for the boy he'd been had died in the arena.

He was dimly aware of darkness, of the constant swaying of a ship, and the fever that burned through him. He thought he heard Velaria talking to him, and her hand held his, though he couldn't seem to open his eyes. She was pleading with him to fight.

Fight for what? He didn't know any more. He'd been forced to kill, over and over, until he craved an end to it.

Burning heat flushed his skin, as if the desert gods had come to claim his body now. Velaria's voice seemed to fade away as the nightmares returned. He flinched when the memory of that blade sliced towards him. In his vision, he fell to his knees, staring at Velaria's horrified face.

It was an accident; he'd known that. And yet, he should have been more aware of Eligor's strategy. He should have guessed the man would put her in an impossible position, one where she had to choose between her life and his.

Footsteps approached, and someone lifted him from the floor. 'Careful,' he heard Velaria say. 'Bring him above.'

He nearly passed out from the pain and didn't understand why they were moving him. The moment they hauled him outside, sunlight blinded his eyes. The scent of salt and wood surrounded him, but he kept his eyes closed. He preferred the darkness to this inferno, and he turned his face away.

'Look at me, Savaş,' Velaria pleaded. 'We're free. We escaped Constantinople, and we're going home.'

But he already knew his body was weak with fever. Death would stretch out its hand to him, and he had to decide whether to take it.

A heaviness weighed upon him, for even if he survived this, there was no place for him to go. Surely, his sister, Morwenna, had gone to the nunnery after losing Robert. His parents were dead, and his home had been claimed by the new Lord Penrith, who treated his serfs like slaves. He couldn't go back to that.

'Savaş,' she said softly. 'We made it out. Don't let that be for nothing.'

His vision adjusted to the light, and at last, he opened his eyes. The ship was not a large one, and in the distance, he could see the shoreline. He turned to Velaria and asked, 'Where are we?'

'Near Italy.'

In her blue eyes, he saw worry blended with relief. Her skin held the rich colour of the sun, and her brown hair gleamed with tints of gold as it spilled over her shoulders, free of the braids. She was as beautiful as the first day he'd met her, and for a moment, he studied her features. Though she was still thin, some of the hollowed hunger had evened out.

She wore a Byzantine robe of creamy white, and it contrasted against the rich hue of her hair. The floral scent of her skin allured him.

'We still have a long journey before us,' she admitted. 'Almost a year. The winds have been good, and Lord Staunton says we'll be home faster if we go by sea.' Her voice broke off, and she asked, 'Savaş, I'm so sorry for what I did. I never meant to hurt you.'

'I know. But it doesn't matter any more.' He leaned back against the ship, staring up at the sky. Now, at least, he understood why she'd brought him here. The sight of land and sea did lift his spirits, even if they were still at the beginning of their journey.

'I wish I could take it back.' Her voice held regret as she continued, 'I made the wrong decision, and you almost died from it.'

He said nothing, for the fierce pain was only subdued by sleeping potions. Though he didn't blame her, he suspected his fighting skills would never be the same. And what did that mean for his future? In the past, he'd always imagined finding his sister.

Or even Piers, Robert's half brother, who had helped teach him to fight. Once, Brian had considered hiring out his sword to earn a living because he was confident in his skills. But now? He didn't know.

'What will you do when you reach Ardennes?' he asked Velaria.

She shrugged. 'I suppose I'll have to face my family.' But instead of joy upon her face, uncertainty lined her expression. 'What about you? Will you try to find your sister?'

He nodded. 'I will travel to Colford Abbey where I left her. I think Morwenna is likely at the nunnery at Saint Michael's Well.'

Though the memory of his sister should have brought him comfort, instead, the guilt returned. Not only because of what he'd done to Robert—but from the realisation that he'd abandoned her. He'd been only fifteen, but that was no excuse. He'd acted like a coward, and she deserved a brother who could protect her—not someone who had left her behind.

Restlessness gnawed at him with the uncertainty of what his life would become now. He had no money, no land. Nothing at all. He needed a new purpose. When he glanced over at Velaria, he saw the fragile hope in her eyes.

'If you need a place to stay, you are welcome at Ardennes.'

Her offer took him by surprise, for he'd not expected it. For a moment, he considered whether it would be the right thing to do. She'd suggested it because they were friends. And yet, he recognised the greater implications. Whether or not she wanted it, her father would probably arrange a marriage for her. And he didn't want to be there when that happened.

Brian didn't understand the knot of emotion that tangled up within him when it came to Velaria. He cared about her and wanted her to find happiness. They had shared a bond of captivity that no one else understood. Both of them had fought to survive, and even now, he felt the shadow of the past year. His body was broken, and he had no idea whether he would heal from these wounds or the inner ones no one could see.

It wasn't right to follow her to Ardennes, not when he had nothing to offer. He needed time to rebuild his life and fortune. And as he studied her face, he made a silent vow that he would do whatever was necessary to become the man of honour he should have been.

If the fever didn't take him first.

Autumn

Velaria stared out at the Mediterranean Sea and the sun dipping below the horizon. Colours of orange and red blazed across the sky, and she watched as Savaş stood nearby with his hands on the edge of the ship. His wounds had healed, but during the past few months, she hadn't seen him train. Not once.

Their friendship had shifted somehow, and she was afraid to ask why. Although they saw each other every day, no longer did he reach out or embrace her. It was as if they were strangers again—and she didn't like it.

Quietly, she approached until she stood beside him. For a moment, she didn't speak. Her heart beat wildly while she tried to gather the right words. But the stilted silence seemed to stretch on.

'How are you?' she asked at last.

He gave a shrug. 'My shoulder is healing.'

A pang of shame caught her, but she pushed it back. 'Do you…want to train again? I could be your sparring partner.'

He didn't look at her, but she saw the slight shift in his bearing. 'No, I don't think so.'

'It might help,' she offered. 'The healer said it will take time for you to rebuild your strength.'

He said nothing but continued staring off into the distance. It bothered her, for this wasn't at all what she'd expected now that they'd gained their freedom. She'd expected joy and celebration. But this awkwardness…was it because he blamed her for the injury? Although he'd said he didn't, she wasn't so certain any more.

Perhaps honesty was the best way to break down the invisible wall of ice.

'Are you angry with me?' she asked.

'No.' Savaş turned to look at her at last. His dark hair was cut short, his face clean-shaven. In contrast, she'd allowed her hair to grow even longer. She only kept a single braid across the top of her head to keep back the strands that tangled in the wind.

'Then why don't you talk to me any more? We were friends once. At least, I thought we were.' Her face burned with embarrassment, though she forced herself to speak the words that needed to be said.

'You once told me your father is a knight,' Savaş said quietly. 'And your grandfather was an earl.'

She shrugged. 'What does that matter?' To her, they were only her family. Their titles meant nothing at all. But he'd never told her anything about his own family, aside from a few stories about his sister, Morwenna. He never seemed to want to talk about his childhood years, and she'd stopped prying.

'I am a serf,' he admitted. 'My father was a miller.'

His humble background didn't bother her at all. 'You don't behave like a serf,' she admitted.

He turned back to look at the water. 'My father and stepmother were killed during an attack on Penrith. My sister and I were captured, and the earl's son Robert and his half brother, Piers, helped us escape. For nearly two years, the four of us lived on our own.'

She'd never heard him speak of this before. 'How did you survive?'

'We hunted for our food and slept in the ruins of Stansbury,' he answered. 'It was a fortress that once belonged to Robert's father. The roof leaked, and it was freezing in the winter.' A pensive expression slid over his face, as if he missed it. 'But we were free.

'Robert and Piers showed me how to fight. Morwenna, too,' he added. 'For a while, it was better than the life we had before. Morwenna and I—we knew how Robert spoke, how he carried himself, as the son of an earl. I wanted to be like him, so I imitated him. And my sister—she was in love with Robert.'

'Where is he now?' she asked.

A darkness shadowed his face. 'He's dead.' The aching emptiness of his voice made her long to offer what comfort she could.

Without thinking, Velaria drew her arms around him from behind, resting her cheek against his back. The moment she did, he seemed uncomfortable, though he didn't pull her hands away. Instead, he turned around to face her. His blue eyes held a rigid emotion she didn't understand.

'Velaria, we come from different families. When we return to England…everything will change.' His words broke off.

She couldn't believe he was even suggesting that she might turn her back on him because of his family. 'Do you think I care who your parents were? Nothing has changed between us, Savaş. You mean the same to me as you always have.'

Truthfully, he meant even more to her now. But she didn't understand this sudden separation he was imposing.

'It will never be the same,' he admitted. 'You'll go back to being a noblewoman. You will never again be chained or starving. They will keep you safe.'

She realised, then, that he planned to leave her. The heat in her face blazed, and though she didn't want to say it, she saw no other choice. 'I always believed we would stay together.' Her voice was thick, rimmed with the weight of emotion.

His knuckles grazed the edge of her cheek. She couldn't read his expression or what he was feeling, but the farewell in his eyes broke her apart.

'I will never forget this past year,' he said. 'Or you, Velaria.'

She felt as if she were standing on the edge of a crumbling cliff, and she tried in vain to hold back the feelings in her heart. He didn't want her in the same way she wanted him. And he was trying to be kind about it in the best way he knew how.

All she could do was nod before she turned to walk away. Tears streamed down her cheeks, though she kept her back straight as she left him. It was her own fault for opening her heart to him. The moment she'd struck him down, she'd known that what she felt for this man went far beyond friendship.

But her worst mistake was thinking that he felt the same. Now it was completely clear that he had never considered a future between them.

And it simply broke her heart.

Late spring

It seemed like a lifetime had passed since he'd last seen England. Brian rode beside Velaria on horseback, but with every mile, tension rose higher within him. Soon enough, he was supposed to return to the young man he'd been before—a serf without even a roof over his head.

He struggled with the fate that lay ahead of him, for it no longer fit with the man he'd been in Constantinople— a fighter and a champion. He craved a different life now, one where he had the freedom to defend those weaker than himself. It wasn't enough to farm a plot of land and pay rents to his overlord.

It's not who you are any more, a voice inside warned.

He knew that. And yet, he didn't know how to create a new life for himself. He could try hiring out his sword, but his shoulder still had not regained its full movement. His injury had healed slowly, and despite the angry red scar, his fighting skills would never be the same. There was a strong chance he would lose against the wrong opponent, and he didn't want Velaria to know about it.

His other choice was to join the monks at the abbey. At least then he would have food and shelter, along with endless days of prayer and atonement. He'd been responsible for the deaths of so many men during the past year. Perhaps this was the right path for him now, to give his life in service.

And yet…he couldn't deny that what he really wanted was Velaria. He'd struggled during the long voyage to set his desires aside. He could never ask her to give up the life of a noblewoman to live with him. It wasn't right or fair. She hadn't touched him again, nor had he touched her. He was fully aware that he had nothing to offer—at least, not yet—and he didn't want her to look upon him with pity.

Until he found a way to lift himself out of poverty, he'd vowed to keep his distance.

They rode alongside one another, and as the miles passed, he noticed Velaria's demeanour turning quiet. Although she ought to be excited about returning home, her expression held worry as they approached Ardennes. Lord Staunton had continued travelling to his lands in the southwest, leaving them to finish their journey without him. In a way, Brian was grateful to have these last few days alone with Velaria.

'It feels strange to be back in England, doesn't it? Without the sun and the desert,' he remarked. Though it wasn't much of a conversation, it was all he could offer.

'It does,' she agreed. 'I don't know how to feel any more.' For a moment, she stopped her horse, staring off into the distance.

'Aren't you happy to be home?' he asked. He'd never stopped to wonder whether her family had treated her well. He'd always assumed that since she was the granddaughter of an earl, she'd had everything she'd ever wanted. But now, he wondered if he'd been wrong.

She took a deep breath and admitted, 'The last time I was here, I ran away from Ardennes.'

Her words startled him, and he brought his horse alongside hers. 'Why?' Had her parents harmed her in some way? Or was there another reason?

She didn't meet his gaze, and her cheeks flushed with colour. 'Because I fell in love with a handsome knight who asked me to wed him.'

It wasn't at all what he'd expected her to say, and the sudden flare of jealousy caught him unawares. He'd always assumed that there was no one waiting for her at home since she'd never spoken of anyone else. After all the conversations they'd had during the long nights, Brian wondered what other secrets she'd kept. Then again, he'd done the same, hadn't he?

Though he wanted to ask more questions, he forced himself to hold back and let her continue.

'My father refused to give his blessing,' she continued. 'And so, I ran away with Sir Drogan. We were planning to marry in secret.'

Every muscle within him tensed. 'And…did you? Wed him?' God above, she was so young when she was taken captive.

'I had planned to,' she murmured. Her face had gone crimson, and she bit her lower lip. 'His father was in the king's court, and Drogan promised that we would live among royalty in a life I could only dream of. But instead, after we—' She didn't finish the sentence but closed her eyes with a pained expression. '—Drogan no longer wanted to wed me.'

A darkness gripped him at her confession, for he guessed

what she hadn't said. The knight had seduced and discarded her afterwards. And he could only imagine how her parents had reacted when they'd learned of it.

A surge of anger came over him that a knight would discard a woman like Velaria. She hadn't deserved to be treated like that. 'You couldn't have been more than—'

'Fifteen,' she finished. 'Aye. I was a foolish maiden who saw nothing but a handsome face and empty promises. I mistakenly believed he was in love with me just as I loved him.'

A tightness caught in his chest. 'Why didn't you tell me of this?'

'I was too embarrassed.' She looked away, and he realised his tone had been harsher than he'd intended.

'I'm sorry.' But he knew, just as she did, that the words meant little and wouldn't change the past.

'Afterwards, Drogan…left me behind and rejoined his father at court. I was taken by a group of travelling merchants who sold me into slavery. I never saw my family again.'

He felt the pain in her voice as an echo within him. All he could do was take her hand in his. Her palm was like ice, and he realised how afraid she was.

'They will be glad to see you,' he predicted.

'I'm not the same woman I was before.' Her face paled. 'No one understands what we endured.'

But he did. More than anyone else, he knew what she had survived. He gripped her hand in silent comfort. 'We have to move forward from what happened. Our past does not define who we are.'

'I know.' Her voice came out as a whisper, and at last, she raised her chin. Her blue eyes held a blend of worry and hope, and in the sunlight, her brown hair gleamed.

At last, she urged her horse onward. He followed, and soon, the towers of Ardennes came into view. Although it had only been about two years since she'd left, he saw her clench the reins tighter.

'You're safe now,' he offered quietly.

'Safe.' She repeated the word and turned back to face him. 'I hardly know what that word means.'

To be truthful, neither did he. But all he could say was, 'You can go back to the life you had before.'

'And what if that's not what I want any more?' She tried to brave a smile and admitted, 'I want to see my family, aye. But I worry about who they want me to be. That woman isn't real.' Her voice held the weight of emotion, as if she were holding back tears. 'Will you stay for a while, Savaş?'

'I need to find out what happened to my sister,' he said softly. Then, he added, 'You're going to be all right, Velaria. I promise.'

She rubbed her wrists where the manacle scars remained. 'I want to believe that.'

But he already knew it wasn't true for either of them. Even now, he awakened with nightmares, his mouth dry, his body covered in sweat. He remembered every person he'd killed in the arena, and never again could he go back to the young man he'd been before. Just as Velaria was nothing at all like the girl she'd left behind.

'I'll watch over you until you're inside the gates,' he promised.

She appeared dismayed at his answer. 'You won't come inside? At least share a meal with us and take shelter for the night.'

Her offer tempted him, but he couldn't let himself falter. 'If I ride hard, I can reach Colford Abbey on the morrow by nightfall.'

She tried again and ventured, 'Are you that weary of my presence that you won't stay one last night?'

She didn't understand. Not at all. When he drew his horse closer, his eyes burned into hers. 'I can't, and you know it, Velaria.' His voice was rough, and he shielded every emotion from her.

'Why?' she asked.

For a long moment, he simply stared at her. It was as if he were memorising her features, capturing a memory. 'Because if I stay one night, I won't leave. And we both know that a woman like you—the daughter of a knight—must wed a man of means. I have nothing to give you. Not even a home.'

She stared at him as if he'd sliced her in half with a blade. And in truth, he felt the same. It took everything in him to do the right thing and let her go.

One day, it might be different. He might find a way to lift himself up and come back for her. But it wasn't fair or right to ask her to wait for him.

Her eyes filled with tears, and his own throat tightened. Brian reached out to touch her cheek, and he leaned in close. More than anything, he wanted to kiss her. He wanted to claim her mouth and teach her what it meant to feel pleasure instead of humiliation.

Not that he knew anything about how to touch a woman. Yet, if he ever had the chance, he would spend hours cherishing her and learning what pleased her.

Endless moments drifted by, and he rested his forehead against hers while his hand slid to her nape. 'Farewell, Velaria. Walk with God.'

She let the tears fall, but he forced himself to turn away and go. It was the hardest thing he'd ever done.

* * *

Velaria watched him ride a short distance away, but he kept his promise and waited on the hillside. Somehow, this joyful moment of returning home was now shadowed by loss. Still, she forced herself to continue riding forward. She wiped the tears away, telling herself that it was always going to be this way. He had his life, and she had hers. There would be time to weep when she was alone in her bedchamber tonight. And so, she gathered the remnants of her pride and turned back. Just before she reached the gates, she lifted her hand to him in farewell.

He answered the gesture by raising his own hand. And still, he waited. For a moment, she watched, still trying to gather her emotions. Then she took a deep breath and stared up at the castle of Ardennes.

It seemed almost unreal to be home again. Velaria remembered her grandsire as a man with a sharp tongue but a gentle heart. She missed him even now. His estate was vast, and after the earl had died, the lands were given to his daughters Honora and Katherine, Velaria's mother. Honora's second husband had been Irish, so she had gone with him across the sea and left Ardennes to her sister. Velaria had spent most of her life here, except for a few years of fostering in Ireland with Honora's extended family, the MacEgans.

Velaria squared her shoulders and rode up to the gates. For a moment, the guard stared at her in disbelief. Most likely he didn't recognise her from the foreign gown she wore and her sun-tanned skin.

'Are you going to let me see my family, or do you intend to stop me?' she enquired.

'My lady—I—yes, they will be so glad to see you.' The guard lifted his spear away and she continued riding into the inner bailey. The familiar castle grounds lifted her spirits, though she was aware of how strange she must look to them.

She dismounted and gave her horse to a stable lad who clearly didn't recognise her. For a moment, she turned slowly, drinking in the sight of home. She saw the familiar walls she'd climbed as a girl until her mother had scolded her for it. And there were the slick stone steps that she'd fallen down more than once after a rainfall. She took a deep breath, then another.

When she glanced up, she saw Katherine standing at the top of that staircase. Shock and joy flooded her mother's face, and a moment later, Katherine practically flew down the stairs to crush Velaria into a hug.

'Oh, my daughter, you're home. Thank the blessed saints.' Already, she was weeping, and Velaria clung to her mother, feeling her own sobs breaking forth. She hadn't seen Katherine in years, and she would have given anything to take back the mistakes she'd made.

'I'm so sorry—' she tried to say.

But Katherine held her face between her hands and kissed her cheeks. 'The past is gone. All that matters is you're alive and here.' Her mother gripped her fiercely, and the love that poured forth was enough to break down every last emotion.

Velaria wept, not only from relief at being home, but also from the burden of the past years of captivity and travelling so far from home. She clung to her mother, welcoming the familiar arms of someone who loved her.

A part of her wished that she could have embraced Savaş one last time. She hadn't forgotten the stolen moments between them, and a heaviness weighed on her with the knowledge that she likely wouldn't see him again. Part of her had hoped that he would want to stay with her, that somehow the invisible barrier between them would drop. Yet, the moment he'd seen her family's estate it reinforced his belief that he had nothing to offer.

She didn't care about wealth or lands…but she understood his pride. In Constantinople, he'd been revered as a champion among men. His strength and fighting skills were legendary.

But here, he could not see his value. And the thought of being without him hurt in a way she'd never expected.

In another moment, her father came forward, and she gripped him tightly. It seemed that the years she'd been gone had carved more lines into his face, and Ademar breathed a sigh of relief. 'Velaria, thank God y-you've returned. Are you hurt?'

She shook her head, for her wounds were not ones he could see. 'I'm all right. But a little hungry.'

He smiled then, and his blue eyes warmed. 'W-we will have a f-feast then, to celebrate your return.'

Her father's familiar stutter warmed her heart, for she'd missed it. Despite it, no one dared to mock Ademar, for he was taller than most men and had been one of the strongest fighters in his younger years.

'On the morrow,' she said. 'I'll eat a simple meal for now and rest, if I may.' She didn't think her stomach could handle too much rich food, since they had only eaten simple foods on the journey here. And the thought of sleeping in her own bed was a welcome respite.

'Of course.' Her father kept one arm around her and the other around his wife as he walked with them up the stairs.

'Where are Phillip and Beatrice?' Velaria asked.

'Your brother is at Dolwyth,' Katherine said. 'Beatrice is with her new husband, and she now lives in the north.'

Though she'd wanted to see them, Velaria supposed there was time for that later. She released a sigh, and when her father opened the door to the Hall, she turned back a moment. From her vantage point at the top of the stairs, she could see beyond the outer curtain wall to the green hills of England.

And it took everything she had to turn back to her family and walk into a home that no longer felt like her own.

Chapter Four

It took longer than he'd anticipated before he reached Colford Abbey. Robert's uncle had been the abbot there, and Brian hadn't seen him in years. He'd been grateful when Father Oswold had offered him food and shelter.

He'd joined the monks at prayers and then sat across from the abbot while he ate a simple meal of bread, cheese, and roasted vegetables. 'It's good to see you again, Father Oswold.'

'You're very welcome,' the abbot answered. 'I must admit, I didn't expect to see you again after you left with the crusaders.'

'By the time I arrived at Constantinople, the battle was already over,' Brian admitted. He didn't share the news of his captivity, though he saw the abbot eyeing the red scar that ran from his neck to his shoulder. 'I was hoping you could help me find Morwenna.' The last time he'd seen his sister, the abbot had spoken of sending her to the nunnery at Saint Michael's Well.

'Morwenna?' The abbot paused a moment and said, 'Do you mean to say that you've not seen her since you left?'

'I've heard nothing.' He straightened and said, 'I would have returned sooner, if I could have.'

'She's at Castle Dunbough in Ireland,' Father Oswold

answered. 'With my nephew Robert, whom you remember. They were married a few years ago.'

Robert was alive? For a moment, he could hardly believe the abbot's words. For so long, Brian had grieved for his friend, despising himself for his role in Robert's death. His reason for journeying across the world had been penance.

But now? It was as if he'd received the gift of absolution. The knowledge lifted the invisible burden of guilt, and thankfulness flooded through him. Even more, there was a sense of joy at the thought of his sister's happiness. She had married the man she'd loved for so long.

'How did this happen?'

The abbot bade him to sit down. 'It's a long story. But I heard their marriage vows myself. Morwenna truly wished you could have been there.' Father Oswold's face softened at the memory. 'She was a lovely bride. I've heard they have a son now.'

'I'm so glad to hear it.' He tried to keep his voice even, but inwardly, he was in shock. In the time he'd spent fighting and trying to escape, his sister had brought a child into the world. It hardly seemed possible. 'Why do they live in Ireland and not at Penrith?' Robert had been the heir to the lands until the king had deposed his father. His friend had been fighting to win his lands back, despite his half brother Piers's claim.

'Robert gave up Penrith to Piers,' the abbot answered. 'Piers married the new earl's daughter, and the two of them live there now.

'As for Ireland—' The abbot paused a moment. 'Robert saved King John's life and earned his favour. His estate at Dunbough was his reward for it.' Father Oswold looked as if he wanted to say more, but he held back. 'Will you travel to join them?'

'I'll need to earn enough silver for the journey, but yes.' He needed to apologise to Robert and find a way to make up for what he'd done. Perhaps his friend would allow him to join the ranks of his guards or let him help train the men. That is, if Brian ever regained his fighting skills.

For a moment, it felt as if the ground had shifted beneath him. For so long, he'd lived each day with the desire to atone for his sins. And now, he could finally let go of the past.

What did that mean now? He couldn't imagine returning to the life he had known as a serf. After the years in captivity, he craved freedom and the chance to make his own choices. He intended to forge a different life, one where he could provide for a wife and family. And he was no longer willing to settle for less.

The problem was, he couldn't get Velaria out of his mind. It was a useless dream, one entirely out of his reach.

Had Velaria's parents welcomed her home? Was she content and cared for? Though he'd believed it was the right course of action to leave, he regretted not staying one more night at her side. She had been with him for so long, it felt strange and lonely without her.

'I agree that you should go to Ireland, Brian. Find your sister and Robert.' The abbot's face grew concerned and he added, 'But…there is…something you should know about your parents. And especially your father.'

He turned back to the abbot, who seemed uncomfortable. 'What do you mean?'

'Your father was not the miller. Nor was his wife your mother.'

A tightness caught his chest. Years ago, when Morwenna had returned to the ruins of the mill, she'd brought back a gown and a golden chain that had once belonged to their mother. But despite his sister's belief that Eldreth had secretly been from a noble family, it seemed more likely that the woman had stolen the gown and chain.

He pushed back the uneasiness and tensed, for the abbot had the answers he sought. 'Who were my parents?'

Father Oswold paused. 'You'd better sit down.'

Lady Katherine stood upon the parapet of Ardennes, watching over her daughter in the courtyard below. Her husband, Sir Ademar, came up behind her and rested his palms upon her shoulders.

'Are you all right?' he asked gently.

She rested her hand upon his. 'I am, yes. But Velaria is not.' During the past fortnight, she'd watched as her daughter picked at her food. There was a sense that the young woman was barely aware of her surroundings. She had a hollow look in her eyes that belied her sun-warmed skin. Although she went outside often and spent most of her days sitting on the stairs, Katherine had the sense that her daughter was waiting on something. Or someone.

'She's home safe. Eventually, she'll g-get better.'

'I'm not so certain about that.' Katherine turned back to her husband. 'She used to watch the men training for hours, don't you remember? She reminded me so much of Honora.' Her older sister had been highly skilled with a sword, and Velaria had learned her own fighting skills from her aunt. 'But now she seems to avoid the practice field. I haven't seen her touch a sword even once.'

Ademar gave a nod. 'I asked her if she wanted to train w-with me, but she refused.'

'She won't talk about Constantinople,' Katherine said. 'I don't want to think of what she must have endured.' She squeezed his hand in hers. 'We have to help her somehow. But I don't know what to do.'

'What if we send her to Laochre…f-for a time?' Ademar suggested. 'She c-could visit with her cousins and the MacEgans.'

Katherine shook her head. 'I only just got our daughter back. Don't ask me to send her away again.'

Her husband pulled her into his strong arms, and she rested her face against his heart. 'We could go with her to visit your s-sister. You needn't be apart.'

She breathed a little easier at that and nodded.

'Do we know anything about her travelling c-companion?' Ademar asked.

Katherine hadn't heard anything. 'Velaria said she had an escort, but she told us nothing about the man except that he returned to Colford Abbey.' But the more she thought of it, the more it seemed that Velaria often looked towards the hills. Katherine was fairly certain she remembered seeing a single rider who had waited in the distance before he'd left.

Ademar kept her in his embrace and stroked her back, offering comfort. 'Perhaps I should travel to Colford and s-speak with him. Her escort might know more about wh-what happened.'

She closed her eyes and breathed deeply before she pulled back. 'I'm not certain I want to know what she endured. I just want her to be well and whole again, Ademar. She barely eats, and I see the sadness in her eyes.'

'I'll m-make the arrangements,' he promised. 'If he was her f-friend, he may know what to do. We c-cannot help her unless we know the truth.'

He was right. And Katherine sensed that if she pressed too hard, Velaria would only lock herself away even more. 'I'll try to find out his name.'

Ademar kissed her lightly, and she rested her forehead against his. Though they had been married for a long time, and the years had turned their hair grey, she still found him as handsome as ever.

'Have faith,' he said gently. 'And I'll make p-plans to leave on the morrow.'

Velaria sat at the top of the stairs that led to the parapets, breathing in the cool spring air. A few trees had begun to bud, and she drank in the sight of her surroundings. After being imprisoned in the darkness and forced to kill in the arena for so long, she was grateful for every moment of her freedom.

And still she watched the hills, wondering if Savaş would ever return. She told herself that eventually, she would forget the horrors of Constantinople, and the memory of him would fade. Did he feel as lost as she did?

She felt like a ship tossing on the waves, travelling but going nowhere. Somehow during the past year, she'd gone from being a warrior to becoming a shadow. And she hated the feeling of helplessness.

Part of it was because of Savaş, if she were honest with herself. During their imprisonment, she'd always believed there was something more between them. She'd held fast to the hope that they would remain together. But now, just as before, a man she cared about had left her behind.

And it hurt so much to know it.

Footsteps sounded behind her, and she turned to see her mother. Katherine smiled and came to sit beside her. 'How are you, Velaria?'

'I am well,' she answered, though they both knew it was a lie.

Her mother gave a nod and stared off at the horizon. Velaria knew she wanted to talk with her about something, but she had no idea what it was.

'When you returned to Ardennes, who brought you here?' Katherine asked. 'You weren't truly alone, were you?'

She shook her head. 'Lord Alexander Berys of Staunton helped us escape Constantinople. He travelled with us for a time, and Brian of Penrith escorted me here.'

Her mother inclined her head, acknowledging their names. 'Your father and I thought we should reward them for bringing you home safely. Do you know how we could find them?'

A sudden tightness filled her, but Velaria answered, 'Brian left to find his sister. He thought she might be at the nunnery at Saint Michael's Well.'

'He wasn't planning to return to Penrith?' Katherine asked.

'I don't know. He said he would stop at Colford Abbey while he looked for his sister. I'm not certain beyond that.' She gripped her hands together, trying to ignore the tangle of feelings inside her.

'Was he a captive, like you?' Her mother's voice was soft but all too knowing.

'He was.' She stood from the stairs and started to walk down them. The need to abandon the conversation was too strong. 'That's all I know, I'm sorry.' She hurried towards the bottom of the stairs, only to find her father's soldiers training. The ringing of swords brought a thin sweat upon her skin, and she felt her throat closing up with the terrible memories.

Ever since she'd returned, she was far too sensitive to the sound of fighting. There had been a time when she'd been fascinated by the soldiers—and truthfully part of it had been their muscular, hewn bodies that had attracted her adolescent feelings. But now she could hardly bear to watch them. It only evoked memories of the arena.

She'd abandoned the trews and tunics she'd worn years ago, in favour of long gowns. She wore her hair unbraided, around her shoulders and covered by a veil, as if doing so would eradicate the woman she'd been only a year ago.

It seemed like an entire lifetime had passed, and she had barely managed to reach the castle gates before her mother caught up to her.

'There's no need to run from me,' Katherine said. 'I only wanted to talk.'

Velaria glanced behind her, waiting for her mother to catch up, before she walked through the gates and over the wooden bridge to the grounds outside the castle. 'I just… need to take a walk. I need to escape these walls.'

'We could walk through the woods like we used to,' Katherine offered.

She shrugged, walking down the familiar pathway. Guilt caused her to slow her pace when her mother struggled to keep up.

'Velaria, your father and I have been talking about your future,' Katherine began.

Invisible ice flooded through her skin as she realised what they meant. They intended to arrange a marriage for her. The thought brought a surge of panic, and she choked back her protests.

Breathe, she told herself. *They cannot force you to do anything.*

When she said nothing, Katherine continued, 'Your brother plans to take a wife soon, and when he does, your father and I intend to move back to Ademar's lands at Dolwyth Phillip will begin learning how to govern Ardennes.

And I know…you'll want a home of your own. Have you given thought to it?'

And there it was—the true reason for the conversation. Though Katherine meant well, the very thought of marriage seemed impossible.

'I was held captive for two years, Mother,' she murmured. 'I have no wish to marry. I could not be a wife to any man after what I endured.' The thought of surrendering to a man's touch or submitting to his will was another form of captivity. Velaria gripped her arms, staring at the forest that lay before them.

Katherine stepped forward and took her hand. Tears gleamed in her eyes. 'Would that I could have spared you that suffering.'

'It was my own fault. If I had not run away with Sir Drogan—'

'Your father could have stopped it,' Katherine admitted. 'I was the one who convinced him to wait. I wanted to believe that you were right, that he loved you. I thought perhaps—' Her words broke off, and she wiped her eyes.

'He took my virtue and abandoned me,' Velaria said. 'He was exactly the sort of man you thought he was. I was too young and foolish to recognise it.' Her voice came out harsher than she'd intended, but she raised her chin. 'But I am old enough to know that I don't want to marry, nor do I wish to be a bride of the Church. I don't think I can be obedient to anyone. Not now.'

More than anything, she needed control over her life, over everything she did. It was the only thing that kept her from shattering inside.

'Tell me about Brian of Penrith,' her mother interjected. 'Did he protect you on the journey?'

The tightness locked up within her again, and she faced

her mother. 'He did, yes.' But he'd also made it clear that he didn't want to see her again. Not when he had nothing to give. She understood his pride, and perhaps by leaving her behind, it was his own way of healing from the captivity they'd endured.

'It must have been difficult travelling alone with men,' Katherine said. 'I hope Brian never made you feel uncomfortable or unsafe.'

'Oh, no, he would never—' she started to say and then realised she'd fallen neatly into her mother's trap. 'We were friends,' Velaria amended.

'I am glad to hear it.' But there was a gleam in her mother's eye that she didn't like.

To her credit, Katherine didn't push but instead offered, 'I am glad you are home again.' She reached out and squeezed Velaria's hand. 'And your father and I both want you to find happiness.'

'I will,' she insisted. 'I just need time.'

But from the expression on her mother's face, she suspected that her parents were up to something. 'Velaria, we made a mistake the last time you wanted to choose a husband.'

'No, *I* was the one who made a mistake,' she corrected. 'You saw the sort of man Sir Drogan was, but I was too young to know it.' With a shrug, she said, 'If I do not marry anyone, it won't happen again.'

'That isn't a choice,' Katherine said softly. 'Your father intends that you should marry. And I agree with him.'

Velaria grew incredulous that they would even consider such a thing. She had hardly been home for more than a fortnight, and already they were trying to make decisions for her.

'I will not,' she insisted.

'You will have a choice,' Katherine said gently. 'There are several noblemen from good families who would make you an excellent husband. We will send word, and—'

'No,' she repeated.

At that, her mother lifted her chin. Velaria recognised that look in her eyes, of a mother who did not appreciate disobedience. But then, too, her mother had married the man she'd always wanted, and Ademar adored her. To Katherine, marriage was joyful, and the sacrament had given her everything.

'We can grant you a little more time,' Katherine said. 'But do not ask me to stand aside and watch you wither away.' Her mother squeezed her hand. 'I see the way you don't eat. I see the shadows under your eyes, and I know you do not sleep.' Tears filled Katherine's eyes, and she brought Velaria's hand to her heart. 'Don't ask me to step aside and watch you slowly die. I will not do it. Your father and I love you, and if that means making difficult decisions to save you from your grief, then we will not hesitate to intervene. Even if you despise us for it.'

She had no answer to give her mother, for anything she said would only make her sound childish and defiant. Then, too, her own weariness cloaked her with the pain of loss. She didn't know how to go on or how to put the pieces of her life back together.

Her mother paused a moment and then said, 'Your aunt Honora invited us to share Bealtaine with them in a few weeks in Ireland. We will travel together, and it will give you the chance to meet other noblemen, if you wish. There will be other Normans there, as well, including the families of Queen Isabel and Lady Genevieve. And you'll see your cousins.' Katherine offered a warm smile, as if the journey would offer consolation.

Velaria gave a shrug, hardly caring one way or the other. But inwardly, she vowed that no matter what her parents wanted, she would never marry any man.

Ireland, one month later

In the distance, Laochre Castle towered high above the vivid green lands. Herds of sheep grazed within enclosures beside freshly ploughed fields while beyond it, the blue sea gleamed like a bold sapphire. Brian was weary of the time he'd spent sailing from England—and yet, now, he felt an air of anticipation.

Within a matter of weeks, his fate had shifted. Velaria's father had come to see him at Colford Abbey, demanding answers about Constantinople.

'I need to know what h-happened to my daughter,' Sir Ademar had said. *'I w-want answers.'*

Brian had faced the knight squarely and stared back. *'Ask Velaria. She will tell you what she wants you to know.'* He had no intention of betraying her confidence, even if her father was trying to help.

Sir Ademar's expression had held fury before he'd taken a breath and calmed himself. *'She's suffering, and I d-don't know how to help her.'*

Although Brian had recognised the worry on the man's face, he'd wanted to know more. *'Tell me.'*

The knight had hesitated. After a pause, he'd said, *'She hardly eats. She doesn't s-sleep well. It's like she's b-become a shadow.'*

Brian understood exactly what Velaria was feeling. They'd gone hungry for so long, it was difficult to imagine always having enough food to eat. And the nightmares haunted him, just as they did her.

'I'll come with you to Ardennes,' he'd told her father.

He needed to see her again—especially now. Not only for her sake, but because his own life had shifted since he'd learned about his father.

The abbot's story had shocked him, and Brian still didn't know how to feel about it. All his life, he'd been nothing but a serf, whereas Robert and his half brother, Piers, had been strong warriors and the sons of an earl. And although the two men had treated him like an equal brother, he'd always remained in their shadow.

Until now.

He could still hardly believe Father Oswold's revelation, for it seemed impossible. And even if it were true, that his bloodline was more than that of a miller's son, it didn't change the fact that he was still a bastard.

If he dared approach his true father, the man was likely to deny Brian as his son. He wouldn't want anything to do with him or might believe he'd only come with the intent of demanding an inheritance.

But there was a chance of living a different life. He couldn't deny that, if he had the opportunity, he wanted Velaria at his side. And now, he had the chance to change their fate.

'I don't think y-you should see my daughter again,' the knight had admitted. *'It will only bring bad m-memories.'*

'You came to me because I have the answers you seek,' Brian had pressed. *'I can help if you take me to her.'*

The knight hadn't answered at first. Then, *'Tell me what you c-can.'*

Brian had met his gaze evenly. He could share the challenges both of them had faced without betraying her confidence.

'We were forced to fight every three days,' he admitted.

'Kadir chose our opponents, and we fought in the arena.' He'd raised his eyes to her father. *'We fought to the death.'*

The knight's expression had tightened. *'And you did nothing to s-stop it?'*

'We survived and escaped. No one else did.' He'd lowered his voice and added, *'Not a day goes by that we don't remember those we were forced to kill.'*

For a long time, Sir Ademar had stared back at him, waiting for him to say more.

Brian had straightened and said, *'Anything else is her story to tell. Not mine.'*

The knight had studied him once again, as if to assess his honour. Then he'd asked, *'Do you still w-wish to help her?'*

Brian hadn't hesitated. *'I do, yes.'*

Sir Ademar had continued, *'Your sister lives in Ireland, doesn't she?'*

He must have spoken with Father Oswold, Brian had realised.

'She lives in the north with her husband.'

The knight had given a nod. From the resolute expression on his face, he had made his own plans.

'We plan to take Velaria to Ireland for a c-celebration at Bealtaine. My wife has family there, and while we are at Laochre, it is our w-wish that Velaria choose a husband and be married. If you can convince her to w-wed a suitable nobleman, I will provide you with a horse and travelling supplies. You will also be p-paid in silver.'

The thought of Velaria marrying another man had sent a flare of jealousy within him. Although he had nothing to offer yet, Brian couldn't stand aside and watch her wed someone else.

'And what if I offer for her hand in marriage?'

Her father's expression had grown guarded. *'I will not*

give her hand in m-marriage to just any man. You must have l-lands and a means of supporting her.' He'd paused and asked, *'Who is your father?'*

Brian held back the truth, for the knight likely wouldn't believe him. *'I never knew my father. I was raised by a miller and his wife.'*

The knight had sent him a knowing look. *'Then you cannot provide the life she deserves.'*

Not yet. But one day, Brian vowed. He would confront his father, though he didn't know if the man would acknowledge or help him. He might not want another son or worse, he might not believe him.

He suppressed the thought. For now, he would seek help from Morwenna and Robert.

'Your task is to c-convince Velaria to agree to wed a suitable man,' Ademar had offered, *'though she has already said she will not marry.'* He'd stared hard at Brian. *'I understand that she suffered in Constantinople. But we will no longer stand b-back and watch her fade into nothing. If an arranged marriage will bring back Velaria's h-happiness, then that is what we will do.'*

Brian hadn't argued, though he would never allow Velaria to be forced into anything.

And so, he had made the journey here, for her sake and for his. Whether she wanted it or not, he intended to protect Velaria.

He'd been given a second chance to forge a different life. He intended to seize it and build his own fortune, even if that meant changing himself in whatever way was necessary. He simply had to convince her father that he was an honourable man of worth—and Velaria needed to know that any marriage between them would offer freedom, with no demands.

As he rode closer, he realised that Laochre was one of the largest castles he'd ever seen. Made of limestone, the outer curtain wall appeared to be twelve feet high, and guards patrolled the parapets. Four square towers stood on every corner of the castle.

Brian had heard the stories of the legendary MacEgan King Patrick and his Norman bride, Queen Isabel. They had built one of the strongest fortresses along the southern coast of Ireland, and they still controlled most of the region since several of the MacEgan brothers dwelled nearby.

It seemed strange to be invited to a place such as this. The last time he'd seen a castle was at Penrith, and even there, he'd been nothing but a serf. The familiar doubts intruded, and for a moment, he questioned what he was doing. He knew no one here, save Velaria and her father. It felt like trespassing, and he hardly knew what to say to the guards. The voices of doubt taunted him with his past, despite his warrior training.

But he straightened his posture and rode towards the gates, telling himself that he did possess noble blood—even if he was a bastard. He had to become someone else and act like a nobleman's son, even if it felt like a lie.

He hoped Sir Ademar and Lady Katherine had made arrangements for a place for him to stay. Possibly he could sleep on the floor of the Great Chamber or even in the stables. But as he stared at the vast holdings, it reminded him of how little he had in comparison.

When he reached the gate, he gave his name, and the taller guard gave a nod before he spoke in Irish to the other soldier. He led Brian inside and motioned for him to wait. Within moments, an older man with a long white beard came forward to greet him while a stable lad took his horse.

'It's welcome you are,' the man greeted him, speaking

his language. 'I am Brendan MacEgan, steward of Laochre Castle. Follow me, and I will show you to your chamber. Lady Katherine and Sir Ademar told us to expect you.'

'My chamber?' He'd never imagined he would have a place of his own to sleep.

The man nodded. 'We have a wing of the castle devoted to guests. The rooms are quite small, but I hope you'll find it comfortable.'

Brian walked behind the steward, studying the inner bailey. There were training grounds on one side, while women worked on dyeing cloth, laying out blue and green lengths of wool to dry in the sun on the opposite side.

'You may join the king and queen for a meal within the hour,' the steward said. 'Choose a place at one of the lower tables. Sir Ademar and Lady Katherine bade me to tell you that they will not acknowledge your presence. They do not wish for Velaria to be aware that they brought you here.'

'I understand.'

The steward led him up the stairs and down a narrow hallway. He opened up the last door, and inside the chamber stood a single bed and a low chair. A narrow slit in the stone wall served as a window that looked down on the inner bailey. Although the room was tiny, Brian was grateful for their hospitality.

He set down his belongings, and the steward added, 'You may explore the castle and the grounds as you wish. King Patrick and Queen Isabel will be wanting to meet you during the noontide meal.'

He thanked the man, and when he was alone, he walked over to the window. For a time, he studied the MacEgan soldiers, surprised to see a group of women training alongside them. An older woman stopped to correct a few of the younger girls and then observed as they practised their fighting.

Brian wondered if she was one of Velaria's relatives. Perhaps this was the woman who had trained her to fight. He recognised a few of the motions Velaria had used in battle.

His gaze moved across the inner bailey, and when Brian could not see much farther, he decided to venture out on the parapets for a better view. He left his quarters and once he was outside, he saw another staircase leading above. He found a spot to observe the others, and after studying the courtyard, he finally saw her.

For a moment, he hardly recognised Velaria. She sat atop the opposite staircase, her brown hair covered with a veil while she wore a gown with a long green overdress. Around her shoulders, she wore a loose wrap. But her face and shoulders were painfully thin, as if she were still in prison.

A full moon had passed since he'd left her at Ardennes—and he was starting to realise that it had been a mistake to leave her behind. She hadn't healed any more than he had.

No one would guess this beautiful woman had wielded a sword and killed to survive. Brian recognised the emptiness in her eyes, the sense that she was here—but not really here. He'd experienced the sensation himself while they were on their voyage home.

There was a sense of being disconnected from the world, and he remembered feeling as if he didn't belong anywhere. He'd been unable to fight while his body healed, and the only person who'd understood the helplessness and isolation had been Velaria. It was she who had kept him steady during those months of endless sailing, and he owed her the same.

His earlier thoughts of remaining hidden weren't possible any more. He didn't care what her parents had asked of him—he couldn't let her fade away any longer.

Slowly, Brian walked along the narrow pathway, making his way towards her. As he drew closer, he saw that Velaria kept her gaze away from the fighting but stared over at the women who were busy dyeing cloth and directing the children to help.

He continued walking until he drew near, and then he moved silently behind her. For a moment, he considered what to say. She would demand to know why he was here, and he already had reasons prepared.

'I'm surprised you aren't fighting among the soldiers,' he said at last. Within seconds, she spun around with her dagger aimed at his throat.

There she was, the girl who knew how to defend herself from anyone and anything. 'It's good to see you haven't forgotten how to wield a blade.'

'By the gods. I could have—' Her voice broke off. Before Velaria could say another word, he crushed her into an embrace, pulling her back into the shadows. She gripped him hard, her body trembling. And when he pulled back, emotions flooded her eyes.

'What are you doing here, Savaş?' she asked. The nickname was a reminder of the fighter he'd been, and he held her waist for a moment.

'My sister is in Ireland,' he answered. 'I learned that your family was coming to visit the MacEgan tribe, and I wanted to see how you are.' It was one of many half-truths he'd invented. He kept his hands at her waist while he eyed her gown. 'I'm not used to seeing you dressed like a knight's daughter.'

Her face flushed, and she took a step back from him. It was as if she'd suddenly realised she'd thrown herself into his arms. 'How are you? And your shoulder, is it continuing to heal?'

'It's better than it was.' But he had no intention of telling her the full truth about his injury. 'Will you walk with me?'

Velaria nodded. 'Of course. We have a little time until the meal.'

She led him down the stairs, and they crossed through the inner bailey, past the fighters, until they came to the barbican gate. She greeted the guards, and Brian remained at her side while they left the castle grounds, crossing over a bridge. A small village stood a short distance beyond it.

'The MacEgans will celebrate Bealtaine on the morrow, but the competitions will begin tonight,' she remarked. 'My family and I were invited to share in their celebration.' With a glance behind her, she added, 'I haven't seen so many preparations since I was younger. There will be games and feasting for days afterward.'

He slowed his pace and reached for her wrist. 'You don't look as if you've been feasting.'

Her face paled, and she shrugged. 'I've tried. But sometimes—I'm just not hungry. Or it hurts to eat.' She pulled her hand back and stared ahead at the dirt path before she looked back at him. 'You look good, Savaş.' Her cheeks grew flushed when she gave the compliment.

He gave a nod to acknowledge her words and then said, 'You're still having the nightmares, aren't you?'

She flinched but lowered her head. 'Most nights, yes. I try to sleep, but—' She shook her head. 'I still see the faces of the people I killed. I despise myself for the woman I had to become, but I can't change what happened.'

'We did what we had to do,' he said quietly.

'I know that. But it's hard.' She shielded her eyes against the sun and looked back at Laochre Castle. The limestone walls were shadowed against the horizon.

'I don't feel as if I deserve to live a life like this,' she admitted. 'They were innocent men and women, and I slaughtered them.'

'You're alive,' he said quietly. 'And no, you won't ever forget what happened. All you can do is move forward.'

Velaria exhaled a shuddering breath. 'My parents want me to marry and start over.'

He hid his own reaction, though he knew her father's intentions already. 'What do *you* want, Velaria?'

She met his gaze and thought a moment. 'I want to be the girl I used to be. The one who was happy.'

Although he understood her wish, there was a darkness in her voice—almost as if she didn't believe it could ever happen.

They reached the edge of the village, and Velaria started walking up one of the trails up a hillside. The pathway was steep, and he could see that stacks of peat and wood had been arranged at the top of the hill for a large bonfire.

She sat down on the hillside near the unlit fire and stared off at the horizon. He joined her, his shoulder pressed against hers. For a moment, it reminded him of the nights after their battles, when they would sit against one another in the darkness. In moments like those, they'd simply been glad to be alive.

The afternoon sun rose high above them, and she lifted her face to it. Velaria was beautiful, just as she'd always been. But beneath the surface, the shadows and darkness loomed, threatening to pull her down. He'd fought them back himself, time and again. It was easier to shut it all out, to bury it deep.

There wasn't enough time to heal these wounds. And although he wanted to find his sister—and perhaps even his true father if he dared—he also knew he couldn't leave Velaria behind.

'What if you helped train the women fighters here?' he asked. 'You could teach them how to defend themselves. I saw an older woman working with them.'

She ventured a smile. 'You saw my aunt Honora. She is visiting for Bealtaine, along with her husband, Ewan MacEgan.' Then her smile faded. 'I don't want to fight any more, Savaş. I can't.'

He understood the memories she didn't want to face. 'You know a great deal more than they do about fighting.'

She shook her head. 'God willing, I'll never touch a sword again.'

He didn't want her to descend back into the darkness of their past, so he offered his hand as they sat on the hillside. 'Tell me about your family's Irish customs at Bealtaine.'

At that, her mood shifted, and she said, 'I've only seen it once or twice, when I was a girl. The men and women will light the fires at night. They drive the cattle between the fires to bless them as they go into the summer pastures.'

He kept her hand in his, and her face grew wistful as she imagined it. 'My cousin Alanna believes in fairy lore. She will tell fortunes and there will be games and feasting. Then later—' Her voice broke off, and she flushed.

'Later what?' he questioned. When she didn't answer at first, he guessed, 'Men and women pair off, don't they?'

Velaria nodded. 'There used to be an older festival where a maiden was chosen to represent the goddess. She would lie with a chosen man, and it would bless the fertility of the land.' She gripped his hand and stared off into the distance. 'We still choose a man and a woman, but I don't think they lie together any more. My aunt Aileen spoke of it once.'

Below them, Brian saw people starting to walk towards the castle keep. 'I was told that King Patrick and Queen Isabel wanted me to say hello. Will you introduce me to them?'

'Of course.' She pulled her hand away and lifted her skirts as they began to walk down the hillside. The wind slid against her veil, pushing it back. In the afternoon sunlight, her brown hair gleamed.

On impulse, he lifted her veil away. 'Why do you wear this, Velaria?'

'Because ladies are supposed to cover their hair.' She tried to take it back, but he held it out of her way.

'You're in Ireland now. Why not be like the other young women? Take down your hair and be free.'

'I spent many years rebelling against my mother's rules. She despaired because I was always taking my brother's armour and coming home with blood and bruises.' A hint of a smile crossed her face. 'Perhaps I want to wear the gowns and veils now.'

Because wearing the clothing of a noblewoman was far removed from the young woman she'd been in Constantinople. Brian supposed it made sense, and he gave back the veil.

'I always liked your hair, even though you kept it braided,' he admitted.

'If it hadn't been, it could have been used against me.' She covered her hair and secured the veil with a narrow band.

'I am glad you didn't cut it.' For a moment, he wondered how long it was. She'd only kept it down past her shoulders in Constantinople, but it seemed to be down to the middle of her back now.

'And I am glad you shaved off your beard,' she teased, reaching out to touch his face. 'I know you hated how long it grew in our prison.'

The moment her hand cupped his cheek, something stirred within him. Though she hadn't meant anything by it, he couldn't deny the rise of interest as he remembered her hands massaging his shoulders at night, after a battle. He met her gaze and covered her hand with his own. He gripped it lightly, waiting to see what she would do.

Embarrassment coloured her face, and she pulled her hand away. 'We should hurry. The meal will be starting soon, and I'll introduce you to the king and queen.'

'And your own family,' he suggested. 'I would like to meet them.'

'I—' She seemed unsettled by the idea and offered, 'I suppose you could.'

She quickened her pace to walk down the hillside, and he caught her elbow gently. 'Velaria, wait.' She turned back, and he continued, 'I don't want to remember the past or speak of Constantinople again. Not while I'm here. Let us simply enjoy the festival.'

She nodded in agreement. 'As friends.' Something shifted within her then, and it did seem that she was willing to push back the shadows for a time.

'Aye. As friends.' He took her hand and looped it in his arm.

But as he walked alongside her, he sensed that she would have to confront her nightmares and her worst fears before she could heal.

And so would he.

Chapter Five

Although she was glad Savaş had come to see her, Velaria was entirely too aware of the knowing looks that passed among the people as they walked to one of the lower tables. Her father, in particular, tensed at the sight of him, though Ademar didn't approach them.

She didn't understand what had changed. Savaş had refused to spend one more night at her side after he'd escorted her to Ardennes. He'd sworn that he couldn't.

And yet now he'd discovered that her family was at Laochre and had decided to visit? His sister lived in the north, so why had he come so far south? Something didn't make sense, for she'd heard nothing from him in all these weeks. What had changed?

Part of her didn't want to question it. He would only be here for a little while, so what did it matter? He could share Bealtaine with her, and then he would leave again.

Her smile grew strained at the thought. Although Savaş sat beside her and offered her portions of food, she still couldn't tolerate very much of it. He must have noticed her lack of appetite, but thankfully, he didn't remark on it.

In contrast, it was as if Savaş couldn't get enough to eat. He had started to regain more strength, and his face was fuller. She couldn't deny her own fascination with the transformation. His skin held the deep colour of the sun, the same as hers. But his face held a strength and intensity that stole her breath. A sudden flare of interest caught her at the memory of his fleeting kiss in the arena.

She told herself it had only been a gesture for the crowd during their last fight. It had meant nothing to him, for he hadn't kissed her since. Better to lock the memory away and remember that he did not think of her beyond friendship and never had.

And still, she wondered why he had journeyed here.

Her thoughts were interrupted when the king and queen left the dais and came over to speak with them. Queen Isabel's face held the soft lines of time, creasing wrinkles against her eyes and mouth as she smiled warmly. She leaned against her husband as they drew close and said, 'We are so glad to see you safely returned to us, Velaria.'

'I am happy to be back with my family,' she answered, accepting the queen's embrace. 'May I introduce you to Brian of Penrith? His sister lives at Dunbough with her husband, and he will travel there soon.'

Then Queen Isabel turned and said, 'I bid you welcome, Brian.' Then she turned and said, 'And this is Patrick, my husband.'

'Your Grace,' he started to say, but the king only laughed and shook his head.

'Neither Isabel nor I care much for titles. Patrick will do.'

Even so, Brian bowed his head.

'I know Velaria's parents are grateful that you brought her home safely,' the king said. 'As are we.'

Isabel smiled and added, 'I hope you will stay with us throughout our Bealtaine celebration.'

'For a time,' he agreed. 'And then I will travel north to find my sister.'

It was a reminder that Velaria needed to hear. He wasn't going to stay. She'd accepted that already. And yet, her wayward heart couldn't stop thinking of Savaş as she imagined a future that would never be.

You're behaving like a coward, her brain reminded her.

But then, that was what she'd become, wasn't it? A shadow with no life at all, no reason to fight. Something stirred within her that felt like shame. This wasn't the woman she'd been before. She didn't like this person, not at all.

There had been a time when men and women feared her, when she had been one of their greatest fighters. And not a single person here, except Savaş, knew it.

It was as if something shifted inside her, with the realisation that Kadir and his men had broken her. They had turned her from a warrior into a maiden.

Her hands clenched in her skirts with restlessness, for she had no idea what to do now.

'You are welcome at Laochre,' Queen Isabel was saying to Savaş. 'If you need anything at all, you've only to ask.'

He bowed again, and after they'd gone, he turned back to her. Before he could speak, her parents approached. Although her mother's face held warmth, her father appeared uneasy.

'You must be Brian of Penrith,' Katherine said with a smile, reaching for his hands. 'I am so glad to meet you at last.'

'Lady Katherine.' He bowed before her, and Velaria didn't miss her mother's knowing smile.

'You should have stayed with us for a few days,' Katherine chided. 'At the very least, we wanted to thank you for bringing our daughter home.' She smiled and added, 'This is my husband, Sir Ademar.'

Her father gave a curt nod and then offered to Brian, 'Would you walk with m-me a moment? I would like to hear more about C-Constantinople.'

From the look in his eyes, it appeared that her father fully intended to interrogate Savaş. 'Another time, Father,' she started to say. 'He's only just arrived.'

But Brian relented and said, 'I would be glad to tell you more.' He followed Ademar away from the tables of food towards the large doors at the end of the Great Chamber.

'Why is Father wanting to speak with Brian alone?' she demanded of her mother. 'They've only just met.'

Katherine only smiled. 'I'm certain he has his reasons. But Brian *is* rather handsome, isn't he?'

It made her wonder if her mother was attempting to bring them together. Although part of her did care for Savaş, she couldn't forget that he had refused her on the ship. 'Mother, he is not my suitor, so do not interfere.'

But her mother sent her a sidelong look. 'Would you want him to be?'

Her face turned crimson, and she shook her head.

Not like this. Not out of pity.

'I've already told you, I don't intend to marry anyone.'

'We will see.' Her mother clearly wasn't listening, likely because she had a romantic heart. 'There will be many visitors for Bealtaine,' Katherine continued. 'My sister tells me that you will have your choice of suitors.' She reached out and took Velaria's hand. 'Honora has invited many noblemen, both Irish and Norman. At least consider each of them.'

Her expression shifted from gentleness to one of determination. 'But if you do not choose someone soon, your father will choose. And I agree with him. A new beginning with a home of your own is the best thing for you.'

No. She would never allow herself to be forced into marriage. But even if she protested again, her mother wouldn't listen. Instead, she told Katherine, 'I am going to return to my chamber.'

She passed through the Great Chamber and up the winding stairs to the room she shared with her cousin. Thankfully, Mairead wasn't there, but she saw something else that made her stop short. It was a *colc* sword that someone had left behind.

Though it conjured memories of the fighter she'd been, the very sight of the weapon made her breath catch. It was a physical reminder of the past, and for a moment, Velaria faltered. Why would anyone leave it here for her?

Carefully, she picked it up by the hilt. The balance of the weapon was excellent, and it felt like another part of herself. Which was a dangerous thought, she decided as she placed it atop a wooden chest.

She glanced outside the window and saw men and women bringing more wood and peat to the hills for the fires. An ache caught within her heart, a restless questioning of who she was now. She wished she knew where to go or what to do.

The door burst open, and out of sheer instinct, she seized the weapon and held it in a fighting stance.

But it was only her cousin. 'Look at you.' Mairead beamed with pride. 'You terrify me, Velaria.'

She laid the weapon against the window again. 'Who left this sword here?'

'Most likely Aunt Honora. There will be competitions tonight. She probably wants you to show off your skills.'

Mairead was only a year younger than herself, and she crossed her arms, sending her a pointed look. 'Who is that man who just arrived? I saw you introducing him to your family.'

'Brian of Penrith,' she answered. 'He and I were captives in Constantinople together.'

'He's yours then?' There was a hint of interest in Mairead's voice.

'We are friends,' was all she said. In truth, she didn't know what Savaş was to her any more. But an ache caught within her body, a yearning that she couldn't quite push away.

It was clear that her cousin was quite fascinated with him. 'So, you won't mind if I...talk to him during Bealtaine?'

There was a slight prickle within her, which was ridiculous. Instead, Velaria said, 'No, it's all right.' She forced herself to say the words, although inwardly, her feelings about it were tangled up.

Mairead smiled warmly. 'Oh, good. Father has been asking me to consider possible suitors.'

'Mine, too.' Velaria sighed. 'It's one of the reasons why they brought me here.'

Her cousin's eyes turned interested. 'You don't look happy about it. Don't you want to be married?'

Velaria thought back to the night she'd shared with Drogan and shuddered. 'No, I don't.'

'Well, *I* do,' Mairead said, 'I want to be in love.' She let out a sigh of her own. 'But my father and brother are impossible. No man is good enough for them.' She cast another look at Velaria. 'But your friend *is* quite handsome.'

A fiercely protective urge came over her, and Velaria bit back the desire to tell her cousin no. Instead, she told her, 'You should know that Brian does not have a title or lands.'

It felt petty to say it, and yet Mairead was the daughter of the king and queen. She would be expected to marry another king or, at the very least, a high-ranking nobleman.

'My father has enough land for us, if need be,' she answered. 'And I need not make a decision so soon.' Her cousin sat down in a chair, smiling brightly. 'I do love Bealtaine. It's one of my favourite festivals.'

'And why is that?' Velaria said.

'Oh, I think you already know,' Mairead teased. 'I want to know who will become the Horned One and who will be the goddess.'

'The competitions,' Velaria guessed. Tonight, the men would fight for the honour of becoming the Horned One. On the morrow would be the women's competition and the bonfires.

Mairead winked at Velaria. 'The first night is still my favourite. Is there anything more fun than to watch the handsome men?'

Once, she would have agreed with her cousin. But now Velaria didn't think she could watch them for fear of the memories.

'I don't think Brian of Penrith will be among the competitors,' she told her cousin.

'I think you're wrong.' Mairead stood and took her hand. 'Look outside. They are gathering the men now.'

Velaria rose and went over to the window. Outside, she could see dozens of men in a small crowd while another warrior gave instructions.

'I cannot see him.'

'He's there, I promise you,' Mairead insisted. 'And after our meal this evening, we can watch. Perhaps you'll find the man you're meant to marry.'

'I have no intention of marrying anyone,' Velaria said.

'We'll see.' Mairead's eyes sparkled with anticipation.

'You're late,' Sir Ademar accused Brian. 'Velaria's best chance to f-find a suitor to wed is during Bealtaine.'

'She's not ready.' He'd recognised the bleakness in Velaria's eyes, as if she had lost herself in the nightmares of the past. He knew exactly what that was like. For months on their journey here, he'd awakened night after night with his own visions of horror. Only cold discipline had helped him lock the bad dreams away. And he knew she suffered the same.

'None of you understands what she's endured,' Brian shot back. 'The last thing she needs is to be forced into marriage.'

'You agreed to t-talk to her,' Sir Ademar warned. 'Your task is to c-convince her to wed, and we expect you to keep that bargain.'

He knew her father was only trying to help, but Brian hadn't given up on the idea of a marriage between them, despite his poverty. He couldn't imagine standing aside while Velaria wed someone else. No. He couldn't do it. But earlier, when he'd voiced his own offer to wed her, the knight had dismissed the idea.

He thought of telling Sir Ademar about his bloodline, but until he'd gained his father's acceptance, it meant nothing. They would only think he was lying for his own gain.

'I will talk with her.' He faced the knight, letting him think what he would.

Her father stared back at him and gave a nod. 'See that you do.' Then the man added, 'But you should know—if Velaria does not choose a husband within the next few d-days, I will choose someone for her.'

The thought of one of those men touching her was like an invisible blade to his skin. No one else would understand Velaria the way he did. 'It's too soon for that,' Brian argued.

Sir Ademar's face was rigid with resolve. 'I will not

stand aside and watch my daughter grow frail and die. Find a way to convince her to live again.'

Brian faced her father and didn't back down. 'I will. But give her more time and the freedom she deserves.'

From the look on the knight's face, he had no intention of backing down. If anything, he appeared even more resolute.

After Sir Ademar left, Brian tried to find Velaria since she hadn't been among the ladies. When the men gathered for the competitions, he finally saw her. She wore a blue gown with a white veil and stood beside a young woman of a similar age. He learned that the maiden was Mairead MacEgan, the only daughter of Queen Isabel and King Patrick.

An older warrior spoke to him in Irish, before he switched into the Norman tongue. 'Are you joining in the competitions?' he asked. The man's blond hair was shot with grey, but mischief brewed in his eyes.

'I hadn't planned on it.'

'Yes, you are.' The warrior seized him by the arm. 'It would be an insult to your hosts if you did not.'

Though Brian hadn't considered it in that way, the warrior was right. 'What sort of competitions are they?'

'The usual,' he remarked. 'Wrestling. Archery. Sword fighting.' His gaze moved towards the red scar that ran from Brian's shoulder to the base of his throat. 'You look as if you've seen battle before.'

'I fought in Constantinople.' Though he led the man to believe it was during the Crusade, it wasn't entirely a lie. He regarded the warrior and saw that the man's right hand was deeply scarred. 'It seems you've done some fighting yourself.'

'Indeed.' The warrior flexed his hand. 'After this injury, my wife cared for me. I would have lost the hand, were it not for Aileen.' He paused a moment and said, 'I am Connor MacEgan.'

Brian introduced himself and studied the man. There was no trace of anger or regret in Connor, despite his injury. He'd accepted his fate and had made the most of it.

'I don't know if I should join the competitions,' Brian admitted. 'My injury has healed, but my skills are...not the same.'

Connor inclined his head. 'You should go and see my wife. Aileen's healing skills are legendary. But in the meantime, there's no harm in finding out what you can still do. And what you can't.'

The man's suggestion held merit. It had been over a year since he'd fought an opponent, and Brian didn't know his limitations. But this might be the opportunity to learn whether the injury had caused irreparable damage. None of the MacEgans knew of his skills.

'I suppose you are right.'

Connor smiled. 'Of course I am. Strip off your tunic and go join the others.' He gave Brian a slight shove towards the men.

He removed his tunic and set it aside while he joined the fighters. One of the men was speaking Irish, presumable giving the rules of competition. Brian didn't understand a word of it, but when the man had finished, the others gave a cheer of approval.

During the first round of archery, his shoulder wouldn't allow him to pull back the bow as far as he wanted, but he did well enough and at least struck the target each time. Another man bested them all.

Brian searched the crowd for another glimpse of Velaria, but she had disappeared with her cousin. It wasn't surprising, given her aversion to fighting.

He continued on to the next round, which was wrestling. His opponent was lean and muscular, and for a moment, Brian took his measure. He suspected the man would be fast, and sure enough, he barely sidestepped as the man lunged. When he grappled with his opponent, it felt good to push back with the strength he had left.

But in his mind, the past and present overlapped. He remembered an early battle when his opponent had disarmed him, leaving him with nothing but his bare hands and his wits as weapons. Then, just as now, he slipped into a place of calm where the only thing that mattered was survival.

Until the man twisted his arm. Pain knifed through his shoulder, and Brian barely managed to push back. He gritted past the discomfort and used his forearm to cut off his opponent's airway. The man dropped down, and Brian managed to pin him.

Although he'd won the match, the victory meant little, for he was still unable to fight at his full strength. It had only been good fortune that he was able to change positions and win.

If he had been back in the fighting pits, he would have been killed—and the thought was sobering. If he'd been at his full strength, no man here could have bested him. And it was frustrating to know that he wasn't the same champion he'd been before.

He glanced up at the stairs and finally saw Velaria again. Her complexion was pale, and he could see that she wasn't enjoying the competitions at all. When she disappeared back inside the castle keep, he slipped inside to follow her.

She stood on the far side of the Great Chamber, pretending to listen to the music an older woman played on the harp. But he could see the unsettled air about her. She appeared shaken up by what she'd watched, even though it had hardly been more than contests.

Brian wanted to distract her, and so he walked forward and touched her shoulder. When Velaria glanced up at him, her face flushed. Then he remembered he still wasn't wearing a tunic, which might be the reason for her discomfort.

'Did you need something?' she asked.

'Will you walk with me?' At her hesitation, he added, 'To the parapets.'

She gave a nod and joined him. He rested his palm against her spine, guiding her away from the people.

'I didn't realise you were competing among the other men,' she began.

'Only as a courtesy to the king and queen.' And to find out what skills he now lacked. He'd already decided to consult with Connor's wife on the morrow. Though he didn't suppose the healer could do anything for an old wound, there was no harm in asking.

'Are you…going to continue fighting?' She appeared uncertain about it.

'I might. I still have the sword competition left.' He didn't miss her slight shudder. When she said nothing more, he added, 'I hope you'll show them your skills on the morrow. Not a woman here could defeat you.'

She said nothing, but her expression had turned grim. Brian reached for her hand and led her up another staircase. Below them, the competitions continued, but she turned her back and stared out at the sea in the distance. 'It's beautiful here,' she said softly.

'It is.' He didn't take his gaze from her, even as he questioned what he was even doing. He'd sworn to help Velaria overcome the nightmares that haunted her still. Perhaps he could convince her to join him at his sister's home. But he already knew her father would not abandon the idea of a marriage for her.

'Why did you come to Ireland?' she asked. Beneath her tone, he heard the edge of suspicion. 'After you left Ardennes, I thought I would never see you again.'

He gave a nod. 'I thought it was better to stay away from you.'

Her face turned crimson, and she looked away. 'I know you don't want more than friendship between us. And truly, I understand that—'

'That's not why I left.'

He stood beside her, and she startled him when she leaned in close. With the quiet invitation, he drew his arm around her waist, and she rested her cheek against his chest as they both stared out at the darkened horizon. The touch of her skin against his was an invitation he couldn't deny. He removed the veil and let it fall away while he stroked her brown hair.

'Then why did you?' she whispered.

His skin heated beneath the palm of her hand, and he wished he were wearing a tunic. Though she likely thought nothing of it, he was entirely conscious of her skin against his. His body craved her touch, though he tried to force it back. But it felt good to hold her in his arms again.

'I left because I'm not the sort of man your family wants you to wed. I have nothing to give.'

In his embrace, he could feel her tension. 'I'm not going to be married, Savaş. Not to anyone.'

Her unspoken words were, *Not even to you.*

A darkness caught within him, but he understood her reasons. 'He's going to try to force a marriage if you don't choose someone.'

'Then I will run away again,' she said softly. 'I won't be any man's prisoner. Especially not as a wife.'

She wasn't going to change her mind—that much was evident. But he wondered if other reasons haunted her. She had never spoken of the night Kadir had taken her captive. A tightness caught in his chest at the thought of her suffering—not only that night but also when she'd run away with Sir Drogan.

Brian wanted to ease that pain, to show her that touch did not have to be a violation. But he didn't know if she would ever want to face that fear again.

She turned back to the competitions, and he kept her in his embrace, standing behind with his arms encircling her.

Then he leaned his mouth against her throat. 'No one will ever force you into something you don't want, Velaria. I promise you that.' His lips grazed the side of her neck, and gooseflesh rose upon her skin.

'I know,' she whispered.

Within his embrace, he felt the tremor of her body. And he realised, then, that it was the fighting that bothered her. He held her slender body against his, and she touched his hands, leaning back. 'You don't like to watch them, do you?'

She didn't answer. But when he pulled back to look at her, he saw that her eyes were closed.

'These competitions aren't the same as the battles we fought.'

'I know,' she repeated. 'But I still don't want to watch them.' Her voice was the barest whisper as he moved her long braid to the side of her shoulder.

He understood that—and yet, he suspected that overcoming her fears meant facing them. Perhaps even wielding a sword once again.

'What are you doing?' she asked, as he began to massage her shoulders.

'Distracting you.' He caressed her arms, and without thinking, he lowered his mouth to her nape. She gripped his arms, a soft sigh escaping. He kissed a path up the column of her throat while he continued kneading her skin.

'Savaş,' she whispered. The single word was enough to make him stop. In his embrace, she turned to face him. He held steady and unmoving, though he craved more from her.

'That day in the arena,' she said. 'It was the first and only time you kissed me, until now.'

'I know.' He pulled her hair aside and rested his hand against her nape. 'Did it bother you?'

She met his gaze evenly. 'I don't know why you waited so long.'

Her words flared his interest, and he bent to kiss the opposite side of her neck. 'It wasn't because I didn't want to.'

Beneath his mouth, he sensed her tension. The thought of exploring the rest of her bare skin with his mouth was arousing, and he tried not to think of what lay beneath her gown.

'I remember the nights we eased each other's pain after a fight,' she said quietly. 'I've missed it.'

'So have I.'

But Velaria surprised him when she pushed his hands away and moved behind him. This time, he watched the fighting while her hands moved upon his shoulders. She knew exactly where the pressure points were, and he groaned in thanks at the massage.

'This is dangerous, Velaria,' he told her.

'Why?' Her voice was barely above a whisper.

Because he didn't trust himself not to touch her. He craved her hands upon his skin, and right now, he ached to be with her.

'Because you're making me want what I can't have.' He turned to face her, bringing her palms back up to his heart.

Her blue eyes stared into his, and she straightened. 'Good.'

And with that, she took his face between her hands and stood on tiptoe to kiss him.

Velaria knew why Savaş had brought her here, though she'd already given up on the idea of ever wanting to watch anyone fight again. But the distraction he'd offered had been a taste of forbidden fruit she hadn't known she'd craved. She'd missed his touch and the way he'd massaged the aching tension in her shoulders.

She didn't know why she'd kissed him. Perhaps it had been impulse, or a need to know whether she'd imagined the attraction between them. Or maybe it was a way to push back the memories she'd locked away, the ones she could never face again.

He was gentle with her, cupping her cheek while he took her offering. His mouth was soft, an invitation instead of a claiming.

But right now, she was even more aware that he stood half-naked before her. Though she'd touched his bare shoulders before, she'd forgotten what it was to trace every line of sinewy muscle. He was stronger than she'd ever imagined, and she lost herself for a moment. Her body warmed, and she grew sensitive to his mouth upon hers.

His kiss coaxed her to respond, and she was caught up in the sensations that poured through her. No man had ever kissed her in this way before, as if she were his reason for breathing. For a moment, she savoured his mouth on hers, feeling her body respond.

Until her fingers grazed the ragged edge of the scar

she'd given him. Velaria jolted and pulled away, suddenly realising what it was.

She didn't know how he'd survived such a wound. It was a miracle he'd lived at all. The weight of guilt flooded through her, and she took a step back. 'I'm keeping you from the competitions. You—you should go and join the others.'

His gaze remained steady, revealing none of his thoughts. Was that pity in his eyes? She looked away, and he gave back her veil before he walked down the stairs. Her fingers were shaking as she put her veil and circlet back in place. Only after he was gone did she turn back.

What are you doing? she demanded of herself.

It was as if someone had seized her and shaken her out of the hazy dream she'd been living. She had allowed her fears to take over, changing her into a spineless coward.

These were only training competitions, meant to allow the men to test themselves and for entertainment. Although she couldn't quite push away the fear, she forced herself to walk down the stairs. One step first, then the other. When she reached the bottom of the stairs, she found Mairead waiting.

'There you are, Velaria! I've been looking for you.' Her cousin took her hand and led her deeper into the crowd.

'What is it?' she tried to ask, but Mairead continued guiding her past all the people. She saw Savaş standing among the men waiting for the sword competitions, and a lump caught in her throat.

He'll be fine, she reassured herself.

But even now, her mouth was swollen from the kiss she'd taken from him.

'Where are you taking me?' she asked Mairead as they went up the stairs and into the Great Chamber.

'Alanna is waiting for us,' her cousin said with a bright smile.

Velaria suppressed a groan. Their older cousin Alanna enjoyed telling fortunes and making love charms. It was harmless fun, she supposed, but Mairead was more than eager to hear her own future.

When they reached the main hearth, Velaria saw a circle of stools. Her cousin Alanna sat before a low table across from another young maiden.

'Velaria,' Alanna said warmly, rising from her seat. She welcomed her with an embrace. 'It's so good to see you again.'

Alanna turned back to the young girl. 'Take the blossoms you've chosen and weave them into a crown. If you rise at dawn, look through the centre, and you may see the face of the man you will marry.'

The maiden stared at her in awe. 'I—I will. Thank you, Alanna.' She took the flowers she'd chosen and one of the rowan twigs, before she retreated among the other women.

Then Alanna turned back to them. 'Which of you would like to go first?'

Mairead sent her an encouraging look, but Velaria deferred. 'Let Mairead go first.'

'As you wish.'

Her cousin knelt at the low table, and Alanna set several small branches before her—Velaria recognised whitethorn and rowan, but then Alanna named the others as sycamore, elder, and hazel. 'First, choose the wood for your May crown. Place your hands upon each one and one will call to you.'

Dutifully, Mairead rested her fingers on each of the flexible branches until she stopped at the elder. 'This one, I think.'

Alanna reached out and rested her hands atop Mairead's. She closed her eyes and said, 'The elder will protect you from evil, yes. But you will need a strong guardian.'

'My husband?' Mairead asked quietly.

'You will meet him soon,' Alanna said. 'But not here. He is not one of us.' She pulled back her hands, and Velaria saw a trace of unease in the woman's face. Almost as if she saw something she didn't want Mairead to know.

She withdrew several sprigs of dried flowers, a few tree blossoms, and greenery. 'Now choose what you will weave into your elder crown.'

'Where will I meet him?' Mairead insisted.

But Alanna's face turned firm. 'Choose.' Mairead appeared disappointed, but she selected gorse, dried heather, and yellow primrose.

'Weave them into your May crown,' Alanna said.

'And look through it at dawn?' Mairead predicted.

Alanna shook her head. 'You will wear your crown two days' hence, just after sunrise. And stay with Velaria.'

Mairead's expression turned confused. 'But that's after Bealtaine. And it's not what you told Sinead.'

Alanna offered no explanation, but she nodded to Velaria. 'It's your turn now.'

Mairead took her branches and flowers, frowning as she took her place upon one of the stools. Velaria saw her mother, Katherine, had joined them and was standing just beyond the circle of women.

Though she didn't truly believe in Alanna's superstitions, she would never insult her cousin by saying so. Instead, she took her place at the low table while Alanna laid out the different branches, just as she'd done before.

But strangely, the woman reached out and took both of her hands, turning them over to study her palms. Though

Velaria's calluses had healed during the past year, it almost seemed as if Alanna could still see them.

'You have journeyed far, but your travels are not over.' The older woman released her hands, but Velaria saw the worry behind her eyes. Then Alanna stared off into the distance, a troubled expression on her face as she fell silent.

Velaria ventured, 'Should I choose a wood?'

Once again, there was no answer, so she touched each of the different branches. Of course, none of them called to her, but the rowan felt light and springy, so she chose it. It would be easier to weave a May crown from it.

'What about her husband?' Mairead interrupted. 'Tell Velaria about how she will meet him.'

Alanna appeared uncomfortable once again. 'There is darkness around you. Darkness and death.' She shuddered, gripping the edges of her *brat* as if an invisible wind had made her cold.

A chill rose over Velaria's skin at her cousin's prediction. She sensed that Alanna had reached into her worst secrets, and when her cousin stared at her, there was fear in her expression. 'You will not find the happiness you seek.'

Velaria faced her and stared back into her cousin's eyes. The prediction seemed as true as she could possibly imagine, and all around her, she heard the sighs of dismay from the other women. But she sensed that Alanna was not finished speaking.

'Not until you face what you fear most and overcome it,' her cousin finished. 'You must take your sword into the darkness and accept what you are.'

From behind, a woman's hands touched her shoulders. Her mother interrupted, 'I think that's enough. Velaria, choose some flowers, and make your crown.' To Alanna, she warned, 'This is not the time or place to tell such a fortune.'

Though Velaria knew Katherine was only trying to protect her, her cheeks burned with embarrassment that everyone had heard about the death surrounding her. Her cousin's prophecy bothered her deeply, for it was as if Alanna could see the truth inside her. And now several of the young maidens eyed her with fear.

'Take your rowan branches and weave them,' Alanna finished.

'What about the flowers?' Mairead started to ask.

But her cousin only shook her head. 'She will get her own flowers later.'

Velaria took the handful of rowan branches, but she wished she had never agreed to let Alanna tell her fortune. Her mother asked quietly, 'Are you all right?'

'You needn't worry. Alanna's predictions don't always come true.' Velaria attempted a weak smile and then pressed the rowan branches into her mother's hands. 'I don't feel like weaving a wreath any more.'

She started to leave the Great Chamber, but Mairead caught up to her and linked her arm with hers. 'It's going to be all right, Velaria.'

Her false smile faded at her cousin's kindness. She didn't know what to say, but Mairead guided her back outside.

'I know what will lift your spirits.' As they passed a servant, she handed Velaria a cup of mead and took one for herself.

'Where are we going?' she asked Mairead.

Her cousin led her through the crowd. 'You'll see.'

Velaria took a sip from her cup, and the fermented honey drink was stronger than she'd expected. Still, it was delicious. By the time they reached the small dais, her cousin refilled her mead and guided her to sit down beside her.

Below, the men were still competing in the different games, but Mairead pointed to another group. The men had stripped to their waists, and in the firelight, their bodies gleamed. She realised then that it was a strength contest. Each man would take turns lifting large stones, which made their muscles flex, revealing every carved line and sinew.

'Now, this is much better,' Mairead said. 'What a view.'

A laugh caught in her throat as Velaria finished her second cup. She was starting to feel warm, and there was a faint buzzing in her ears when her cousin handed her a third drink.

She was beginning to realise that she should have eaten more food earlier, but the mead was so pleasant, she didn't care any more. What did it matter if she never found love or a husband? She could enjoy the wonderful view before her, could she not?

'Savaş is more handsome,' she remarked to Mairead.

'Who?'

'Brian,' she corrected. 'But I call him Savaş. It means "war" in the Byzantine language.' She gestured with her cup, and some of the mead spilled. 'You should have seen him fight. No one ever defeated him.'

'Not once?' Mairead asked.

She shook her head. 'If he'd been defeated, he would be dead. The same as me.'

Her cousin's expression turned fearful, but Velaria gestured with her cup. 'We fought opponents in an arena to the death. Every three days, I never knew if I would survive by nightfall.'

'I never knew,' Mairead whispered. 'I'm so sorry. Thank God you were rescued.'

Darker memories tried to surface, but Velaria drained her cup to push them away. Now she was well and truly dizzy. But despite it all, she found herself asking, 'Where is Savaş?'

'I think he just finished a sword fight,' Mairead said. She sent a sidelong look towards her. 'You care for him, don't you?'

'He is my friend.' But she already knew the boundary between them was slipping. The intimate touch of his mouth against her throat had overwhelmed her, and she couldn't deny that the kiss had kindled more intense feelings. He'd warned her already that it was dangerous to imagine a future. But if he didn't want to be with her, why had he come to Laochre? Was this simply meant to be another farewell?

He is leaving, Velaria reminded herself. He would go north to his sister's home, and she probably wouldn't see him again. It was better to keep her distance.

Chapter Six

Brian flexed his shoulder, reaching back towards the dull ache from his wound. He hadn't won any of the competitions last night, just as he'd suspected. But this day, he'd decided to speak with Connor's wife, Aileen, to see what he could do to regain his full range of motion.

He noticed that the king had gathered a group of men together within the Great Chamber. From their age and appearance, he had a feeling they were the king's brothers. He recognised Connor among them.

Though it wasn't his place to eavesdrop, the men appeared concerned about something. And when Brian heard the mention of King John, he couldn't stop himself from moving in closer.

'Is the king returning to Ireland?' Connor was asking.

'I believe so. Sir Ademar spoke of large forces gathering in England.' Patrick's tone revealed a trace of frustration. 'We think John is bringing an army to suppress some of the Normans in the north, likely Walter de Lacy or William de Braose. But we don't know when they will come.'

'If they are already gathering, then mayhap by early summer,' Connor said.

The thought of King John's presence unnerved Brian for many reasons—but he'd never expected the king to invade.

He needed to travel north to warn Morwenna and Robert. But since the king's forces were not here yet, there was still time to make decisions.

One of the men, who towered among the others, crossed his arms. 'Will the king come to Laochre?'

'He might,' Patrick answered. 'We have enough Norman allies between Isabel and Genevieve's families. But even so, I want our forces doubled. We will need men at Ennisleigh to keep watch for ships. After our Bealtaine celebration tonight, I want our people guarded at all times.'

They began discussing their defences, but Brian's mind shifted to his sister's safety. He needed to travel north as soon as possible—and yet, Sir Ademar had demanded that he stay until after Bealtaine, for Velaria's sake. He was torn between protecting his family and protecting her.

He had no doubt that they would pressure her to marry even more if he left her behind. But if he took Velaria with him, her father would send soldiers to bring her back. They would never allow it.

Then, too, he questioned the strength of his fighting skills if they encountered a threat. Although Velaria was a strong fighter in her own right, she hadn't wielded a blade in nearly a year. He needed to believe that he could defend both of them, if needed. And that meant healing his shoulder.

Brian quietly left the men and asked one of the servants where to find the healer Aileen. He learned that Connor's wife was in the solarium with several other ladies. Although he didn't know if anything could be done—he walked up the spiral stairs to ask.

The moment he entered the solarium, all conversation ceased. One of the ladies asked, 'Were you looking for Velaria?'

'I was looking for the healer Aileen,' he corrected.

A woman with dark and silvery hair stood. 'I am Aileen.' She turned to the others and said, 'I will return in a little while.' To Brian, she said, 'I suppose you were among the competitors last night.'

'I was, aye.' He followed her down the hallway to a different room. She opened the door and inside he saw a table with a mortar and pestle, dried herbs, and bandages. He saw a pallet on the floor and a tall stool beside the table.

She motioned for him to sit down and then regarded him. 'Where were you injured?'

He loosened the laces of his tunic and raised it over his head. 'Your husband, Connor, suggested you might be able to help me with this. It's an old injury, but my sword fighting skills haven't been the same since.'

Her expression turned pensive. 'And you discovered this last night, did you?'

'I have not faced an opponent in the past year,' he admitted. Despite the training exercises he'd done, he hadn't realised it was this bad until now.

'Raise both of your arms above your head,' she commanded. He obeyed but could not lift his right arm as high as his left.

'Move your left arm in a circle from front to back. Then I want to see your right arm.'

Just as before, his right arm could only move so far. She pulled and pushed at his shoulder, pressing her hands against the muscle as she moved it.

'You're lucky to be alive,' she said. 'After an injury like this, you could easily have bled to death.'

'I am fortunate,' he agreed, 'but I want to know if there is any way to regain my old fighting skills.'

'There are stretching movements you can do,' she said.

After she moved his arm again, she said honestly, 'But I think it would be best if you learned how to fight with your left hand.'

Though he should have expected this, it wasn't the answer he'd wanted to hear.

Even so, he asked her to show him the stretching motions. While she did, she asked, 'Why do you wish to fight again?'

'I was once the best fighter in Constantinople,' he admitted. 'And now I don't know if I can protect anyone. Especially those I care about.'

'Where is your family now?' she asked. Gently, she pressed his arm back, stretching the muscle until it grew uncomfortable.

'My sister and her husband live in the north, at Dunbough. I am travelling to meet them there.'

'And your parents?' she asked.

'I have never met them,' he answered honestly. Although he sensed that he soon would, if Morwenna had anything to do with it. Unrest brewed within him, making him question what lay ahead.

Aileen released his arm and then asked him, 'Is it necessary for you to fight again? Or is there something else you can do?'

He understood what she was implying. But in truth, he had no interest in farming or tending sheep. When he'd faced opponents in the arena, the people had cheered his name. But the price of being a champion was the guilt of the lives he'd taken.

No, he didn't want to become a killer once again. But he did need to know that he could defend his loved ones, regardless of the danger. He met her gaze and answered honestly, 'I need to know that I can defend my family and friends.' Regardless of his bloodline, he'd been born into poverty. His sword skills were all he possessed. 'It's the only way I can prove my worth.'

Her smile tightened. 'And do you think my husband is not a man of worth since he can no longer use one of his hands?'

'That's not what I said.'

'No, but it's what you believe.' She stepped back and re-garded him. 'Think about what it is you truly want, Brian. There are many ways to be a man of honour. Find yours.'

That night, the king's son, Liam, returned to Laochre with his wife, Adriana, and four of their children. Velaria hadn't seen them in years, but Liam gave her a hard em-brace. 'I am glad to see you again. My father told me you returned from Constantinople.'

She gave a slight nod, and Adriana caught her in an em-brace. 'We will talk later. Liam and I…we've been to the Holy Land.' In the woman's eyes, Velaria felt a connection, one she'd never imagined. Without saying the words, her cousin's wife seemed to understand what she'd endured.

Unexpected emotions struck her, and for a moment, Ve-laria couldn't find any words to say. When she glanced up, she saw Savaş standing across the room. He'd kept himself apart from the others, but when he saw her silent plea, he crossed over to her side.

After he reached her side, Velaria introduced him. 'This is Brian of Penrith. We were both held captive in Constan-tinople.' Then she nodded to her cousins. 'This is King Patrick's son and heir, Liam, along with his wife, Adriana.'

'And our loud, ill-behaved children, of course,' Adriana said with a smile, reaching out to pull two of them apart.

The young boy glared at his younger sister. 'Stop *following* me. I said I don't want to play.'

'I wasn't following. I don't even like you!'

'Enough,' Liam said.

Velaria met Savaş's look and saw the amusement in his eyes. Though she'd been around children all her life, it was a sudden reminder of her father's demand to find a husband and start her own family.

A coldness slid over her spine, and Savaş's hand brushed against hers. The warmth of his hand eased her fear, though she doubted if anyone else was aware of it.

The young girl started to cry, and Liam pulled her into his arms. 'If you're crying, Gabriella, I suppose that means you're too tired for the festivities tonight.'

Immediately, the girl's eyes widened, and she blinked at her father. 'I can stay awake.'

'Are you certain?' He sent her a doubtful look, but she bobbed her head.

'Yes, Papa.'

'Good. Then leave your brother alone.' He ruffled her hair and set her down. 'Go and see your grandmother. She might have ribbons for you.' Gabriella hurried towards the queen, and Isabel caught her in her arms.

Adriana turned back to them and said, 'The women's competitions are tonight. Will you join them?'

'No, I—I don't think so,' she said. Although the contests were harmless, like archery and foot races, Velaria had no desire to be noticed by anyone. It would only increase the chances of her mother and father pursuing more marriage offers for her.

'Why not?' Liam asked.

'I…don't want everyone watching me,' she said. Though that was part of it, it wasn't the only reason. She didn't want to be in any kind of arena with others surrounding her. The very idea brought back memories she didn't want to face— of the other women and men who had died. A wave of sorrow and guilt passed over her.

'Would you be willing to help the other women and set up some of the games?' Adriana asked. 'Many of them will be very nervous to compete. You could reassure them.'

'All right.' The answer surprised even her, but the idea of helping others felt good.

Adriana smiled warmly. 'I'm glad. After I've settled the children, come and join me on the training field.'

Liam walked away with his wife, leaving them alone. Velaria turned to Savaş and saw a distant expression on his face. 'Is something wrong?'

He led her outside again and said, 'I overheard that King John is bringing an army of men from England to Ireland. Some of the noblemen in the north have rebelled against him.' The tension in his posture was evident. 'My sister and her husband live there.'

Which meant he would be leaving soon. She'd known it, but she hadn't been prepared for the sinking feeling in her heart. For a moment, she didn't know what to say. She couldn't ask him to abandon his family during a time of need, despite her own desire for him to stay.

'What will you do?'

He let out a breath. 'Fight alongside them. Do everything I can to protect my sister and her family.'

Although she understood his reasons—and she'd have done the same for her own family—she couldn't help but feel left behind once again. Part of her yearned to go with him. She had no desire to remain here so her father could arrange a marriage she didn't want. Nor did she want to seem pathetic, like a woman chasing after a man.

But Savaş confused her with his actions. He'd kissed her last night, implying that he wanted more between them. And despite her hesitation, she forced herself to voice the question. 'Do you want me to come with you?'

'Your father would never allow it,' he started to say.

But that was only an excuse. The answer was no, he didn't want her to accompany him. And somehow, a flare of anger caught her. Savaş kept pulling her close and then pushing her away. Despite her own emotions, she was tired of feeling as if she weren't enough. She hadn't been enough for Drogan—he'd stolen her innocence and had discarded her. And despite spending two years with Savaş, he still kept her at arms' length.

She'd had her fill of it.

Velaria kept her voice bright, revealing none of the pain beneath it. 'Then I bid you a good journey when you travel north.'

She squared her shoulders and turned to walk away from him. Inwardly, she was trembling with the force of her frustration. Restless energy rose within her, and she strode towards the training field. Every time she was around Savaş, her emotions seemed to crumble apart.

She had nearly reached the field when he caught up to her. 'Velaria, wait.'

He caught her by the arm, and she wrenched her hand away. 'Do not touch me.'

He raised his hands and backed off. 'I don't want to put you in danger. The king's army—'

'I faced danger every single day we were in captivity. But we faced it together,' she shot back. 'It's clear that you want to be on your own. So go. I don't need to be shielded from the world. I know exactly how cruel it can be.'

He looked as if she'd struck him. But he met her gaze and

said, 'There are things you don't know about me, Velaria. And I don't know how it will change my future.'

Her anger was still blinding her, for she already knew that future didn't include her. 'Keep your secrets, Savaş. They don't affect me at all.'

'And what if they do?' he demanded. He reached up to touch the side of her face, offering a slight caress that slid deep within her skin, making her crave more. And she hated herself for the weakness.

She kept her pride and informed him, 'My family wants me to marry. If I want a different life, all I have to do is say yes.'

His expression turned hard as he accepted her silent challenge. 'Do you want to wed any of those men?' When she gave no reply, he caught her by the waist and pulled her close. 'Not one of them knows the kind of hell we walked through and survived. They don't know—and never will know—what it was like.'

She was taken aback by his sudden touch. Though she wanted to succumb to the embrace, to rest her head against his heartbeat, she forced herself to hold back. Slowly, she extricated herself from him, keeping her eyes fixed on his face. She'd made him angry, and it matched her own mood.

'But you don't want me by your side, do you?' Her voice turned quiet as she waited for him to deny it. When he said nothing, she added, 'If you're wanting to leave, Savaş, I won't stop you.'

Before sundown that night, every fire in the kingdom was extinguished, and groups of men herded the cattle between the hills. Each farmer walked the perimeter of his lands, stopping at the four directions of east, south, west, and north to plant a seed and sprinkle ashes and water upon each. Brian joined the men and women atop the hill of Amadán, watching as Liam lit one of the Bealtaine fires. Within moments, the flames blazed in the night sky, followed by another fire on the opposite hill, which was lit by King Patrick. Below them, the cattle passed between the hills while a priest raised his arms high to give a blessing.

He looked for Velaria, but she'd been avoiding him ever since their argument. Though he'd wanted to tell her the truth about his heritage and share the burden of that secret, he was well aware that his father might deny him.

If he asked her to wed him, it would be the same as before. Her father would refuse the match, and how could he ask her to run away from her family again? Velaria deserved better than that. And the last thing Brian wanted was to pin his hopes on his own father, a man who didn't even know he'd fathered him.

He had to either find the strength to let her go—or convince her father that he was a man worthy of her.

Brian reached for one of the torches, and he joined the others in lighting it within the Bealtaine fires. On the opposite hillside, the others did the same, and slowly, a row of gleaming lights illuminated the darkness.

'Let us go and light the hearth fires,' Liam proclaimed. They began walking down the hillside, and children joined them with candles. Liam lit one of them for his oldest son, who carried it solemnly before he helped his younger siblings light their candles.

The lights stretched out from the hills, leading all the way to Laochre Castle. As Brian walked among the others, he saw more lights gleaming upon a nearby island.

There was a sense of anticipation among the people, and as they reached the castle grounds, the scent of roasted meat and delicious foods filled the air. As the two crowds of people blended together, carrying torches and candles, Brian searched for a sign of Velaria.

Although he couldn't find her, he did see her father standing tall among the others. Ademar met his gaze with a nod, and Brian approached the man. 'Good Bealtaine to you,' he greeted Ademar.

'And to you.' The knight's expression remained stoic as he waited for Brian to continue.

'I came to ask that you grant more time to Velaria,' he began. 'She refuses to consider marriage.'

Her father's demeanour shifted into his own stubbornness. 'Sometimes decisions must b-be made for a daughter's own good. She will be better f-for it.'

'She should have the right to choose,' Brian argued.

'And so she will. Tonight, after the champion of the w-women's competition is announced,' Ademar said.

It was clear that the knight was unwilling to relent. His demeanour was that of a protective father who intended to see to his daughter's future. But the thought of Velaria being trapped with a husband who would expect her to submit to him and bear children kindled a dark jealousy within him.

Brian would do everything in his power to protect her from an unwanted union. She deserved better than to be trapped in another set of invisible chains.

All around them, the MacEgans continued past with their torches and candles, and Ademar joined them. They reached the inner bailey with the others, and on the other side, he saw Lady Katherine standing with her sister, Honora.

But before the women walked towards them, Ademar turned back. His blue eyes flared, and he said, 'If you plan to ask Velaria to w-wed, the answer is no.'

Brian stared back at Ademar in a silent challenge of his own. 'As you said before—that choice is hers.'

Before the women could reach them, Brian made his way through the crowd towards the opposite side. Inwardly, his thoughts were a churning storm of unspoken plans. He needed to talk with Velaria again. She was angry with him—there was no doubt of that. But she needed to understand that if he brought her with him, it would cause an uproar with her family. Her father would send soldiers, which would only deepen the conflict.

The priest gathered at the front of the dais to offer prayers for the coming summer. The king and queen joined him, along with their daughter, Mairead. She wore a crown of wood, woven with dried flowers, while several other maidens wore similar May crowns.

These were the maidens who had decided to join in tonight's competitions, but Velaria was not among them. After the priest had finished the blessing, the maidens walked towards the different events, and it was then that he saw her standing apart from the others.

This time, she had removed her veil, and she stood among the others. Her hair was bound back from her forehead, but it hung to the middle of her back in soft waves. The sight of her brought an ache within him.

Brian was fully aware that he wasn't the only man watching Velaria. Though he didn't speak the Irish language, he'd seen several warriors drawing closer to watch the competitions. Several had their attention fixed upon her, and many of them would try to win her hand in marriage. His fists clenched at the thought.

He wondered if he should damn the consequences and simply ask her. He had the means of helping her escape a marriage she didn't want. All he had to do was give her the choice.

The women began their competition, and Brian moved

towards them. Although he'd caught Mairead sending him a few interested looks, his concentration was still upon Velaria.

He pushed his way past the crowd of people until he reached her side. She stood beside a stone wall and was congratulating the young woman who had won the foot race. When she turned and saw him, her expression tensed.

'Could we talk for a moment?' he asked.

'I have nothing to say to you.' She started to walk away, but he reached out to her arm. Though he'd only meant to stop her, she twisted away in a defensive movement that was familiar. Without thinking, he spun her around and pinned her against the wall. The moment their bodies touched, heat blazed through him, even as fury brewed in her eyes.

'Savaş, let go of me.'

At first, he meant to do exactly that. But the closeness of her body against his was a reminder of what he truly desired. He couldn't deny that he wanted Velaria more than the next breath. And the softness of her body against his evoked a craving that drew him to the edge of need.

'Your father plans to announce your betrothal tonight,' he cautioned.

'He can say whatever he likes. I will not wed a man of his choosing.' Her anger turned fierce, and she said, 'We're attracting attention. If you don't release me now, the men will—'

'You know exactly how to free yourself,' he challenged. 'Do it.'

Her expression shifted. 'I don't know what you're trying to prove, but—'

'Or have you forgotten how?' He leaned in close, waiting to see if she remembered her training.

A moment later, she shoved him back and twisted in his

arms, seizing the blade at his waist. She stood in a defensive stance, her temper flaring. 'Don't try to force me to fight, Savaş. I won't do it.'

'Your father will give you a choice of suitors,' he countered, circling her as he stayed clear of his own dagger. 'But if you do not choose, he will choose for you, in front of everyone. I came to warn you.'

He waited for her to lower her defences while she considered what he'd said. But the moment he seized her wrist to steal back his blade, she spun again and kicked him back. Whether or not she was aware of it, several onlookers encircled them to watch. Even the maidens had ceased their foot race, turning back to them. But Velaria seemed unaware.

'I won't do it.'

Brian tried to redirect her into a corner, and instead, she shifted her direction, cornering him instead. He hid his smile, for this was the fighter he knew.

'He believes he knows what is best for you,' he countered. Slowly, he guided her towards the centre of the circle.

He was trying to provoke her, wanting her to unleash the tight control. She was one of the greatest fighters he'd ever met, and he didn't want her to subdue that part of herself. If that meant pushing her to remember who she was, so be it.

Velaria cursed, and then he made his move, diving towards her and knocking her off her feet. There was a shout from someone, but he ignored it as she rolled over and pinned him to the ground with his own blade at his throat. There was a look of triumph in her eyes, but he knew her too well.

Brian held her wrist as he sat up, his stomach muscles flexing. Her legs were straddled across his, and he gritted his teeth as desire flared through him. He held her in his arms and stood before he disarmed her and tossed the dagger away.

'What are you doing?' she demanded. Her face had turned crimson, but she didn't struggle or try to break free of him.

'I tried to convince your father to let you have your freedom. But he refused.' Brian kept his arms around her and gently lowered her to the ground.

'So, I think it's best if you wed me instead.'

Velaria stared at him in disbelief. Was he truly offering to marry her? After he'd just told her he was planning to leave her behind? She didn't know what to say, and at first, she simply gaped at him.

His blue eyes darkened. He leaned in against her ear and murmured, 'You said you would run away if your father tried to force you to marry. But you won't have to leave if you wed me. I would grant you whatever freedom you wish. I would not demand that you share my bed or ask you to be a wife to me in anything but name.'

Then it was a shadow of a marriage. She didn't know what was worse—to take whatever bargain he offered or to hold the remnants of her pride and refuse. Her mind was troubled with confusion, and he reached out for her hand. 'Think upon it. It is another choice you can consider.'

And with that, he released her and walked away.

It took only moments before her father reached her side. 'Are you all right?' He glanced back at Savaş with unveiled fury. It seemed that Ademar fully intended to go after him to avenge her honour.

'I am,' she said. But to avoid her father causing more bloodshed, she lied, 'It was only a demonstration to the other women of how to avoid an attack.'

When Ademar didn't seem to believe her, she lifted her

chin in silent defiance. 'Father, he did not harm me. I promise you that.'

The knight met her gaze with stubbornness of his own. 'Three men have offered a generous bride p-price for you. Avar of Gall Tír, Eamon Ó Phelan, and w-we also had an offer from Blaine de Renalt. Any of them w-would treat you well.'

'Why do you keep insisting that marriage will make me happy?' she asked softly. 'I've said no already. If you try to force me to wed, I will leave.'

'You need a new p-purpose,' he said softly. 'Someone to l-look after so you'll stop thinking about the past. Perhaps children of your own.'

There was love beneath his intentions, and for that reason, she stopped arguing. 'I'll look after you and Mother,' she answered. 'It's enough for me.'

'We want more for you.' He embraced her lightly. 'Th-think on it, Velaria.'

She hugged him back and then went to join the other women. Along the way, she thought of what Savaş had said. His offer of marriage was born of pity, nothing more.

Although he'd kissed her back the other night, *she* had been the one to kiss him first. It would break her heart every day to look at him and know that she wasn't truly wanted. But more than that, she sensed that there was a great deal he wasn't telling her. One moment, he behaved as if her family's wealth intimidated him—and the next, he was asking her to wed. Something had changed, but what?

Adriana stepped over to Velaria's side and took her arm. 'Thank you for your help this eventide. I am grateful for it.' She led her away from the competitions, and Velaria remained at her side.

'I wanted to ask how you are,' Adriana said. 'I know

how…difficult it was when Liam and I were at Acre with King Richard's forces.' Her voice held a trace of a shadow when she spoke of it. 'So much bloodshed.'

'It was difficult,' Velaria agreed. 'Sometimes, I thought we would never make it out alive.' A heaviness weighed upon her, though she tried to force it back. Tonight was the first moment she'd started to feel useful. And perhaps that was what was missing—a chance to fill the hours.

'It's good that you have each other,' Adriana said. 'I don't know that I would have survived without Liam. He stood by me through everything.'

'Oh, we don't—' Her words broke off, for she didn't want Adriana to believe she and Savaş were more than companions. Not when she didn't know herself what they were to one another.

The woman's expression held understanding, but she added, 'He came to Laochre for your sake. And it's clear that he cares from the way he watches over you.'

Velaria didn't truly believe that. She was saved from having to answer when Adriana directed several servants to help put away the straw targets and the bows and arrows. The woman was constantly in motion, silently guiding the Bealtaine preparations while her husband, Liam, spoke to the people. King Patrick and Queen Isabel were still present, but they both hung back, watching.

Before Adriana could continue on, Velaria stopped her. 'Has something happened tonight with the king and queen?'

The woman paused a moment and admitted, 'Patrick has considered stepping down as king. Liam has to prove he is worthy to take the throne. As do I.'

There was a thread of anxiety in her voice, and Velaria felt the need to reassure her. 'You're ready. I believe that.'

Adriana ventured a slight smile. 'I hope so.'

* * *

The two champions were led to stand near a large bush made of whitethorn, and children held bright ribbons, flowers, and other trinkets. They came forward to decorate the May bush, and soon enough, the bush was filled with colourful adornments, including a few dyed eggshells.

After that, pipers began to play, and several dancers led a procession throughout the inner bailey. An older woman began passing out iron nails to each of the people as protection against the fairy folk.

Velaria had disappeared among the people, but Brian took one of the nails, tucking it within a fold of his cloak. Torches illuminated the space, and all around him, he heard the sound of laughter and music.

Liam stepped forward in front of his father, King Patrick, and raised his hands to gain their attention. The song finished playing, and soon, the crowd turned to hear him speak. 'We bid you a blessed Bealtaine on this night. May your fields be fertile, and your families have good fortune in the coming year.' He invited the two champions to join him upon the dais, and the young man and woman received another blessing. Adriana then joined her husband and invited the others to join in the Bealtaine feast.

Brian walked through the crowd, searching for Velaria, but she seemed to have disappeared once again. He was about to walk in the opposite direction when Velaria's aunt Honora and another man approached. The man kept his arm around her, and though his face showed the lines of age, his build was that of an exceptionally strong warrior.

'My wife has been wanting to meet you,' the man said. 'I am Ewan MacEgan. And this is Honora. I believe you're already acquainted with our niece.'

Although his tone was light and easy, Brian didn't miss

the hint of warning. He introduced himself before he turned to Honora and said, 'You should know that your training saved Velaria's life. If you had not taught her to wield a sword, she would not be alive today.'

For a moment, a flash of emotion crossed the woman's face. Then, she gave a nod of acknowledgement. 'I've always thought that every woman should be able to defend herself.'

'Velaria did well. And she saved my life,' Brian said.

Ewan's expression twisted when he glanced at the scar that ran from Brian's shoulder to his neck. 'It looks as if she tried to take it from you.'

With a shrug, he added, 'I suppose there are times she wishes she hadn't pulled back her sword. I've been known to irritate her.'

Ewan's hearty laugh surprised him. 'My wife has felt the same way many times.'

'Every day,' Honora agreed. But she leaned over and kissed her husband.

The easy affection between them was something Brian had never imagined was possible. But part of him wanted to have the same companionship of a wife.

He'd made the marriage offer to Velaria as a form of sanctuary—yet he couldn't deny that he wanted her. If she agreed to wed him, it might change everything between them, even though he would honour her wishes if she wanted to remain untouched.

'How is she?' Honora asked quietly. 'I've not seen her fight since she arrived. At least, not until she pulled a blade on you just now.'

Ewan was still smiling. 'I enjoyed watching that fight. It reminded me of my beloved wife when we first met.' He winked at Honora.

'Why did Velaria fight you?' Honora's voice held a trace of accusation, and he could fully imagine her wielding a knife against him. 'What did you do?'

He didn't know how to answer that. 'Velaria was angry with me,' he hedged.

'Well, that was clear enough.' Honora rolled her eyes. Then she turned serious. 'What happened to her in Constantinople? She's not the girl I once knew. She never wore gowns or veils in the past.'

'She's trying to forget our days of captivity,' he answered. 'By becoming someone else.'

'What did you say that made her so angry?' Ewan asked.

He was saved from having to answer when he saw Sir Ademar approach the dais. He was joined by his wife, Katherine, and the king, though King Patrick appeared somewhat uneasy about it. It appeared that the knight intended to keep his promise of announcing a betrothal for Velaria.

And something within him snapped. Brian pushed his way through the gathering crowd. Velaria was nowhere to be found, which he supposed was her own way of avoiding the situation. But once her father made the announcement, it might cause difficulty with the bridegroom he'd chosen, especially when Velaria refused. Brian hurried past the onlookers until he was nearly at the dais.

'Bealtaine is a time f-for joyful celebration,' Sir Ademar began. 'And I am p-pleased to share that my daughter Velaria will be betrothed this night.' Lady Katherine touched her husband's elbow and leaned in to whisper to him. But the knight stiffened and continued. 'She has chosen—'

'Me,' Brian called out. '*I* am Velaria's betrothed husband.'

There was a stir within the crowd, as if he'd interrupted plans that had already been made. But Brian didn't care.

This was about keeping Velaria safe and protecting her from a marriage she didn't want.

But then, the crowd applauded, and soon enough, they continued on with their feasting. Sir Ademar appeared furious at Brian's interference, and as soon as he climbed the dais, the tall knight caught his arm. 'I said already that y-you would not be permitted to m-marry my daughter.' His face held anger, and he regarded Brian. 'We p-paid you to come to Ireland to help our daughter. Not to w-wed her.'

It was then that Brian saw Velaria had come towards them and was now staring at him with shock. She'd clearly overheard her father's words, and hurt broke over her face.

'You have no future to offer her,' the knight continued. 'I will not p-permit it.'

But Brian straightened and regarded both her father and the king. 'Our future is yet to be determined. I will wed her and bring her north to my sister at Dunbough.'

'Velaria deserves b-better than the son of a miller,' Ademar said quietly.

An uneasiness slid within him, but Brian forced himself to stand his ground. He hadn't intended to reveal the truth, but he saw no other choice. If he went along with their assumption, they would never allow him to take care of Velaria. And he simply couldn't watch her be imprisoned or held captive by a husband who would never understand what she'd endured.

'I am not the son of a miller,' he said quietly. He raised his eyes to regard both Sir Ademar and his wife. 'I am the bastard son of King John of England.'

Chapter Seven

For a moment, Velaria could only stare at Savaş. A thousand emotions roiled within her, and at first, she was convinced that his words were a lie. He would have told her if he were the son of a king. Not once had he mentioned it in the past.

It must have been a falsehood of some kind, just a means of getting her father to agree to…whatever Savaş was offering. Not a true marriage, certainly.

But worse than the lie was her father's claim that he had paid Savaş to come here. She didn't want to believe it. And yet, it seemed entirely probable that he would have taken her father's offer of horses and supplies. He had no other way to gain passage here.

'Velaria,' her father interrupted. 'Is this t-true?' The expression on his face held anger, but it was nothing compared to her own fury.

She had already warned Ademar that she didn't plan to marry anyone. But her father had already dismissed her decision as if he already knew what was best for her. He had no idea what she'd survived already, and it was clear that he would not let this go. Why couldn't he simply accept her answer?

Her own frustration was so tight, she could hardly

breathe. 'I am going to speak with him alone before I make a decision.' Not because she had any intention of agreeing to this marriage, but because she wanted to find out Savaş's intentions. It was time for brutal honesty between them. And after that conversation, she didn't know whether she would go through with a false marriage or not. Savaş knew of her desire for freedom and had said he would grant it.

He took her hand in his and led her from the dais. She walked alongside him and up the stairs towards the guest chambers. Although she sensed her father's disapproval, her mother's face held worry as well.

But Velaria didn't know how *she* felt. For so long, she had avoided discussing any sort of future for them— especially after he'd gently pushed her away on the journey home. Even now, it felt like an arrangement, not a desire to be with her. And she dreaded the thought of marrying a man she cared about who didn't feel the same way in return.

Savaş took a torch from a sconce and opened a door that led to a tiny, narrow space with a single bed. He lit a brazier and an oil lamp before returning the torch to the sconce outside. After he closed the door behind him, he met her gaze.

'I want your full honesty,' she began. 'No lies between us.'

'All right,' he agreed. 'But for every question I answer in honesty, you must do the same.'

She nodded. There was no reason to hide anything any more.

Savaş leaned against the stone wall and studied her. In the glow of the lamplight, his face was shadowed and lean. Her attention was fixed upon his mouth as she remembered the kiss. His expression narrowed, and there was an intangible heat that rose up between them. She didn't truly understand it, but she remembered how it felt to have his hands upon her skin.

'Did my father pay you to come to Laochre?' she asked.

He gave a nod. 'He did. Your parents were worried about you, and I lacked the means of travelling to my sister's home without their help.'

Even though Velaria had guessed as much, it felt like a spike driven within her heart. For Savaş never would have come here had it not been for their coins. He truly *had* left her, with no intent of returning.

Was there ever anything between us? she wondered.

Or had that been a lie?

He took a step closer to her. Then another. She resisted the urge to step away from him, for she didn't want to seem as if she were running away. Yet, his physical presence unnerved her. His blue eyes stared into hers, piercing through her fumbling excuses.

'Do I frighten you?'

Yes. But not because she thought he would hurt her—it was because of the volatile feelings he conjured within her. And the heart-wrenching truth that he had only come to Ireland because of payment, not because he wanted to see her.

'No,' she lied.

When Savaş took another step forward, he caught her waist with one arm. He held her so lightly—and yet, her body flinched without meaning to.

'You're trembling.' He cupped her cheek, sliding his warm palm downward to her throat. She could almost imagine his bare skin upon hers, and the image evoked a shuddering response.

'What is it you want, Velaria?' His voice was the slightest murmur, and her heart began to pound. She was entirely aware of his body so close to hers and the raw expression in his eyes.

Heat and need blazed upon her, and she didn't understand the feelings he conjured within. Why was he doing this to her?

Her body ached, and she felt as if she were standing upon the edge of a vast ocean that threatened to pull her under. With reluctance, she pulled away.

'I want the freedom to do as I wish,' she answered honestly. 'I am weary of being told what to do.'

Even in this, she felt like a pawn. Her father wanted her to be married, and she didn't know what Savaş wanted from her. She forced herself to face him. 'Why did you tell my father you are the son of the king?'

He met her gaze. 'After I went to the abbey, I learned of it from Father Oswold.' He didn't offer anything more, though she wanted answers. He seemed uncomfortable, but when she searched his expression, it didn't seem to be a lie.

'How is this possible—' she started to ask.

'My sister knows more than me. But the priest said it was true.'

It occurred to her that if she were to marry him, it would give King John yet another strong alliance with her family. Which might give Savaş what he wanted—to be recognised by the king as his son.

She took a step back. She needed a moment to gather her thoughts and make a decision.

He didn't push for more but asked, 'Is there another reason you don't want to marry anyone, Velaria?' She didn't know what to tell him, but then he continued, 'Is it because of what happened on the day Kadir took you from our prison cell?' His voice had turned grim, shadowed in darkness.

Velaria's face flamed with embarrassment, for she'd never wanted to remember that day. 'Why would you ask me this?'

'Because I need to understand.'

'I don't want to answer,' she shot back. The memory still haunted her, even now.

'Is that the reason you're afraid of me?' he pressed again. 'Because of Kadir's men?'

Hot tears burned in her eyes, and she turned away. It was clear that he already believed the worst, that the men had violated her. And although they had wanted to, she'd fought them off. Kadir's punishment—the severe beating—had likely saved her from rape.

'Do not ask me about that night again,' she warned. Inwardly, she felt as if the slightest word would cause her courage to shatter.

He came up behind her and drew his arms around her waist. He offered wordless comfort, and it was all she could do not to start crying. 'Your wounds may be invisible, but they're still bleeding,' he said quietly. 'Let me help you heal from what you endured.'

The tears did break free then, but she didn't turn around. Nor did she pull away from his embrace.

'I don't need or want your pity,' she whispered.

His embrace tightened around her. 'It's not pity, Velaria. You took care of me for nearly a year while I was healing. Let me do the same for you.'

Deep inside, she was aching. She wanted so badly to admit the truth to him, that she already knew he didn't want her. A marriage between them would only hurt more, making her long for something she couldn't have.

She didn't understand the rising feelings of yearning, but she forced herself to break away. If for no other reason than to protect her heart.

'I don't know what you want from me,' she said, turning her face away.

'I want to protect you.' He touched her cheek, caressing it with his knuckle. 'We suffered together in that prison, and I won't let your father force you into a marriage where the same thing happens.

'If you wed me, I'll grant you the freedom you want,' he swore. 'I would never hurt you. Not ever.'

He still persisted in this idea of a false marriage, not understanding that she wanted it to be real. She wanted him to look upon her as if she were precious, and she wanted to be loved. But both of them were so broken after Constantinople, it was a foolish dream.

'I need to travel north to my sister,' he began. 'Come with me, and you need not worry about your father any more. And I'll get the answers I need about my own father.'

'And when the king comes to Ireland?' she ventured.

'I don't know. I need to face him and tell him who I am.'

But she didn't miss the thread of doubt in his voice. There was a chance that the king could deny him or ignore his existence. And then what?

It seemed that the ground between them was shifting, and she was afraid of what that meant. But when she studied him closely, it made her wonder if Savaş had his own invisible wounds that would not heal. There were shadows beneath his eyes, as if he struggled in sleep. Though he put up a brave face, like a man who had faced his nightmares and overcome them, she wondered if that was actually true.

'I need to think,' she said. 'I can't give you an answer just now.'

'What about your father?' There was an edge to his voice, one she didn't understand. But he was right— Ademar had already proven his stubbornness, and he wasn't about to let go of this idea.

'He won't listen,' she admitted. 'And I don't know if he believes what you said about the king.'

Savaş met her gaze. 'You could leave with me,' he offered. 'Before he tries to announce your betrothal to someone else.'

Though it was a reasonable offer, she still knew he didn't truly want her. If there was any way out of this mess, any way at all to avoid being trapped into marriage, she had to try.

'No,' she said softly. 'I won't be forced into a marriage neither of us wants.'

And with that, she turned and left.

The next morning

'Are you certain you want to do this, Mairead?' Velaria asked. To be honest, she wasn't disappointed to be leaving Laochre this morn. She'd avoided her parents for the rest of last night, not wanting to give them an answer.

So, when her cousin had asked her to slip out of the castle before dawn, Velaria had been glad to agree. It offered her the time she needed to make her decision about the betrothal. Savaş's offer had been made in haste, and though he'd claimed he didn't want a true marriage, she didn't want him to look upon her with distaste or pity.

Mairead had wanted to walk, claiming that it was easier to slip away with no one noticing if they did not ride horses. Which was true enough. Even so, Velaria wasn't certain she agreed with her cousin's desire to go alone. It was never wise for women to travel without a guard, but she could also see Mairead's reasoning that there was no one here as far as the eye could see.

The morning dawned clear, and the air was cool. Velaria trudged up the hillside of Amadán, thankful for the freedom they could enjoy this early in the day.

Mairead had brought her May crown with her, and Velaria sensed this secret journey was somehow connected to Alanna's prophecy. And her cousin desperately wanted something to cling to.

It was a fair distance from the castle, and the journey to the top of the hill wasn't easy. Velaria breathed in the crisp air and drew her *brat* closer around her shoulders. Her cousin had woven the dried primrose and heather blossoms into the elder crown that she carried in one hand.

'Alanna said I would meet my future husband in two days,' Mairead announced. 'And I want to find him before my brother interferes.' She exchanged a glance with Velaria. 'Liam is the most overprotective man I've ever known. The only person worse is my father.'

'They want you to be happy,' Velaria reassured her. But she understood her cousin's complaints. Her own brother, Phillip, had been unbearable when they were growing up. The only difference between them was that Mairead wanted a husband, whereas Velaria wanted to avoid marriage.

'I intend to follow Alanna's suggestion,' her cousin said. 'It will work. I'm confident that she speaks the truth.' Then Mairead's face fell a moment later when she remembered that Alanna had given a very different prediction to Velaria. 'I mean, her prophecy for me was probably true. She doesn't know you that well. Mayhap yours was wrong.'

Velaria shook her head and shrugged. 'I didn't make a crown, so it doesn't matter.'

Mairead let out a sigh. 'I suppose you're right.' But her cheeks flushed as if she hadn't thought before she'd spoken.

They continued walking uphill until they reached the summit. Mairead turned back to her and smiled.

'What are you going to do?' Velaria asked. She didn't understand her cousin's superstitions. But her question was answered when Mairead held the circlet of branches up to the sun for a moment. She closed her eyes and murmured in Irish, words that Velaria didn't understand.

Then she slowly lowered the circlet and glanced back at her cousin. 'It's just a blessing. Now we'll return to the bottom of the hill.' Mairead squared her shoulders as if she fully expected her future husband to be waiting there.

Velaria didn't believe that anything had really happened, but she saw no harm in letting her cousin dream of a future. The morning sunlight was bright, despite the chill.

'I'm glad you came to visit, Cousin,' Mairead said. Her dark hair hung down to the centre of her back in a long braid, and she placed the May crown upon her head. 'I pray that you will find your own happiness.'

Velaria murmured words of agreement though she didn't know what her own happiness would look like any more.

Her cousin seemed to notice her sudden silence and prompted, 'Tell me more about Brian of Penrith.' With a sly smile, Mairead added, 'Is it true that you're now betrothed?'

In spite of herself, Velaria felt her cheeks burn. 'I—I haven't decided yet.'

Mairead linked her arm in Velaria's as they trudged downhill. 'What was it like when you were with him in Constantinople?'

Though she recognised that her cousin was trying to pry out more information, her tone had shifted to one of sympathy.

'He was all I had when we were held captive together,' Velaria admitted. Those nights seemed so long ago. And yet, she would never forget them.

'It sounds as if you meant a great deal to him, as well.'

Velaria couldn't find the right words and simply shrugged. She didn't really know how Savaş felt about her—especially now.

As they reached the pathway, Velaria heard the sound of men speaking the Norman language. Out of instinct, she put her arm back to push Mairead behind her. She raised her finger to her lips and stared down below.

Mairead's eyes widened. 'The love charm actually worked,' she whispered. 'I wanted to believe it, but—'

'Wait.' Velaria shielded her eyes against the sunlight and inhaled sharply. On the other side of the hill where the sea gleamed, she saw the glint of armour. And she suspected the men below had come to scout the area.

She bit back a curse that they'd come alone. Turning back, she murmured to Mairead, 'Was your mother expecting guests?'

Mairead shrugged. 'There are always guests at Bealtaine.' She ventured a soft smile. 'Velaria, I think Alanna was right. I don't know who these men are, but...what if one of them is the man I'm destined to marry?'

She didn't believe that for a moment. There were nearly a dozen men, fully armed with spears and swords. They were not here to visit—they were invaders.

'We need to go back to Laochre, Mairead. Before we're seen.' Now she wished that she'd armed herself with the *colc* sword. Her only weapon was an eating knife, which was worth nothing at all.

Her mind blurred between past and present, as if she were once again in the arena, fighting an enemy. She took a moment to gain her bearings. It was better if they returned to the top of the hill to gain a better view of where it was safe to descend. She held her cousin's arm and ordered, 'Climb back up. We need to see who these men are and find out how we can safely return to the castle.'

Mairead turned serious then. 'You think they will harm us? We've done nothing wrong.'

Was her cousin truly that innocent? Velaria nodded. 'You're the daughter of an Irish king, Mairead,' she pointed out. 'We should have brought a guard with us.' Already she was regretting the decision to indulge her cousin's romantic dreams of a suitor.

'No one in this region would dare harm me,' Mairead said. 'My uncles and aunts own even more land beyond my father's.' She appeared uncertain and confused. 'But… I feel certain that this is connected to what Alanna told me. It's part of the prophecy.'

'Those are Norman soldiers, not Irish,' Velaria said. 'And if they find two women alone with no escort…' She closed her eyes, trying to push back the rise of nausea.

Mairead paled. 'I—I suppose you're right.'

Velaria took her cousin's arm and commanded, 'Follow me.' They hurried to climb back up the hillside, but just as they were reaching the top, six men caught up to them. Five wore chainmail armour while the sixth man had armour trimmed with gold. But it was their knowing smiles that stopped her short.

Velaria knew if she didn't protect Mairead, both of them would be at the mercy of these men. Never again.

'Mairead, stay behind me,' Velaria ordered. She was grateful when her cousin obeyed.

'What a pleasant diversion,' one of the men said, his eye on Mairead. 'We didn't expect to find such lovely flowers waiting to be picked.'

'Velaria.' The panic and warning in her cousin's voice was evident.

'Stay back,' she murmured again. A strange calm descended over her. She would allow none of these men to lay a hand on her cousin. She had done this before, and she knew the role she had to play.

Strangely, the idea of touching a weapon wasn't so terrible. Not when it meant protecting her cousin.

Just as before, she pretended to be weak and helpless. 'Please, don't hurt us.' She kept her voice fearful, even as she took a step closer to the man who appeared the weakest among them. He had already set aside his shield, which was his mistake.

All she had to do was seize his sword.

Brian had been careful to give Velaria time to consider the possible betrothal. Though he was aware of her reluctance, he'd decided not to push her for more. If nothing else, he could bring her north with him and give her the chance to avoid a marriage she didn't want. But there was always the chance that she would refuse him—or that her father would try to stop them.

An invisible fist gripped him at the thought of Velaria being forced to wed another man. They had survived this long together, and he couldn't consider leaving her behind. Not this time.

The sound of shouting caught Brian's attention. He heard the guards calling out near the barbican gate, and he walked closer to get a better look. Then he saw Velaria.

Her arms were covered in blood. He started running, not knowing if she was wounded. But he recognised the cool expression of fury on her face and knew the blood was not hers.

Why had she fought? She'd sworn she never wanted to touch a sword again. Yet, he could already see the weapon strapped to her side, a man's broadsword. Someone shouted for a healer as she dismounted.

Brian hurried to her side, and she stared at him. It was then that he saw the shock in her eyes, a blend of terror and victory.

'What happened?' he demanded. 'Are you hurt?'

She shook her head, and within moments, Connor, Liam, and King Patrick reached her.

'Tell me what happened,' the king demanded. From the bleak expression on his face, it was clear he already suspected the worst.

Velaria's mouth tightened, but she faced him. 'The Normans have taken Mairead. I tried to stop them—but there were too many. I—I couldn't fight them all.'

Patrick expelled a curse and gave orders for soldiers to gather. 'Why were you out alone together?'

The fury in his voice seemed to startle her. 'I—'

She had no time to finish answering his question before the king prompted, 'Where did the soldiers ride, Velaria?'

'North,' she answered. 'They went north.'

The king commanded dozens of men to begin a search party. Though it seemed like chaos, the soldiers gathered weapons and armour, until a large force rode outside the gates.

'I should go with them,' Velaria insisted.

'You will not,' a man said. When Brian turned, he saw Sir Ademar arming himself among the others. His expression was grim when he regarded his daughter. 'You're s-staying here with your mother.'

'Father, I need to help,' she insisted. 'It's my fault they took her.'

But the knight shook his head before his expression turned quiet and sympathetic. 'It would b-bring back memories you don't want to face.' He reached out and squeezed her shoulder. 'We'll find her. I p-promise.'

From the stricken look on Velaria's face, Brian knew if she stayed behind, she would retreat even further into the shadowed woman she'd become. 'Come with me,' he said. 'We'll clean off the blood.'

But she glanced back at her father and the other soldiers. 'There's no time,' she insisted. 'We have to find her.'

He took her hands in his and leaned in close to murmur, 'We will hunt them down, Velaria. I promise you that.' Her blue eyes met his, and he gave a slight smile. 'We'll arm ourselves and travel separately from the others. If the Normans haven't taken her far, the MacEgans will find her. Or we will.'

His words seemed to get through to her, and at last, she nodded. He led her to the small chamber the MacEgans had given to him. Once they were inside, he guided her to put her hands into a basin while he poured water over them. While he did, he noticed that her hands were still shaking.

'What happened?' he asked quietly while he bathed her hands in the water, washing away the blood.

'Mairead wanted to go to Amadán,' she began. 'Our cousin Alanna predicted that she would find her future husband at dawn this morning. She—she believed her.' Velaria closed her eyes, and a shudder crossed over her. 'I don't really know what happened. It was like the arena again.' She took a deep breath and expelled the air slowly. 'It doesn't seem real that they took her.'

He dried her hands with a cloth and asked, 'How many men did you face?'

'Six.' Her voice sounded dull. 'I…hardly remember what happened. I attacked before they could make the first move. But two of them took Mairead when I was surrounded. I didn't have a choice but to fight.'

He drew her into a hard embrace, offering what comfort he could. When he released her, he asked, 'Did you kill the others?'

Slowly, she nodded. 'It happened so fast.' A flush coloured her cheeks, and she averted her gaze. 'I never wanted to be that woman or wield a sword again. But if I hadn't—'

Her words broke off, as if she struggled to come to terms with her decision.

Brian met her gaze squarely. 'You did what you had to do to escape. And because of it, both of you survived.'

He fully understood her guilt and knew what it was to feel as if your soul was damned and no one would forgive you for your sins. To ease her, he added, 'If you hadn't killed them, they would have hurt both of you.'

'They were scouts, Savaş. They weren't travelling to Laochre—they were here for another reason.'

He suspected these men had been sent by King John. But he still didn't know the monarch's intentions or whether his family would be harmed by their forces.

'Were any of them noblemen?' he asked quietly. 'Out of those you killed?'

She didn't look at him, but she inclined her head. 'One had chainmail armour trimmed in gold.'

Which was a yes. He didn't know what to think of that, for there could be consequences for her actions. He could only hope that the nobleman was one of the king's enemies.

He reached out and traced the line of her cheek. 'We'll find Mairead and bring her back. I swear it.'

She covered his hand with her own and admitted, 'I told them she was an Irish princess, and I pray to God they believed me.'

He understood why—it was likely the only means of protecting Mairead from being defiled.

'I'll get the horses and weapons if you'll gather the travelling supplies,' he offered.

She nodded, but before she could pull away, he took her face between his hands and said, 'It's going to be all right, Velaria.'

She didn't move, and he saw the aching emotion on her face. 'I never wanted to kill anyone again.'

He understood that. And yet, the world had forged both of them into steel weapons. Whether they wanted to be or not.

They rode swiftly, and both of them were heavily armed. Despite the nightmares of the past, Velaria hadn't protested when Savaş had given her a sword. She'd chosen leather armour to wear and braided her hair back in the same way she'd worn it in the arena. Though she felt a sense of cold fear, she straightened her spine and tried to behave as if she had courage and determination.

It was a familiar mask that she wore to push back her fear. And she noticed that Savaş had done the same. He wore chainmail armour, and a broadsword hung at his waist. His hair was already cropped short, and on his face she saw the determination of a man who anticipated battle.

It took her aback to see him the way he'd been in Constantinople. And she couldn't deny her own fascination with this warrior. Unlike her father, Savaş hadn't hesitated to let her come and fight alongside him. He trusted her skills, even though she hadn't fought in nearly a year. And he accepted that as part of her.

She led him on horseback in the direction the men had gone. At first, it was easy to track the Normans as they passed the hill of Amadán. But as they travelled farther afield, the tracks seemed to separate. She didn't know where they had taken Mairead, and for a moment, she studied the horizon, searching for a glimpse of the soldiers.

Most of the MacEgans had gone in the direction of the larger group, but she wasn't convinced it was the right choice. Her instincts warned that Mairead had been taken by only a few men. Savaş drew his horse beside hers and asked, 'Which way?'

'It looks like most of the MacEgans went in the other direction, but there are a few who went towards the forest.'

'What do you want to do?' he asked.

She hesitated. 'Mairead would leave a trail of some kind.' Her cousin was accustomed to defending herself, and she believed the young woman would find a way to let her father know where she was. 'I think we should follow the smaller set of tracks. But we'll look along the path for anything unusual.'

They continued riding into the forest, though they were forced to slow their pace because of the trees. Velaria's gaze remained intent upon the ground, but she wasn't certain what they would find. At one point, the horse tracks disappeared, and she guessed they had gone through the stream.

Savaş raised his hand and drew his horse to a stop. He pointed towards the opposite side of the stream where a sprig of dried gorse rested on the ground. 'Look over there.'

The flowers from the May crown, Velaria realised. She crossed the water and let out a breath of relief. They had chosen the correct path. She started to continue through the trees, but Savaş stopped her. 'Wait. Let me alert the others.'

She had no desire to wait, not when Mairead could be anywhere by now. They had already taken enough time as it was. Before she could argue, Savaş caught the reins of her horse.

'I have faith in our fighting skills,' he said. 'But we need the numbers to win. And I won't risk her life or yours.'

There was an air of possession in his voice that made her heart stumble. 'I just don't want to lose time. I feel as if I should have followed her instead of coming to Laochre. If we don't find her...'

'We have most of the MacEgans searching. She *will* be found.' He released the reins of her horse. 'Give me just a moment, and I'll bring them this way.'

Without waiting for her agreement, he urged his horse towards the others. Velaria studied the gorse flowers, praying that her cousin had left more of a trail. It was the only trace of her they'd found.

Her own guilt weighed heavily upon her that she hadn't been strong enough or swift enough to conquer all her opponents. It had been a combination of luck, recklessness, and the element of surprise that had helped her defeat four of them.

King Patrick was right—they should have brought guards with them. It had been foolish and arrogant to imagine that no one would harm them.

And now her cousin might be suffering at their hands. Velaria bit her lip as she continued with her horse towards the edge of the forest, but she didn't leave the shelter of the trees. Instead, she shielded her eyes against the morning sunlight and scanned the grasses for any trace of horses. The horse tracks seemed to weave in one direction, then another.

Within moments, she heard more horses approaching behind her. When she glanced around, she saw that Savaş had arrived with the others, along with her uncle Ewan and aunt Honora. His expression was grim, though he relaxed somewhat when he realised she'd stopped to consider the direction.

After a moment of studying the tracks, Velaria said, 'These tracks lead towards the coast. The others go back towards the hill, travelling north.' She glanced back at Savaş. 'What do you think?'

He met her gaze. 'If I had stolen an Irish princess whose

family owns most of the land in this region, I would take her by boat. It's not as easy to track.'

'It's possible,' Ewan agreed. 'Patrick has an island fortress, and there are always boats nearby. It wouldn't be hard to steal one.'

'We should ride towards the coast,' Velaria suggested. 'If they've gone by boat, we might see them.'

She urged her horse onward, and Savaş joined at her side. They galloped hard towards the edge of the land, and soon enough, she spied tracks that continued downhill to the strand.

And there, they saw two horses and a fallen May wreath.

Chapter Eight

Brian rode alongside Velaria, while Ewan and Honora joined them. Ewan gave orders for the other men to go and alert the king and the remaining MacEgan soldiers.

'We need a boat,' Brian said.

The man gave a grim nod, and he spoke with Honora for a moment. 'There *were* boats here earlier. At least two. But now…' He shook his head. 'We'll have to go back closer to Laochre.'

Which would take even more time. Brian turned back to Velaria, who had gone pale. She was staring out at the water and then at the island fortress of Ennisleigh across from Laochre Castle.

'What is it?' he asked her.

She pointed out at the waves. 'Look there.'

He followed the direction and saw a body floating in the water. Without thinking, he crossed himself. But Velaria was already walking into the waves, heedless of the cold water.

'Velaria, no.' He joined her, and the vicious chill of the water sliced through him. But she continued to venture closer to the body.

She meant to identify the man, he realised.

Velaria reached for the first man's hair and raised it up

enough to look at his face. Then she dropped it and stepped back. 'He was one of our attackers.'

Brian judged that it hadn't been very long since the man's death. He started to drag the body from the water, but before he got far, he saw the second body floating on the waves.

'Velaria—' He pointed to the other man as he released the first.

She crossed her arms as she trudged deeper into the water. Soon enough, she reached the second man and raised his face to look at it.

'But that man wasn't the second,' she said. 'I don't know who he is.'

Just as before, Brian helped bring the body to shore, but afterwards, they both stared in all directions, praying there would be no sign of the king's daughter. Thankfully, there was nothing.

'What do you think happened to Mairead?' he ventured.

Velaria started to shiver the moment she left the water. 'I suspect she defended herself. Or someone else defended her.' Although her tone was matter-of-fact, Brian sensed the uncertainty beneath it. Her teeth began to chatter from the cold, and his own body was numb from the frigid water.

When they reached her aunt and uncle on the shoreline, Velaria told them, 'I think we should search Ennisleigh.'

'I agree,' Ewan said. 'There are guards posted at the tower at all times. If Mairead left these shores by boat, they would have seen her from the island.'

After they returned to their horses, the other MacEgans arrived to join them. Ewan quickly related their findings to the king and his son, offering the fallen May wreath as evidence. Liam took the wreath, and after a discussion with his father, they agreed to search Ennisleigh and send boats out in several directions.

Brian joined his horse alongside Velaria's. For a time, she said nothing but merely followed the larger group. He could see in her posture, in her weariness, that she still blamed herself.

'We'll go with them,' he told her. 'And learn what they saw.'

She gave a nod of agreement, but he could tell that she was still uneasy about it. After finding the bodies, he didn't blame her.

'Or would you rather return to Laochre and change into dry clothes?' he suggested.

'No. Not until we've gone to Ennisleigh.' She urged her horse faster, but he could see her clinging to the reins, her shoulders slumped as she tried to ignore the effects of the sea water.

They rode along the water's edge towards the larger pier. But before they reached it, Velaria's father joined them.

'Are you all right?' Ademar asked his daughter. 'Wh- what happened? Why are you h-here? I ordered you to stay at Laochre with your mother.'

'I needed to help Mairead,' Velaria started to say.

'You needed to r-remain safe,' her father snapped. But the knight had no idea what she'd endured. And Brian had no intention of staying silent.

'That's enough,' Brian said coolly. 'Let her be. If she wants to go to Ennisleigh, then I'll take her there.'

'I h-hired you to look after my daughter. Not b-bring her into more danger.'

Before Brian could intervene, Velaria moved her horse between them. 'You had no right to hire anyone,' she told Ademar. 'I didn't need your help then. And I certainly don't need it now.'

Brian saw the frustration in her father's face, of a man who only wanted to heal his daughter.

'Velaria—' Ademar started.

But she moved closer to him and said, 'Stop trying to make decisions for me. No matter what answers I've given, you've never listened.' Her face turned pained, and she said, 'I never should have come home again.'

And with that, she urged her horse into a gallop, leaving them both behind.

Her body wouldn't stop shivering. Velaria ignored the clammy wet clothing as she joined a few other soldiers in one of the boats going to Ennisleigh. When she gazed out at the island fortress, her heart beat faster.

She shouldn't have spoken such cruel words. But she'd been so angry with her father for his stubbornness that she'd blurted them out without thinking.

Now she wondered if she should have held her tongue. Savaş's expression had been unreadable, and she worried what he would think of what she'd said. Even now, her cheeks burned with embarrassment. But her wild emotions transformed into utter relief when she saw Mairead standing beside the stone wall within Ennisleigh. Her hair was tangled, her gown torn, and there was blood on her clothing. But the expression on her face was quiet and steadfast.

Velaria ran to her cousin and embraced her hard. 'Did they hurt you? I'm so sorry, I—'

'I wasn't hurt,' Mairead answered. 'They tried, but...' She paused and held Velaria's gaze for a moment. 'They're dead now.'

She fully recognised that her cousin was hiding something—but what? Within another moment, Mairead was surrounded by her family and uncles. She accepted their hugs, and in the meantime, Velaria studied the fortress, searching for a hint of what had really happened. But she saw nothing, save the guards.

Savaş came up behind her. 'Come inside and get warm, Velaria,' he urged. 'You need to dry out by a fire.'

She nodded and led him up the stone stairs to the small keep. The island fortress was quite small, and when they reached the interior, there was only a single chamber with a large hearth. Velaria walked over to the fire, and Savaş stood beside her while they warmed their hands.

'Mairead wasn't alone,' he predicted.

'No. But whoever saved her is in hiding,' Velaria agreed. 'Mairead isn't a fighter.'

'Not like you.' His voice turned deeper.

'No,' she agreed. 'Not like me.'

In the firelight, his blue eyes watched her with an intensity she didn't understand.

An awkwardness washed over her, and she said quietly, 'I know you want an answer about…a betrothal between us. But I'm not the sort of woman any man wants to marry. Not any more.'

'I didn't offer to wed you out of pity, Velaria.' His voice held a deep timbre that seemed to reach past the invisible barriers she tried to hold between them.

A tightness caught in her chest at his words. 'Why did you, then?'

She was afraid of the answer, especially when he looked away. For a moment, he held back his answer, until at last he said, 'Because I don't want you to ever lose your freedom again. And if I can stop it from happening, I will. You can live your life as you choose.'

She didn't know what to think of his words. It reminded her once again of his earlier offer, of a marriage that was not a true one. And her heart bled at the thought of being married to a man who didn't want her. 'Savaş, I'd rather not marry at all.'

He threaded his hands through her hair, staring into her eyes. 'I know.' An invisible shadow seemed to cross his face. 'But I can give you the freedom you crave.'

She could scarcely breathe from the warmth of his breath upon her cheek. Heat flooded through her, and when he pulled back, he continued. 'And I know your strength. Both here…' He slid his fingers down her skin to her wrist. Then he brought his hand to her heart. 'And here.'

She couldn't speak, for her throat had closed up with unspoken emotions. She wanted to believe him, to lower the defences she held around her heart. But the thought of being vulnerable again, of sharing her heart and her love with anyone, only reminded her of her past failures.

She was saved from an answer when she heard approaching footsteps. Mairead entered the chamber, followed by her father, brother, and uncles. For a moment, Velaria caught her cousin's gaze. Though Mairead's expression remained sober, there seemed to be a hint of defiance within it.

'What happened, Mairead?' she asked.

Her cousin didn't meet her gaze. 'They're dead.' She didn't offer any other explanation, and an uneasy feeling caught in Velaria's stomach.

'Who killed them?' Liam demanded. 'And how many more men were there?'

'Only two,' Mairead whispered. 'And I killed them.'

Velaria didn't believe her at all, and from the look on Patrick's face, neither did he. But why would she lie? When she took a closer look, there was an iron resolution on Mairead's face—almost as if she were protecting someone.

The king gathered his forces together. To his daughter,

he said, 'We will return to Laochre. Your mother will be beside herself with worry.'

Mairead inclined her head in agreement, but as they were leaving, Velaria caught her hand. 'Did the May crown work?' she asked softly so the others wouldn't hear.

A slow smile spread over her cousin's face before she turned away.

As they rowed back to the mainland, Brian was separated from Velaria. Instead, he was surrounded by Connor, Ewan, and Trahern, three of the king's brothers.

'A long day for you, was it?' Connor remarked to Brian.

'Very,' he agreed. But his attention was fixed upon Velaria, who was in a boat with her cousin. He wanted to talk with her more, but she would probably refuse. Her mood had grown subdued, as if troubled thoughts weighed her down. He suspected it was because of their earlier fight.

But now what? He needed to travel north to find Morwenna, and he didn't want to go without Velaria.

'Has she given you an answer yet?' Ewan asked. 'You offered for her, didn't you?'

'I did. And she wants more time to make her decision.'

Ewan settled back with one of the oars. 'We should help him out, Brother. The lad is wanting to marry Velaria, but Ademar plans to marry her off to a high-ranking lord.'

'And why should we get involved?' Trahern mused.

'Because she can't take her eyes off him,' Ewan said. 'And I think 'tis a good match. Honora agrees.'

Connor leaned back in the boat. 'Slow your rowing, then, while we think on it.' He eyed Brian. 'Have you kissed her, then?'

Brian wasn't certain he wanted this conversation at all,

but he wasn't foolish enough to ignore their offer to help. 'A few times.'

'But did she kiss you back?' Ewan prompted.

He sent her uncle a pointed look and a nod.

Trahern's expression shifted into a sly smile. 'Well, then, it sounds as if all she needs is a nudge in the right direction.'

From out of nowhere, Brian felt a sense of uncertainty. 'I promised her that if she agreed to wed me, I would leave her untouched, if that's what she wanted.'

Then men started to laugh, even her uncle Ewan. 'Oh, Danu, he *does* need our help,' Trahern groaned. 'We may as well drop anchor, for we'll be here all night.'

'Are you afraid that she'll steal your virtue, lad?' Connor teased.

His fists tightened, and he glared at the man. Though he'd never been with a woman before, he had no intention of admitting it. For a moment, the idea of swimming back to shore sounded appealing.

But before he could say another word, Trahern turned to his younger brother. 'Ewan, she's your niece. Will he make her a good husband?'

The man turned serious. 'Aye. He allowed her to fight alongside him. I don't know that many other men would willingly let their wives wield a sword.'

'Velaria deserves the right to defend herself,' Brian said. 'I've never met a woman who could fight as well as she can.'

'My wife, Honora, is just as strong,' Ewan said. 'And you're right. A strong woman is worth more than gold. I would give my life for hers, just as she would for me.'

Connor nodded to Brian. 'Seduce her thoroughly, lad, and she won't be arguing about marriage. She'll be eager to wed.'

Ewan's expression darkened. 'I was speaking of marriage, Connor. He'll not be dishonouring my niece.'

His older brother grinned. 'Well, then, he could tempt her in the right direction. Honourably, of course.'

Brian shook his head. 'She was…hurt before.' First by the knight who'd abandoned her and possibly again in Constantinople. 'I'm not about to make her feel uncomfortable.'

'Good lad.' Ewan nodded his head in approval.

Trahern sobered and said, 'Aye, then. In that case, you'll tempt her—but without touching her. Allow her to make the choice.'

Brian said nothing, and Ewan exchanged a glance with his brothers. 'I think we've a wealth of knowledge between us that our young lad needs.'

Brian wasn't at all certain what her uncle was talking about, but Trahern set down the oars. 'All right then. We'll tell you what you're needing to know if you want to win her heart. And if you have any wits about you, lad, you'll not tell her father about this conversation.'

He paused a moment and regarded the men. 'And why would you help me in this?'

Connor smiled. 'Because it's a road we've all travelled, lad.'

Although Brian wasn't at all certain about this, he listened to their advice as they rowed back to the opposite shore. And he began to form a plan of sorts.

The only question was whether it would work.

The following evening, Velaria heard a knock at her door. When she called out for the person to enter, she saw her aunt Honora and her mother, Katherine, standing there.

'Is something wrong?' she asked the women.

Her mother shook her head. 'Not at all. But Honora and I were hoping you would walk with us for a little while.'

It was a strange request, but Velaria reached for a wrap and pulled it around her shoulders. 'All right.' She followed them outside the chamber, wondering if it was something to do with Mairead. 'Did you need something?'

Her mother exchanged a look with her sister but didn't answer at first. Instead, they led her along the hall and down the spiral stairs towards the Great Chamber. 'I wanted to see if *you* were all right.' Katherine's voice dropped to a low whisper. 'After everything that happened with those men who attacked you.'

Her shoulders relaxed when her mother rested her hand on her waist. It was only a mother's concern, and she was grateful for it.

'I'm all right,' she said softly. It was strange to realise that she hadn't even thought about the deaths of those men. Just as she'd done in the arena, she'd locked away every emotion, refusing to think of the death and destruction. She had protected Mairead and wasn't sorry for it.

Velaria lifted her gaze to Honora, knowing her aunt would understand. 'I didn't have a choice in what I did.'

Her aunt reached out to squeeze her hand. 'I know.'

'But there may be…consequences for it,' Katherine said, guiding her outside and into the inner bailey. The night air had grown cool, and torches illuminated the space. Velaria saw guards stationed at every corner of the towers, vigilant over their enemies, and it brought her a sense of security.

Her mother continued, saying, 'The men who died were King John's men, sent on ahead before the king arrives with his own army.'

It didn't surprise her to learn of it, but she still didn't understand why her mother and aunt appeared so serious.

They stopped walking a moment, and Katherine said, 'When they buried the bodies, they learned that one of the men was Terence de Vere, Baron Marwood.'

Ice flooded through Velaria's veins as she made the connection. Though she had never met Lord Marwood before, she'd known his son well enough. Past and present seemed to blur, and she turned to her mother, whose expression had gone pale. Katherine only reached for her hand and squeezed it.

Honora seemed unaware of their reaction and added, 'The baron visited King Patrick on several occasions on behalf of King John.'

Velaria was starting to understand their concern. If the baron had died on King Patrick's lands, then the MacEgans would be held responsible for her actions. But her own thoughts were caught up in what would happen next. There would be severe consequences for what she'd done.

And yet, she held no regret for taking his life. 'They were planning to hurt us,' Velaria said. 'Even the baron.'

'I believe you,' Katherine said. 'But if they learn that you were responsible for killing a nobleman—even though you defended yourself and Mairead—the king may demand a price for it.'

Velaria understood the unspoken threat. Her life could indeed become forfeit for the baron's death—especially if his family sought retribution. And her father did not hold enough power to protect her from the king's wrath.

Katherine looped Velaria's arm in hers. 'But we have a way to keep you safe.' Her aunt joined on her opposite side, and they led her towards the family chapel. Once they were inside, Velaria saw a small altar and a wooden cross upon the wall. Inside, a priest stood waiting. Had he come to hear her confession? Or did they intend for her to seek the sanctuary of the church and join a nunnery? But when she turned around, she saw her father waiting.

His expression was grim, but he came forward and opened his arms. Without really thinking, she went into his embrace as he held her tightly. 'I'm s-sorry for what happened to you, Velaria.' There was no anger in his voice, only the tone of a worried father.

In his arms, she felt like a little girl again, lifted up after she'd fallen and scraped her knee. But this time, his blue eyes were filled with unspoken fear.

She turned to both parents. 'What is happening?' All around her, it seemed that her family was gathering for a reason they had not yet revealed.

'We intend to protect you from the king's wrath,' Katherine said. 'Whether you want it or not, you need to marry.'

Panic rose up in her stomach, and Velaria turned back towards the door—only to see Savaş waiting there.

He was dressed in the same leather armour he'd worn earlier, and behind him stood the rest of the MacEgan brothers and their wives. One by one, the family entered the chapel, and she understood what was happening. They were here to witness a wedding—her own.

'I need to talk to you,' Savaş said quietly.

Her emotions were tangled up inside her, for it felt like an ambush. She'd told everyone she didn't want to marry. And yet, no one was listening. She didn't move. Nor could she breathe when he stepped forward and took her hand in his.

He guided her to the far side of the room and lowered his voice. 'You're in danger. The king will be furious when he learns about Lord Marwood.'

'He won't,' she started to say. But the moment she voiced the words, she remembered the attacker who had escaped.

The soldier would make his way back to the king and the truth might come out.

'We can't stay here any longer,' he said. 'I have to take you north to my sister's home where you'll be safe.'

'Then we'll go,' she murmured. Her voice broke, but she gripped his hand. 'There's no need to wed.'

'Your father demands it for the sake of your honour. He also believes I can intercede with King John if necessary.' His thumb edged her palm, and his eyes met hers. 'Will you let me protect you, Velaria?'

She couldn't speak, for her throat seemed to close up. The truth was, if her family truly forced her into marriage, there was only one man she would consider—the one standing before her.

Her heart pounded, and every muscle in her body tensed. She'd never had time to consider what she wanted, but in Savaş's eyes, she saw the calm face of a man who intended to keep her safe.

Everyone was waiting for her answer. And although she feared being a disappointment to him as a wife, she didn't want to humiliate him in front of everyone by refusing.

All she could do was offer a single nod. The world appeared to freeze in place as he led her outside the chapel to speak their vows before the priest. Someone pressed a crown of rowan, woven with lavender, upon her hair.

Velaria hardly heard a word of the marriage rite, but she was fully aware of the moment when Savaş brushed his mouth against hers in a kiss of peace. The warmth of the kiss slid over her, causing a deep ache of longing. Then he led her back inside the chapel where the priest held the wedding Mass.

She clung to his hand as if it were the only thing holding her upright. The scent of incense filled the space, and dozens of lit candles flickered shadows and light against the stone walls. But he was here beside her, and if his purpose was to guard her from being taken prisoner again, she could accept that.

After the Mass ended, the MacEgans congratulated them both. Queen Isabel invited them back to the Great Chamber for mead, honey cakes, and a small celebration. Savaş rested his hand upon her spine and leaned in. 'How are you feeling?'

'Overwhelmed,' she admitted honestly. 'It doesn't seem real.'

He studied her and added, 'I meant what I said. I will protect you from whatever happens now. But we should leave at dawn to travel north to my sister. We need to be far away from here before the king's men arrive.'

She nodded in agreement, and he led her back into the Great Chamber. To her surprise, she saw flowers and greenery everywhere. Her cousin Mairead wore her finest *léine* and overdress and smiled warmly when she saw them. Beside her stood Adriana. It was clear that both women were responsible for the decorations and the food.

Mairead embraced Velaria and murmured, 'I am glad you agreed to the marriage. You'll be happy together. I know it.' She led them up to the dais, and Velaria took her seat with Savaş beside her.

A servant poured cups of mead, and Velaria drank hers, still feeling uncertain about all of this. One moment, she'd been in her chamber, and the next, she'd become a bride. Part of her thought she ought to be angry or upset at how it had all come about. And yet, when she looked at her new husband, she saw the face of the man who had been by her side during the worst moments of her life. It was Savaş who had kept the broken pieces of her from falling apart. She couldn't name the swirling emotions within her, but part of her felt a sense of unexpected hope.

Was it wrong to feel this way? He'd married her as a means of protection. But would he continue to desire a false marriage, one where they remained apart within the union? She didn't know.

There was music and dancing, and he leaned in. 'We're expected to join them. Will you dance with me?'

She felt awkward about dancing in front of everyone, but she understood that it was expected. 'I'm not very good at it.'

'Neither am I.' But he stood and offered his hand.

Just then, there came the sound of cups pounding against the tables and cheering. Velaria didn't quite understand what was happening, but a moment later, Savaş leaned down and kissed her.

It was not the same kiss of peace from the wedding, but something else entirely. His hands threaded through her hair, and he kissed her as if there was no one else except the two of them. His mouth was hot and hungry, and her own response frightened her with how quickly her body grew heated. Beneath her gown, her breasts tightened, and she ached between her legs. He'd only kissed her like this once before, and it had made her feel vulnerable and desirable.

His tongue threaded with hers, and she clung to him as her cheeks flushed. Never had she imagined he would kiss her like this in front of everyone. But when he broke off the kiss, there was loud approval from the crowd. He led her down into the dancing, and soon enough, they were surrounded by others. She took several missteps, but he lifted her up and held her for a moment.

'I'm glad you agreed to wed me,' he said. But there was a flare of heat in his voice that suddenly made Velaria anxious about the wedding night ahead. A rush of nerves caught her, and she tried to push back the rising uncertainty. Would he expect to consummate the marriage? He'd sworn not to, but what if he'd changed his mind? She didn't know how to feel about it. When she'd lost her innocence to Sir Drogan, it had been awkward, and she hadn't enjoyed it. But perhaps that had been her fault.

She couldn't deny her own attraction to Savaş or the way he made her desire him. But what if the same thing happened, and he no longer wanted her afterwards?

'Velaria,' he said, as he lowered her down. 'Don't be afraid of me.'

'I don't know what I'm supposed to do,' she admitted.

He smiled then, and she couldn't remember the last time she'd seen a true smile on his face. His eyes held her captive, and he said softly, 'Just dance with me.'

Brian was grateful to Connor and Ewan for their help in arranging the wedding, but his own nerves were rising when at last it was time for the wedding night. The king and queen had offered to let them stay at the smaller fortress at Ennisleigh to give them privacy for the night. He couldn't deny that he was grateful to have an actual bed, as opposed to the pallet he'd slept on during the past few days.

But he didn't know whether Velaria would want to consummate the marriage or not. He hadn't told her that King Patrick had said the consummation was necessary to sanctify the marriage. Yet, no one would know the truth if he didn't touch her, for Velaria was not a virgin. He planned to spill a few drops of his own blood upon the sheets as false evidence of her innocence, if need be.

Brian despised the knight who had seduced and abandoned her. In many ways, he wished he could take away her past suffering, but the truth was, *he* was the virgin tonight. And despite all the advice the MacEgan men had offered, he wouldn't touch his new bride if she wanted to be alone.

He rowed the small boat from the mainland towards the fortress, and above them, the stars gleamed. The sea was calm, and he could see how nervous she was from the way she clenched the wooden sides of the boat.

'How are you?' he asked quietly.

'I don't even know. I never imagined that I would be married only a few hours ago.' She pulled the edges of her *brat* around her shoulders, for the night air had grown cooler.

'Neither did I,' he admitted. 'It's hard to believe.' As they drew closer to the island shore, he guided the boat towards the wooden pier. 'But I don't regret it. I would do anything to protect you.'

She shivered and said, 'I only did what I had to. Those men *would* have hurt Mairead and me. But I also never meant to start a war.'

'We won't let that happen,' he said. 'With any luck, no one will know it was you. We'll go north to my sister's home, and we'll be safe there.'

Brian tied off the boat and helped her to the pier. Behind them, the moonlight reflected on the darker waves of the sea. He escorted her inside the fortress and was surprised to find that the king and queen had arranged for more decorations. He didn't remember seeing them the previous night.

A servant brought them to their own private chamber, and inside, there were several candles and lamps to illuminate the darkness. On one table, he found a small repast of bread and cheese, along with a ewer of wine. The hearth had been lit, and a peat fire burned brightly.

But Velaria glanced at the bed and appeared uneasy. He

needed to reassure her that he would never demand something she was unwilling to give.

'Come here,' he bade her gently.

She walked over to stand by the fire, and he removed her *brat*. Then he pulled her into his embrace, and she rested her head against his chest. For a moment, he simply held her, and she did the same. The warmth of the fire was comforting, and he stroked her hair lightly.

'I never imagined I would have a marriage like this,' he admitted. 'Especially after the life I led as a serf. I never dreamed of someone like you—your life was so far above mine.'

She raised her head and regarded him. 'Is that why you pushed me away during our journey home?'

He gave a nod. 'I knew I wasn't good enough for you. It was different in the arena. We were equals then. But in England...' He let his words trail off.

'I'm not the same woman who left England,' she admitted. 'That maiden died when we wore chains.'

He reached for her wrists, turning them over in the firelight. There were still raised lines upon her skin, and he lifted them to his mouth, kissing one and then the other.

'Savaş,' she whispered. 'I don't think I can be the sort of wife you want.'

I'm broken, she almost said.

Even now, though he'd been nothing but gentle, she was afraid of the darker memories. She'd locked them away for so long, refusing to face them. It was easier to pretend that the time in Constantinople had never existed.

'You have nothing to fear from me,' he said. 'I won't do anything you don't want.' He slid his hand against one cheek, and the warmth of his palm upon her skin evoked a yearning that threatened to open the doors of the past.

'Will you let me kiss you?' he asked.

That, at least, she could accept. She lifted her face to his, drawing his mouth down to hers. His lips were firm and coaxing, and she lifted her arms around his neck, welcoming her new husband.

It was so strange to imagine that they were now married—or even that her father had allowed it. She didn't know whether it was because of Savaş's possible relation to the king or because she had finally agreed to wed.

And yet, to her, he was the man who had been her closest friend while they'd been captives. She had needed him then, just as she did now.

His kiss turned hungrier, his tongue sliding against hers. She clung tighter to him, uncertain of the feelings coursing through her. Drogan had kissed her before, but not like this. Not as if she were the very breath he needed to survive.

Savaş kissed her deeply, his hands moving down her spine. Her body was awakening to him, and although it frightened her, she didn't want him to stop, either. His mouth moved to her throat, and her skin erupted in gooseflesh. Her breasts tightened against the linen of her shift, and between her legs, she felt a warmth blooming.

He drew back the neckline of her gown, and it was then that she realised he'd loosened the laces. Her heartbeat pounded, and she wanted to protest. But all he did was bare her shoulder and press his mouth against her skin.

'If you want me to stop at any moment, just say the word,' he told her.

She took a deep breath and admitted, 'I wish I had run away with you, instead of Drogan. I wish I were a virgin this night.'

It embarrassed her that she'd made such a mistake. And even afterwards, she hadn't enjoyed it. She hadn't pleased him, and the lovemaking had been painful and embarrassing. The same thing might happen tonight. And though Savaş might be kind, she was afraid she couldn't be the bride he wanted.

'But if you hadn't run away from home…if you hadn't been sold into slavery, we never would have met,' he said. He tilted her face to look at him. 'We cannot look back on a past that can't be changed. But we can make this marriage whatever you want it to be. We can remain friends. Or it could be something more.'

He was offering her a choice that terrified her. But if she pushed him away, she sensed it would be the same as when they'd been aboard the ship sailing home—distant and cool. It had hurt so much to feel unwanted.

But right now, when she looked into her husband's eyes, she saw a man who *did* desire her. His kiss had awakened her own needs. Perhaps, if she dared to reach out to him, if she wanted something more, he might push the nightmares away. And that meant setting aside her fear and surrendering herself.

Slowly, Velaria lifted away her overdress and stood before him in her shift. His gaze turned heated, but he removed his leather armour and tunic until he stood only in his trews. She stared at the rigid lines that cut across his pectoral muscles and the ridges that led to his waist. He hadn't lost any of his strength, despite the hardships they'd suffered. Uncertainty washed over her, but she forced herself to reach out and touch him.

Beneath her fingers, his skin was warm and hard. She reminded herself that this was Savaş, the warrior who had fought to save her life. Her friend who had spent endless months at her side as they had tried to survive. And now, her husband.

He remained still, allowing her to explore his skin. She studied the reddened scar at his shoulder and stood on tiptoe to kiss it. 'I'm sorry I hurt you,' she whispered.

'I'm not,' he answered. 'It was worth the price of our freedom.' Then he bent down to claim her mouth again.

Once again, his kiss awakened her to a yearning she didn't understand. She clung to him, and the softness of her own curves pressed against his hardened chest. He pulled her close, and it was then that she felt the ridge of his arousal.

Instantly, she froze, afraid to even move. He seemed to sense it, and he relaxed his hold, giving her the power to pull away.

'It's all right,' he said. 'We don't have to consummate the marriage.'

Though she understood he didn't want to pressure her, guilt weighed upon her. Not only because of her past, but also because she wanted to please him.

'I'll—I'll be all right,' she murmured.

From the look in his eyes, she sensed he didn't believe her. For a moment, she couldn't guess what he was thinking. But instead, he took her by the hand and led her over to the bed. He drew back the coverlet and lifted her onto the mattress before guiding her to lie back.

She told herself it would be all right, that he would never hurt her. But instead of covering her body with his own, he moved to the opposite side of the bed. He kept his trews on and got beneath the covers before pulling it over both of them.

Oh, God.

Her thoughts grew bewildered, for she hadn't expected

this at all. She stared at the hearth, feeling dejected that she had caused him to stop.

But then he drew his arm around her waist in silent comfort. 'Goodnight, Velaria,' he murmured as he kissed her shoulder.

She felt the rise of tears, knowing that this wasn't what their wedding night was supposed to be. She had hoped to drive out the demons of the past, but instead, it seemed that their shadows still lingered.

For a moment, she didn't move, didn't breathe. Then it occurred to her that she would have to reach out if she wanted more. She had to show him that she wasn't afraid.

Slowly, she eased back into his arms until her spine nestled against his chest. And she reached back to draw his arms around her in the embrace she wanted.

Her breath caught in her lungs, but she dared to bring his hand to her breast. His palm warmed the linen, and her body ached at the barest touch.

She spoke no words, nor did he. And yet, he caressed her softly. The bud of her nipple rose to his fingertips, and he gently encircled it with his thumb. She bit her lip, startled by the deep feelings that slid between her legs, coaxing her into a feeling that was…strangely pleasant. He adjusted his position and brought his hands around until he cupped both breasts. She held back her gasp of surprise, but she couldn't stop the moan that escaped her when he stroked both nipples at the same time.

She pressed back against his erection and was rewarded by his own intake of breath. Though she ought to be frightened, she was too distracted by the sweetness of his touch.

'You're killing me,' he murmured against her nape. 'I was planning to leave you alone.'

She knew that. And yet, she couldn't deny how good his

hands felt upon her skin. It was nothing at all like the night she'd lost her innocence.

His hands skimmed over the curve of her breasts, down her stomach, and his fingers stilled at the apex of her thighs. Velaria understood his silent question. And for a moment, she considered removing his hand. Yet, nothing he'd done so far had been a demand—only an invitation.

And so, she reached beneath the coverlet and drew up the hem of her shift. Slowly, she removed the linen garment until she was naked in his arms.

Fear slid beneath her skin, but it was the fear that she wouldn't please him. That this night would change their friendship and make it awkward between them.

Savaş tensed behind her, but once again, he made no demands. She settled back against him, and in truth, she didn't know what she wanted. Did she want to consummate the marriage and push past what had happened before? Or was it better to wait?

Dozens of questions and possibilities warred within her mind, but he silenced them all when he cupped her breast with one hand, and his other moved between her legs. The sweetness of his caress against her nipple brought a pleasure that stole her breath. For a moment, her hand tightened upon his heavy thigh in a silent plea for more.

He didn't make demands, but the warmth of his palm against her thighs made her shift against him. Her body was wet with a need she didn't understand.

But then, he slid his hand lower, caressing her intimately. Shock bolted through her, and though she couldn't deny the pleasure of his touch, darker memories assailed her. She couldn't do this. It was too much, too soon.

'Stop,' she whispered, even as she hated herself for speaking the word.

Immediately, he removed his hand from her body. He said nothing at all but moved away until their bodies no longer touched.

And as she huddled in a tight ball, she couldn't stop the silent tears that flowed down her cheeks.

Chapter Nine

The chains encircled his wrists first, before they wrapped around his throat. In the darkness, Brian couldn't breathe, and he fought against the bindings. He struggled to push away his attacker, but he couldn't see who it was.

'Savaş,' a woman's voice said. Her presence was familiar, like a hand reaching out to him. He wasn't aware of his surroundings, and past and present seemed to blur around him. He struggled against the hands trying to hold him down, and it was only when she pressed her body to his that he realised she was naked.

Desire speared through him, and he felt the softness of her breasts against his chest, her hips against his. His body was covered in sweat, his breathing unsteady.

Velaria was here, in his bed. Slowly, reality came back to him, and he stilled.

'You were dreaming,' she said quietly. 'It was just a nightmare.'

His mouth was dry, and he was torn between annoyance at himself for losing control and the fierce desire for his new wife.

'I'm sorry,' he managed. He hadn't wanted her to know about the dreams that still plagued him, even though he knew she understood. It embarrassed him that he'd lost sight of where he was—especially now.

'Do you get those dreams often?' She rested her hand upon his heart, which was still beating rapidly. Although right now, his blood pounded for her as much as the dream. Right now, he could feel every inch of her slim, muscled body. And she had to be aware of his need for her.

'Most nights, I have bad dreams,' he admitted. 'Don't you?' He didn't move, for fear that she would pull away.

'Yes,' she admitted. 'Sometimes it feels like a lifetime ago. And other nights, I still feel the chains. I remember the horrors we faced.'

He took her wrists in his hands, gently caressing them. 'We're safe now.' His hands moved to her bare spine, but he did nothing more than hold her against him. Yestereve, he had frightened her, and he blamed himself for pressing her too soon.

'Savaş, about…our wedding night.' Her voice held shame, something he never wanted her to feel.

He sat up slightly and drew his arms around her. 'I asked too much of you,' he said against her lips. 'You weren't ready.'

'I wanted to be,' she whispered.

He knew that. But he slid his hands down her bottom to her hips, gritting his teeth at the softness of her body upon his. 'We have time.'

She stared at him for a moment and then rolled to her side. He came up behind her, resting his face against her neck.

'That night, when Kadir's men took me—' she started.

His arms tightened around her. 'You don't have to tell me.' He wasn't entirely certain he wanted to know what had happened that night.

She fell silent for a moment but drew his arms closer around her. 'They brought me to a large chamber with four noblemen. Kadir sat with the noblemen in chairs around the room. There was a sunken pool of water in the floor.' Her voice caught a moment, but she continued.

'They stripped my clothing from me and forced me to stand naked before the men.' She let out a slow breath. 'He planned to sell me to one of them as a concubine.'

Brian stroked her hair, but inwardly, he wanted to kill Kadir and every man who had humiliated her. 'I'm sorry.' No woman deserved to be treated like that.

'There were two serving girls who came into the pool,' Velaria said. 'They—they washed me in front of the men, and Kadir invited them to…touch me.' Her body curled inward, and he knew she was crying. Every part of him tensed at her confession, but he simply held her in silent support.

'I thought I could…ignore them and pretend it didn't matter.' Her body trembled against his as she admitted, 'But when the first man touched me, I couldn't pretend it wasn't happening. I used my chains to choke him, and I fought them. I drew blood, and I didn't care.'

'I'm glad you did,' he said quietly. 'I wish I could have killed them for you.'

'I nearly did kill one of them,' she admitted. 'Kadir was furious. He stopped the men from…claiming me. But he ordered me to be beaten while the others watched.'

She shuddered again, gripping the coverlet. 'They—' Her words broke off, but she didn't finish.

'You don't have to say anything else, Velaria.' He turned her to face him and stroked her cheek. 'I will never make demands of you. Nor will I touch you if that's not what you want.'

'I don't want those memories to keep me from having a future,' she admitted. 'I don't want them to hold that victory.' Then she took his hand in hers. 'The only man I want is you.'

* * *

The next morn, Velaria endured the teasing of several of the MacEgan brothers, but it was all with good wishes. Mairead bid her farewell, but the young woman still had a mysterious smile, which made Velaria wonder what she was hiding.

Brian waited with the horses while she embraced her mother and father. Katherine touched her cheek and smiled. 'I hope you will be happy together. Come back to England when you can.'

Velaria gave a nod, and then her father regarded her. 'Brian of Penrith was not the man I would have chosen for you to w-wed. But if you are happy with him, we will f-find a place for both of you at Ardennes.'

'Thank you, Father.' She squeezed his hand, and then Brian helped her on to her horse. She noticed that he had tied a sword to her saddle as a weapon for defence. It didn't bother her to be armed as much as it had before.

King Patrick came forward to say farewell, but instead of bidding them a good journey, he warned, 'I am sending a few of my men with you as escorts for part of your journey. If you see any of the king's men, stay away from them on your journey north. You don't want to be caught between sides.'

'I hope to gain an audience with my father,' Brian said. 'After I've spoken with my sister and her husband.'

'Be cautious,' the king advised. 'If there were witnesses to Lord Marwood's death, they could identify Velaria.'

A chill slid over her at the reminder that one of the men had escaped—one who could identify her to the king.

'I will keep her safe,' Brian vowed. 'With my own life. No one will harm her.'

A softness caught within her heart, for Velaria knew

he meant it. After they said their farewells and continued on the pathway north with their escorts, her husband drew his horse closer.

As she met his gaze, she saw the heated stare and her body seemed to respond to him. She remembered his touch and the way he had made her feel desirable. But she was also ashamed that she had asked him to stop. He had never asked for more than she could give.

Yet, she was frustrated with herself for not being able to give him the sort of marriage he ought to have—the sort of marriage she wanted, too. She promised herself that she would try again.

As they travelled away from Laochre, she stopped to glance back at the coast and the horizon. There were no ships yet, but she worried what would happen when the king's men discovered she was responsible for the deaths of the baron and the others.

Brian seemed to guess her thoughts. 'We'll be far away from here by the time the king and his men arrive.'

Her mood sobered, and she continued riding alongside him. 'Tell me about your sister, Morwenna.'

His face softened. 'She was always protective of me when I was young. We moved from place to place often. I didn't realise until later that we were adopted. But I think Morwenna suspected it.'

'Who is your mother?' she asked.

Brian shook his head. 'I don't know. I'm hoping Morwenna can tell me that when I find her.'

She understood how much he needed answers about his past. And yet, her own thoughts were focused upon an uncertain future. Her father had been sincere in his offer to help them, but she also suspected that Savaş would want to forge his own path. It meant facing King John, eventually. Part of her hoped it wasn't true that he was the king's bastard son. Yet, if he was, then it might offer the protection they needed.

Velaria could feel Savaş's gaze upon her as they rode north. She couldn't deny that her own attention kept shifting towards him. Although she'd lost her courage last night before they could consummate their marriage, she believed Savaş could help her move forward. His touch had conjured the memories she hadn't wanted to face—but perhaps that was what she needed to lay the ghosts to rest.

He'd listened to her when she'd revealed what had happened with Kadir's men. She'd sensed his anger, but it was towards the men, not her. And somehow, confessing her darkest moments had seemed to pull them closer together. Not once had he looked upon her with distaste. Instead, he'd held her all night. The warmth of his skin against hers had brought her a comfort she'd never expected. And in the morning, he'd cut his hand, adding a few drops of his own blood to the sheets to make it seem as if she'd lost her innocence. It was a noble gesture she hadn't anticipated.

The truth was, she wanted a real marriage between them. And she hoped that if she offered herself again, it might heal the jagged memories of the past and make her whole.

Despite their long journey, Savaş's skin had not lost the bronzed colour from Constantinople. She understood his need to feel the sun's warmth and remember that they had their freedom. But when she looked over at her husband as they journeyed, she couldn't deny the flare of attraction. When she stole a glance at his handsome face, she thought of his kiss and his hands upon her.

Savaş caught her staring, and though her cheeks flushed, she saw the answering look in his eyes and the promise of more. She took a deep breath and offered a slight smile.

But the intensity of his gaze seemed to awaken her body until her skin grew sensitive beneath her gown.

They rode alongside one another for hours before Savaş finally raised his hand to stop for the night. He sent their escorts off to hunt, and Velaria started gathering stones for a hearth fire. Before she could finish stacking the wood and kindling, he came up behind her and wrapped his arms around her waist. The gesture of affection was entirely unexpected, but she turned to embrace him.

'I've been wanting to do that for hours,' he murmured.

His words evoked a smile, and she lifted her gaze to his. 'I'm glad you did.'

He kept his hands at her waist and said softly, 'There's something I need to know, Velaria.'

Her heartbeat quickened, but she ventured, 'What is it?'

He bent to her ear, and his warm breath sent a dark shiver through her. 'Do you want a marriage in name only?'

Colour stained her cheeks, but she forced herself to touch his face. 'No,' she breathed. 'I never wanted a marriage like that.' She swallowed hard and admitted, 'I always wanted you, Savaş. But I'm not a virgin any more, and I'm afraid I won't please you.' She couldn't hide the shame in her voice. Drogan had abandoned her after that night, and she couldn't bear the thought of Savaş being disappointed.

And yet, the look in his eyes was fiercely protective. 'What happened to you wasn't your fault,' he insisted. 'And I disagree. If you found no pleasure, then you *are* still a virgin.' His hand moved slowly up her spine, and he said, 'Do you want me to touch you, Velaria?'

His words made her breathless, and she didn't know what to say. She felt self-conscious and uncertain, for she couldn't imagine lying with him while others were nearby.

Before she could ask what he meant, the men returned with rabbits and another had fish.

The MacEgans had provided other food supplies, and Velaria used the meal preparation as a chance to occupy herself and keep her mind off the offer her husband had made. What did he mean she was still a virgin?

She couldn't deny that Savaş made her blood race, that she'd welcomed his kiss. But all she'd ever known of lovemaking was Drogan's fumbling hands and the unwanted caresses of Kadir's men. Her only consolation was that she had saved herself from rape. But what had hurt her most of all was the blow to her pride. Although Kadir had ordered her beaten, the physical pain had been nothing compared to the emotional shame she bore.

One of the men lit the hearth fire, and she cooked the fish and the meat while the others set up their own tents. Savaş had disappeared, and she didn't know where he'd gone. He hadn't set up their tent, so she suspected he'd set it up elsewhere for them to have more privacy.

Her thoughts were a scattered distraction, but after he returned, she was fully aware of her husband's gaze upon her. His very presence made her conscious of his body and his sinewy strength. She remembered the way he had fought at Bealtaine, and she yearned to touch him. The very thought brought a surge of heat within her.

She had barely finished eating when he reached for her hand and drew her to stand. Some of the men sent teasing smiles, and one remarked, 'Sleep well.' But Savaş picked up a torch and handed her a blanket. Then, he led her down a narrow pathway through the woods a short distance away.

'I found a better place for us to sleep,' he said.

Beside a small stream, she saw an abandoned thatched

hut. It was falling apart, and she suspected the roof leaked. Even so, she followed him when he brought her inside.

'We're staying here tonight,' he said. And she understood, then, that he'd wanted to be alone with her. She didn't know if she was ready for this, but she hadn't lied when she'd said she wanted a true marriage between them. Somehow, she would push aside her fear and try to heal the past.

Savaş lit the hearth fire, and she spread out the blanket upon the ground inside the hut. Although there were holes in the roof, Velaria could see the stars appearing in the dark lavender sky above them.

When the fire had taken hold, he unbuckled his sword belt and set it aside. She felt her body go cold with fear, and she tried to avert her gaze.

'You never answered my question earlier,' he said. 'Do you want me to give you pleasure? Or would you rather sleep instead?'

His words aroused her, making her wonder what he meant. 'I don't know what I want,' she murmured, 'except to touch you.'

His gaze warmed, and he removed his tunic to stand bare-chested before her. His shoulder still bore the scar, but it did nothing to diminish his strength.

Savaş took her hand in his and brought it to his heart. Beneath her fingertips, she could feel his massive strength. And when she looked into his eyes, she saw the trust there.

Slowly, she explored his skin with her hands, tracing the stony muscles of his chest, down lower to the ridges of his stomach. His body was warm, and he admitted, 'I am at your mercy, Velaria. Do whatever you will.'

Her hands went motionless, and she took a breath. Part of her feared it was too much like the night she'd been taken prisoner, when the men had touched her against her will. But Savaş had freely invited her hands upon him.

'I don't want to do anything you don't want,' she started to say.

'I want everything.' His voice was husky, laced with his own desire. 'I want your hands upon my skin.'

His words were provocative, and she could feel a shimmering ache between her legs. But it was different, wasn't it? This was her chance to give *him* pleasure. Something within her warmed to the idea.

And so, she came closer and stroked his broad chest, lowering her lips to his skin. He cupped her head against him, sliding back her hair.

'I love seeing your hair free,' he admitted. He caressed the locks, and she brought her mouth to kiss a path towards his nipple. She slid her tongue across it, and he hissed, his hands tensing on her waist.

'You took me by surprise,' he admitted. 'Sorry.' He softened his grip, and then she came up behind him to rub his shoulders. Her fingers found the knots, and she kissed the skin of his back, gently stroking him.

When she reached his waist, she stilled her touch, afraid of going any further.

'Every night you fought, I was afraid you wouldn't return,' he said. 'And the day I was forced to fight you was the moment I feared most.' He tilted her chin up to look at him. 'I would never hurt you, Velaria. Not in a thousand years.'

'I know.' And she wanted to be a true wife to him, more than anything. 'I want to consummate our marriage, Savaş. I'm just…afraid of the way you make me feel.'

He leaned in and rested his forehead against hers. 'Tell me.'

She didn't know how to explain it. 'I feel like I have no control over the way my body responds to your touch. I don't like the feeling of surrendering.'

To her surprise, he smiled. 'I have another idea. If you're willing.'

* * *

Velaria gave a nod, and Brian walked closer to the fire. He never took his eyes from her as he removed the rest of his clothing and stood naked before his wife. Her expression faltered, but she studied him, her gaze taking in all of him. She appeared startled at what he'd done, but he beckoned for her to come closer. Instead, she remained in place, her cheeks blushing.

'Do you trust me?' he asked quietly.

'I do, but—' Her words broke off, and she didn't finish the sentence. It didn't matter, for he understood her hesitation. And although he'd never lain with a woman, he'd received enough advice that he knew what he wanted to do.

This night was about her, about learning her body and what pleased her. And the thought of caressing that silken skin and tasting every part of her was enough to send his desire to the edge.

His wife took a moment to gather her courage, and then she reached back to loosen the laces before she removed her overdress and *léine*. She stood before him in only a thin linen shift, and for a moment, she faltered. 'I'm nervous,' she confessed.

He didn't tease her but instead continued to wait, allowing her to make the decision.

Then at last, she reached down and removed her shift, pulling it over her head. The sight of her naked body stole his breath. Her body was still lean, but it had lost the look of hunger. The sight of her breasts and those long legs held him captive.

He sat down upon the blanket she'd brought and beckoned for her to come and lie beside him. She did, and he drew her body against his, so he nestled against her from behind. Then he took her hand.

'I don't want you to be afraid of me,' he said gently. 'But you are also the only woman I've ever touched.'

Velaria turned to face him, and there was a softness in her expression. She rested her forehead against his in silent acknowledgement before she kissed him softly. The kiss was an offering that humbled him.

When he drew back, he took both of her hands in his. 'I want you to put my hands wherever you want them. If you want me to stop, you need only move my hand.'

In the firelight, her nipples tightened as if his words had aroused her. He ached to touch her, but he forced himself to hold back. Velaria turned around again, pressing her backside against his arousal. Brian suppressed a groan of need, and he sensed that this night would require all his control.

First, Velaria brought his hand to her stomach. He explored her skin with his fingers, gently stroking her. He could feel the tension in her body, and then she moved his hand higher to her breast.

He gently cupped the delicate flesh, learning the shape and size of her. Against his palm, he felt the tight bud of her nipple, and when he moved his hand slightly, she jolted. Immediately, he stopped.

'It's all right,' she said. 'It just felt good, in a way I didn't expect.'

'Tell me,' he encouraged. Gently, he continued caressing her nipple, and he felt her squirm against him.

'When you touch my breast, it makes me ache between my legs,' she admitted.

She guided his hand to the other breast, and he experimented with circling the nipple and pinching it gently. She gasped slightly, but it seemed as if she liked the sensation. With his thumb, he stroked the erect tip, and her body trembled.

She shifted against him, and he held his hand in place when he realised what she'd done. Now, instead of his shaft resting against her bare spine, she had guided his length between her legs. He could feel the slickness of her arousal, and it was all he could do not to move.

As he caressed her nipple, she tightened her legs, squeezing him against her wetness. It was the sweetest torment he'd ever imagined. To distract himself, he kissed her bare shoulder, and she moved again.

He realised then what she wanted. Gently, he extricated himself and rolled to his back. Then he guided her to straddle him on her knees. He put both hands upon her breasts, and as he'd hoped, she pressed herself against his arousal. Her blue eyes were blazing with her own desire, and she inched higher upon his thick length.

'I can hardly breathe,' she admitted. But then she rubbed herself against him, arching slightly. Watching her pleasure herself with his body only heightened his own desire.

'Take what you need from me, Velaria.' He was beyond caring. But he sat up slightly. 'Will you let me kiss you?'

'Yes.' She started to lean down, but he brought his mouth towards her nipple instead.

'Here?' he asked, his breath against the hardened tip.

And when she whispered yes, he tasted heaven.

Chapter Ten

Velaria had never craved anything like this before. Her body was on fire, utterly liquid with desire. Her husband's mouth upon her breast was a pleasure she'd never felt in her life. Drogan had simply stolen her innocence, claiming her and taking what he wanted. It had been over so fast, she'd felt utterly used and discarded.

But Savaş was worshipping her with his mouth and tongue. She was so overwhelmed she could hardly catch her breath. And yet, the feeling of his shaft between her legs was so very good. When she moved against him, it intensified the feeling of his tongue upon her nipple.

In the darkness, his own breathing was as laboured as her own. But she needed him so badly. With Savaş's help, she guided his length inside her until she was fully seated upon him. He had gone so still, she wondered if she shouldn't have done it.

'Do you know how good you feel?' he murmured against her skin. 'You honour me, Velaria.'

He sat up slightly, but the sensation had changed now that he was inside her.

'May I touch you?' he asked. His voice was so hoarse, it sounded as if he was holding on to his own control.

'Yes.' She started to move against him, but when he

touched the hooded flesh above her entrance, sensations of pleasure spiralled through her. She couldn't stop herself from squeezing him, and his breathing shifted into nearly a gasp.

'Did I hurt you?' she whispered.

'No. Did I hurt you?'

She shook her head. 'I wanted more.' He brought his hand back between them, and although she felt awkward, she said, 'Here.' She showed him her most sensitive place, and when he stroked her there, waves of pleasure broke over her. Her breathing hitched, and she began panting with need.

'Don't move,' she begged. 'Keep touching me.'

And thank God, he obeyed. The touch of his thumb caressing her was so intense, she felt her body shudder. Then he began kissing her breast again, and the tremors pushed her to the brink of a pleasure so fierce, it shattered her. Velaria convulsed against him, and then couldn't stop herself from riding his shaft. The pleasure didn't stop, but it seemed right to share it.

She made love to him and saw the expression of raw pleasure on his face when she brought him deep inside and rose up again. He rested his hands on her hips, but not once did he force her. She was crying out, shaking as she quickened her pace. His hands moved to her bottom then, helping her as she took him again and again.

He was rigid inside her, and she looked into his eyes and said, 'I belong to no man but you.'

Her words seemed to drive him over the edge, and when she found her pleasure another time, he went with her, groaning as he spilled his seed inside. She kept him inside her, resting her body upon his, skin to skin.

And as she drifted off to sleep, it felt as if she had reclaimed the lost part of herself.

* * *

The MacEgan escorts stayed with them for another day before they turned back to Laochre. Brian rode alongside Velaria, grateful that their marriage had shifted into the one he had hoped it would be. And yet, he couldn't deny his protective instincts. He wanted to keep his wife in hiding a little longer—at least until he'd gained the king's pardon on Velaria's behalf for the death of Lord Marwood. He still questioned why the baron had travelled into the MacEgan territory with a group of scouts. It was unusual for a nobleman, and it made Brian wonder what the man's true intentions had been, beyond attacking two young women.

'How much farther until we reach Dunbough?' Velaria asked.

'I don't know. But I suspect another day or two.' Trahern MacEgan had sketched out a rough map, and thus far, it had proven useful.

'Do you…plan for us to live there?'

Brian could hear the edge of nervousness in her voice. 'I don't know how long we'll stay,' he admitted. 'It depends on how the king reacts when I find him.' He paused and admitted, 'I suspect my mother was a noblewoman, but I don't know whether the king cared for her. All I know is that she left Morwenna a gown and a pendant.'

'I hope you find her one day,' she offered, 'and that King John acknowledges you as his son.'

'As do I.' Even so, he intended to leave Velaria behind with Morwenna and Robert when he went to speak with the king. He didn't want her threatened by the death of Lord Marwood, and it was safer for her to stay with his family.

She rode alongside him until the afternoon sun rose high above them. There was a silvery grey lake lined with stones, and he suggested, 'We could stop for our meal and let the horses drink and rest.'

Velaria's cheeks flushed as she seemed to guess what he truly wanted. 'If you like.'

Her sudden shyness intensified his desire…and yet, he didn't want to press her for too much, too soon. Instead, he helped her dismount and led both horses over to drink. She gathered wood and tinder to build a fire.

His shoulder had gone stiff from the long ride, so he flexed it, moving his arm to stretch the muscle in the way Aileen had taught him. He was slowly starting to get back more range of motion.

Then he caught his wife watching him, and he stretched again, lifting his arm high and pressing it back. He didn't miss the flush on her cheeks, and he couldn't deny his own interest in her. But first, they needed food. From their belongings, he withdrew a net weighted with small stones.

'Where did you get that?' she asked.

'Your uncle Ewan gave it to us.' It took several tries before he managed to catch a few small fish. By that time, the fire was burning brightly while Velaria tended it. She wore a few braids across her forehead, but most of the long locks hung below her shoulders. In the afternoon sunlight, the wind caught some of the strands, and they framed her face.

'You're staring at me,' she remarked as she stood from the fire.

'Because you're beautiful.' Although she wore a plain green *léine* with an overdress in a darker shade of green, the Irish style of clothing suited her. After he set the fish up to cook, he rinsed his hands and then went to kiss her. Velaria rested her hands upon his chest, but he sensed her tension.

'Did I hurt you last night?' he asked quietly. He'd responded out of pure instinct and didn't know if she was all right.

'No,' she admitted. She appeared flustered and admitted, 'I've never felt like that before with anyone.'

He pulled her hips close to his, and she suddenly seemed nervous again. He told himself it would take time for her to relinquish her fears. He relaxed his hold upon her, and her shoulders seemed to lower in relief.

One day he hoped she would be eager in their marriage bed instead of haunted by nightmares. He kept his embrace loose, and she reached up to touch his cheek.

'What is it?' he asked. Whatever she wanted, he would give it, without question.

Then she hesitated a moment and said, 'I'm only thinking about what lies ahead for us.'

Apprehension tightened her features, and he caught her hands in his. 'What do you mean?'

Her palms were cold, and she lowered her gaze. 'I know you want to visit your sister. But will we stay there? Or go home to England?'

Though it was an honest question, he understood the greater implications. 'I must speak with my father before I can make that decision.'

She paused a moment. 'Don't put all your hopes on King John. What if he denies you as his son?' It was a risk, but before he could answer, she continued, 'I think we should accept help from my father and brother. We could live at Ardennes or Dolwyth… Or perhaps we should go to Staunton. We could find out what happened to Alexander after he freed us.'

Her suggestion about visiting Lord Staunton held merit. 'I agree that we should go and see him after what he did for us.' Brian released her hands. 'But do not be afraid if the king refuses to acknowledge me. I'll find a way to provide for you myself, Velaria.' He wasn't about to live off the goodwill of others. 'I will hire out my sword, if need be.'

'Can you still fight?' Her words were an invisible barb, and he knew her question was about his injury. He gave no reaction and held back every emotion, steeling himself.

'Do you want to spar?' he asked. 'Should I prove myself to you?'

She took another step backwards. 'Savaş, that's not necessary. I only meant that—'

'Train with me,' he insisted. 'We'll make a wager of it.'

She was already shaking her head. 'No. There's no need.'

But he wasn't finished yet. 'Are you afraid to fight any more, Velaria? After all this time?'

'I'm not afraid. But your shoulder…' Her words trailed off.

He realised then that she hadn't been admiring his exercises—she'd recognised his loss of flexibility and motion. But he continued to stretch each day, and already he'd seen an improvement.

Brian strode towards the pack of their belongings and withdrew two swords. He held one out to her. 'Fight me, Velaria. Let me prove myself to you.'

'Why?' She was still entirely unwilling and refused to take the weapon.

'Because for some reason, you seem to think I am still weak after my injury,' he said.

Her expression turned grave. 'You didn't win the sword match on Bealtaine. If that had happened in Constantinople, you'd be dead. And I'm not willing to lose you again.'

Her lack of faith in his fighting skills was an invisible blow he'd never expected. But he would show her the truth—that he was strong enough to win.

'Spar with me, Velaria,' he said. 'If you are victorious, I'll grant you a favour of your choosing.'

His wife seemed to consider it. 'And what if I ask you not to fight again?'

He wouldn't even consider that as an option. But he needed to show her that he could win. 'Do you want to know what I want if I win?'

Velaria met his gaze and asked softly, 'What do you want?'

He took the short sword and tested its weight. Then he eyed his wife. 'I want to learn your body better than my own. I want to spend an entire night discovering how to make you burn with pleasure.'

A surge of liquid heat seemed to flood through her at his words. Velaria was torn between accepting the fight and wondering what it would be like to experience such a night in his arms.

But her greater concern was their future. Savaş was resting all his hopes on a capricious king who had not won the approval of his noblemen. And God help her, she knew he would hire out his sword rather than accept help from her family. His pride was too great for that.

She accepted the sword, testing the weight and balance of the blade. He assumed a fighting stance, but she was not yet ready. Instead, she removed her overdress and *léine* until she stood only in her shift. She needed greater freedom of movement, and the weight of her gown would only hold her back.

She stretched her arms, drawing his attention to her breasts. And when she braided back her hair, she didn't bother to hide the way her shift moulded to her body.

Now she had his full attention as he circled her and said, 'Whoever disarms the other person is the winner.'

She gave a slight intake of breath as she withdrew her own weapon and assumed a fighting stance. 'You can try.'

'Oh, I will,' he said. 'And then I'm going to lay you down and put my mouth upon every inch of your body.' He stripped off his tunic and bared his upper torso.

She went breathless at his words, and for a moment, she faltered. He'd caught her full attention with his ridged muscles and she imagined putting her mouth on him.

Savaş struck out with his weapon, and only instinct brought her own sword up to block him. He wasn't going to fight fair, and from the way he was staring at her, he would do anything to win.

His shoulder was his weakness...but so was his desire for her. She considered how best to attack, and her words became another weapon.

'I remember what it was like to touch you,' she said softly. 'And feel your bare skin against mine.'

He let out a slow breath of air as if he were imagining it. But when she struck hard, he defended the blow.

'When I end this match, I plan to do exactly that.' He moved in closer, but she spun away.

'I want to build a life with you,' she admitted. 'But I don't want you to hire out your sword. I want you to stay with me.' The thought of him leaving her again and taking such a risk was horrifying.

His face tensed, and she moved to a new angle, forcing his weaker shoulder to deflect another strike. 'I don't need the pity of your family, Velaria. I won't take what I haven't earned.'

'Then find another way.' She blocked his next blow, holding it steady. His face was so near to hers, his blue eyes burned with the heat of desire. 'Don't let the king brush you aside.'

'I have no control over his opinion of me.' His voice held

a shadowed darkness, as if she'd struck a different kind of blow. Deep within, Savaş did not believe himself worthy. And now she wished she hadn't spoken of it. He had become legendary within the fighting arena, a fighter whom men feared to face. He had earned that pride.

And she would not take it from him.

She lowered her sword and faced her husband. Then she opened her arms to the man who was quickly stealing her heart.

He dropped his own weapon and caught her up in his embrace. 'I wasn't expecting you to surrender, Velaria.'

'I don't want to fight you,' she answered honestly. Although she was still afraid of intimacy, she was starting to realise that he'd been right. With him, there was only pleasure.

Savaş took her travelling cloak and laid it out on the soft grasses. Then he knelt down and reached for her calves. Slowly, his hands slid up her skin, higher to her thighs, and he pressed his hand between them.

'Open for me,' he commanded.

She obeyed, and still, she was uncertain about what he meant to do. His hand caressed her bare thigh, rising higher towards the centre of her. Already, she was restless, feeling vulnerable to the sweet ache within her. Her knees went weak, and he helped guide her back, his hands trailing her body as he explored her.

As promised, his hands seemed to be everywhere upon her legs, stroking and caressing her skin. She reached out to bring him closer, and he covered her nipple with his mouth, causing her to grip his hair.

'You're sensitive there, aren't you?' he murmured against the erect tip.

'Yes,' she breathed. The heady kiss and the way his tongue swirled over her brought a wetness between her legs. She was shifting beneath him, the pleasure causing her to rise to his touch. She craved her husband, and without thinking, she guided his hand to her intimate flesh. Savaş let out a low growl of approval, and she arched her back in shock when he slid a finger inside her. She nearly came apart when he began caressing her, and she reached down until her hand closed over his erection. He was using the barest rhythm, and his gentleness was driving her over the edge.

'More,' she pleaded, and her own voice was barely recognisable. She felt primal, hardly able to think.

And when he replaced his hand with his tongue, her hands gripped the edges of the cloak, and her body pulsed as he feasted. She couldn't stop the rhythmic panting of her own breath or the pounding of her heart as he discovered how to make her burn.

'Savaş,' she moaned, and he increased the pressure only slightly, driving her closer and closer until she erupted with the force of her release. He never relented, but suckled against her nodule while both of his hands cupped her breasts, caressing her nipples.

Never in her life had she felt such an out-of-control experience, and she was about to guide him inside her when they heard the sound of approaching horses. Her husband quickly covered her with her cloak and adjusted his trews.

There was a small copse of trees, and Velaria seized her sword, just as he did his. It was too late to take their horses, so they simply hid within the trees while the travellers passed by. She saw no armour, and it appeared that the men wore Norman clothing. From their bright colours, she suspected they were noblemen. But who were they? The men rode north in haste, and thankfully it didn't seem that they'd noticed them there.

Savaş stood in front of her, his weapon in hand. She

guessed there were twenty in the travelling party, but again, there appeared to be no threat. Velaria lowered her weapon, and soon enough, he did the same.

Her heart was still beating, and when at last he turned to her, she whispered, 'We weren't finished yet.' Slowly, she exposed herself from the cloak and was rewarded when his face turned pained with rigid desire.

'I don't think—' His words broke off when she loosened his trews and found his erection. The moment her hand closed over him, he lifted her away and pressed her against a tree. 'Never mind. I don't care any more.'

He fitted himself to her wet entrance, and she bit her lip as he slowly sank deep inside. Her legs wrapped around his waist, and his mouth closed over her breast again as he started to move against her.

She was fully conscious of his strength and how he picked her up as if she weighed nothing at all. The sound of horses was starting to fade, and he began to thrust gently. Her body welcomed the intrusion, and she began to move with him, trying to increase the friction.

'Shh,' he urged as a keening cry caught within her. He was unbearably gentle, and the slow, deep thrusts were pressing her towards a wildness she couldn't endure. She started to increase her pace, gripping his shoulders as he took her by the waist. He seemed to understand what she wanted, and he drove himself deep inside over and over.

She covered his mouth with her own, her tongue twining with his as he made love to her. The heady rush of release came barrelling towards her again, but she welcomed it, knowing that he was giving himself to her.

She accepted him in her body, surrendering as they gave and took from one another. When she dared to open her eyes, she saw that he was fighting for control, his body pulsing within her.

'Let go,' she urged. 'It's all right. You won't hurt me.'

And God help her, he did. His breath was ragged as he abandoned caution and took what he needed from her. To her surprise, it wasn't at all frightening—instead, it only intensified her own response until she shattered against him, going utterly liquid while he penetrated and withdrew. He gave a few last deep strokes before he found his own pleasure, and she clung to him, shaking as he did.

There were no words, nothing to describe the feelings she held for this man. And yet, she didn't know what path lay ahead for them or what the future would bring.

They arrived at Dunbough a few days later. Brian saw the large castle on the edge of the coast, and for a moment, raw emotion caught in his throat. It had been so long since he'd seen his sister. For a moment, a sense of uncertainty passed over him.

Velaria seemed to sense his feelings, and she rode up beside him. 'Are you all right?'

He exchanged a glance with her. 'It's been years since I've seen her. I don't know if Morwenna is angry with me for what I did. I abandoned her.'

'You were fifteen,' Velaria said. 'I think she will be glad to see you.'

It wasn't his sister who concerned him as much as her husband. He wasn't at all certain Robert would want to see him again—especially after he'd nearly got the man killed.

Velaria paused a moment and said, 'Do you want to go alone when you meet her first? I can wait here in the forest.'

He hesitated, not really wanting to leave her. And yet, if Robert was still angry with him, it might make her uncomfortable to witness whatever his sister's husband wanted to say.

Though it wasn't his preference, it seemed wise not to bring too many surprises at once. 'Just for a little while,' he said. He uncovered a bow and arrows and handed them to her. 'Take these, in case you need them.' Though they were now on Robert's lands, he wanted his wife to remain well armed. 'I'll return to you soon.'

She caught his hand and leaned close to kiss him. 'I'll be waiting.'

He glanced around, but there was no sign of anyone nearby. She would be safe enough until his return.

He continued riding through the forest and towards the castle. Just as he reached the main path, two men approached him on horseback and spoke in Irish. Though Brian didn't understand their words, he gave his name and added, 'Morwenna is my sister.'

One nodded and rode swiftly towards the castle while the other man motioned him forward. He suspected they were going to tell Robert and Morwenna of his arrival. He kept the pace of his horse slow as he studied the high walls surrounding the castle. A little while later, he saw a man and woman walking outside the gate. From this distance, he guessed it was his sister and Robert. She was holding an infant while she spoke to the man, and beside them stood a young boy.

Brian held his horse steady, staring at them as if he could take back the years that had been stolen from them. He allowed himself to imagine what it would be like if Velaria bore a son or a daughter. The thought evoked a longing he'd never dared to imagine.

And he understood, then, why she no longer wanted him to fight. She didn't want him to leave her alone with their children, never knowing whether he would return.

Just then, his sister seemed to catch sight of him. She started to run, clutching her infant as she did. 'Brian!' she cried out, while tears of joy spilled over her cheeks. 'My brother!'

The ache of happiness that caught him made his own eyes sting. He urged his horse closer, and the sight of his sister filled him with gratitude. She wore a crimson *bliaud* with fitted sleeves and a golden girdle that suited her as Lady of Dunbough.

Robert wore chainmail armour and a dark cloak, and he rested his hand on a young boy's shoulder. It warmed him to know that the man was now his brother in truth. The kind smile on Robert's face filled him with relief and the hope of forgiveness.

Brian dismounted, and he caught Morwenna in an embrace as she wept. Robert took the baby from her, and Brian held his sister close, stroking back her dark hair. The joy on her face mirrored his own. He gripped her hard and finally said, 'I returned to the abbey, and Father Oswold told me where you were.' He glanced over at Robert, and added, 'I thought you were dead on the night we tried to rescue Morwenna. It was my fault.'

Even now, the memory of his reckless actions evoked guilt. He now understood why Robert had tried to stop him, and Brian wished he could go back and change what he'd done.

Robert's expression held forgiveness, and he shook his head. 'No, you were right to attack. I should have done so sooner.' After a pause, he said, 'I only wish you had stayed at the abbey a little longer.'

If he had, he would have learned of Robert's survival. And yet…he wouldn't have left for Constantinople, nor would he have met Velaria. A tightness caught in his chest at the thought.

He drew back from his sister's embrace. 'I never imagined you would give up your lands at Penrith.' For so long, it was all Robert had wanted. He'd spent years training to win back his birthright, and Brian didn't understand why his friend had given up.

'I found something of greater value,' Robert answered, with a smile towards his wife and children. Just then, the baby began to sob, and he put his daughter to his shoulder, soothing her and patting her back.

The sight of the father and infant twisted Brian's own yearning for a family of his own. The thought of a daughter with Velaria's eyes or a son of their own evoked an inner vow. One day, it would happen.

He glanced down at his young nephew, and the child's face held worry. Brian smiled as he knelt down to the boy. 'I am your uncle Brian, young lad. What's your name?'

'Nicholas,' he answered.

The boy appeared uncertain and reached out to his mother. Morwenna smoothed his hair to offer reassurance. 'He's my brother, sweeting. Just as you are Eleanor's brother.'

At that, her son seemed to understand. He tugged his mother's skirts and informed her, 'I need to play.'

'Go on, then.' Brian patted his nephew's shoulder and the boy hurried off, running to join a group of older children. Then he turned to meet Morwenna's gaze. 'You look happy, my sister.'

'I am. More so, now that I know you're safe.'

There was thankfulness in her demeanour, and her husband rested his hand against her spine. 'Have you to come to live with us, Brian?' Robert asked. 'We would be glad to have you stay.'

'I will visit for a time,' he agreed, 'but I have my own

debt to repay.' After he gained an audience with the king, he would take Velaria to visit Lord Staunton and his wife. Then he would decide where to go next.

'What sort of debt?' Morwenna asked. 'Do you need our help?'

Brian shook his head. 'Not one that involves silver. The debt was my life.' And Velaria's. The more he thought of it, the more it felt right to travel to Staunton. Then, at least, he would know whether the baron had made it back safely.

'You have our help, should you need it,' Robert promised. 'Come and join us for a meal.'

Brian glanced back towards the forest, wondering how he should tell them of his sudden marriage to Velaria. He studied their surroundings while they walked together towards the keep. As they passed the people, it was clear that Morwenna and Robert had built Dunbough into a place of prosperity.

Before he could speak to his sister about Velaria, Morwenna turned to them and said, 'I need to feed the baby. I will join you afterwards.'

Robert kissed her, letting his hand linger at her waist as he gave her their daughter. 'I'll be waiting.'

She walked towards a set of spiral stairs, leaving them alone. Brian walked alongside Robert and said, 'If you'll come with me, there's someone I want to introduce to you.'

Robert's expression turned curious. 'Someone?'

'My wife, Velaria.'

At that, his friend brightened. 'And you left her alone? Morwenna will be angry with you for not bringing her with you right away.'

'I wasn't certain you would want to see me,' Brian admitted. 'After what I did, and after I abandoned Morwenna, I deserved to be cast off.'

Robert clapped him on the back. 'We are brothers now, Brian. And the past can remain there.' His smile broadened. 'Now, let us go and fetch your wife so Morwenna can be surprised when we return.'

They walked along the pathway towards the woods, and Brian remarked, 'Father Oswold told me Piers married Lady Gwendoline, the Penrith heiress. How did that come about?'

Robert laughed and said, 'Piers wed her in secret. Her father tried to have him killed, but he won that battle. Now they govern two estates—Penrith and Tilmain.'

It seemed impossible to imagine that Piers had managed such a feat, for he'd been a bastard son, just like himself. But Robert didn't seem at all displeased by the turn of events.

Their path wound downhill towards the trees, and Brian led them back to Velaria. He couldn't stop his smile when he saw her holding a bow with an arrow nocked.

She lowered the weapon as soon as she saw them and offered a chagrined smile as she put the arrow away. 'I didn't know it was you.'

'Velaria, this is my sister's husband, Robert, the Earl of Dunbough.' To Robert he said, 'This is my wife, Velaria of Ardennes.'

She set the bow down and Robert took her hand in greeting. 'I look forward to hearing the story of how the two of you came to be married.' He exchanged a look with Brian. 'I presume you met while you were on Crusade.'

'In a manner of speaking,' he hedged. He pressed his hand to Velaria's spine and led her back towards the path with Robert. She leaned closer to him, and he sensed her apprehension about meeting his family.

He leaned in and said, 'Morwenna and Robert have two children. We have a nephew and a niece you'll want to meet.'

A softness stole over her face. 'I look forward to that.'

Robert led them back to the castle, and along the way he added, 'Now that you've introduced me to your wife, there is someone else here who will want to meet you both.' There was a gleam in his eyes, and he regarded Brian. 'It's your mother.'

Chapter Eleven

Velaria sensed the tension in Savaş though he merely inclined his head. He gripped her hand, and answered, 'I would be glad to meet her.'

'Rochelle came to help with the birth of Eleanor,' Robert said. 'I know this will come as a happy surprise to her.'

At the thought of meeting his mother, Velaria was starting to wish she had worn a nicer gown or had a moment to fix her hair. But there was no time at all before they were escorted upstairs into the solar, where a young woman held an infant in her arms and an older woman sat beside them. Both had dark hair, though the older woman's held strands of silver. The moment the matron saw Savaş, she rose from her chair and hurried forward.

Joy broke over her expression, and she reached out to frame his face with her hands before she pulled him into a fierce embrace. 'Morwenna told me you were here.' She drew back and studied him, saying, 'I am so happy to see you at last, my son. I cannot believe how many years it's been.'

There was a visible change in Savaş's expression, as if he'd never expected to meet his mother for the first time. Though he kept a light smile of welcome on his face, Velaria didn't miss the shock and the deeper emotion behind his gaze.

For a moment, she felt rather like an intruder. Though she wanted her husband to enjoy this reunion moment, she was uncertain of her own place. But before she could take another step back, a hand pressed against her shoulder, moving her forward. It was Robert, and he said, 'Brian has also brought his wife, Velaria of Ardennes, to meet you both.'

'His wife?' A smile broke over the younger woman's face. 'Brian, I'm so happy for you both.' She came forward and embraced Velaria with one arm while holding her daughter. 'I am his sister, Morwenna.' She transferred the infant into Velaria's arms and said, 'And this is our mother, Lady Rochelle of Banmouth.'

Lady Rochelle smiled. 'I am very glad to meet you, Velaria. I know of your family, and I believe I met your grandfather a time or two, years ago.'

Velaria murmured her reply, but her attention was caught by the baby, who was now grabbing her hair with her fist.

'This is your niece, Eleanor,' Morwenna said. 'She was born only two moons ago.'

A softness crept within Velaria to feel the babe in her arms. The sudden surge of yearning startled her, even though she'd held young children before. For so long, she'd lived one day to the next, simply trying to survive. But now she had a husband and the chance to bear a child of their own. She traced the edge of Eleanor's cheek, marvelling at its softness. Unable to stop herself, she kissed the baby's forehead.

Brian brought her over to sit with the women near the fire. He regarded his mother and said, 'I need to know everything about you and my father. Please tell me whatever you can.'

Lady Rochelle's expression grew solemn, but she nodded. 'I had no choice in our union, you must understand. John was a demanding king. He sent my husband, Edmund, off to fight, and then he forced me to share his bed.' She closed her eyes a moment and said, 'When Morwenna was born, I did not know whether she was Edmund's daughter or John's.'

Velaria saw the concern on Brian's face, but he waited for his mother to continue.

'My husband allowed me to keep Morwenna for a time. After the king sent for me a second time, there was no doubt that you were John's son. As punishment, my husband forced me to send you and Morwenna away. I was not allowed to keep you, nor was I allowed to tell the king.' She turned away to stare at the fire, her emotions welling up as tears in her eyes. 'I grieved the loss of both of you, despite everything. You were innocent of my sins.

'But I am so very grateful to have found both of you again. And now, more than ever.' She turned back to Brian and said, 'Will you come and visit my estate at Banmouth?' Her expression turned pained, and she simply said, 'I would like you to meet your younger half brother.'

He reached out and took her hand in his. 'We would be glad to.'

Brian went to speak with Robert, and Morwenna returned to retrieve her baby. 'Will you walk with me, Velaria? I'd like to know you better.'

She gave over the infant and agreed. Morwenna murmured to Robert where they were going, and she gave the baby to a nursemaid before they left the solar. At first, the young woman led her down the stairs and back outside.

'It seems impossible to imagine my little brother being married,' Morwenna said. 'When was your wedding?'

'Hardly more than a sennight ago,' Velaria admitted.

'And he did not invite his own family?' His sister appeared aghast. 'Why not?'

She hesitated, uncertain of how much Savaş wanted to reveal. 'We married in haste.' To soothe his sister, she added, 'Yet, I cannot imagine marrying any other man.'

That seemed to pacify Morwenna, but she said, 'I know my brother. And he appears troubled about something. Did something happen?'

Velaria chose her words carefully. 'He wants to confront his father, King John.'

'He shouldn't,' Morwenna advised. 'John is not a man who cares about us. He only gave Robert command of Dunbough to help subdue the rebellion rising in the north.' She shook her head. 'It took a long time for him to gain the trust of his men here. They despise King John, but they will fight for Robert.'

Her words only underscored the danger, and Velaria was beginning to think it was better if Savaş never confronted John.

They walked inside the inner bailey, where men were training with swords and spears. Velaria averted her gaze, not wanting the memory of fighting to interfere. Even so, she could tell that the soldiers were organised and well trained. A row of shields rested against a wooden platform where their captain was giving them instructions.

'Tell me how you met my brother,' Morwenna started to say.

But before she could answer, her attention was caught by a blur of motion. Her nephew, Nicholas, broke free from an older woman as he ran towards his mother. Without thinking, Velaria darted forward and caught the child before he could reach the fighters sparring with one another. Out of raw instinct, she seized a shield, and seconds later, a blade embedded in the wood where the boy had been standing.

A cry of horror spilled from Morwenna's lips as she took her son from Velaria's arms. 'Nicholas, you could have been killed.'

'Lady Morwenna, it's sorry I am,' the soldier said as he withdrew his blade from the shield. 'Hamish disarmed me, and I lost my sword. Forgive me, I beg of you.'

But Morwenna only gripped her son in her arms, shaking her head as she clutched the boy and regarded Velaria. 'You saved my son's life.'

She stood, still holding the shield. For a moment, she almost couldn't believe what had happened. And yet, she was grateful for her fighting instincts that had saved the boy.

Tears flowed down Morwenna's face, and she said, 'Thank God.' She clutched her child and turned back. 'I don't know how you reached him so fast, but I will always be grateful. Anything you ever need from us, it will be yours.'

Velaria lowered the shield, but her heart was still pounding. It didn't seem to matter how long it had been since her time in the arena. She could never let go of her fighting instincts. For the last few months, she'd set aside her weapons, trying to blot out the past. But now, she was starting to realise that it would always be a part of her.

And perhaps that was a good thing.

One month later

Brian reached across the bed, but only empty sheets remained. He turned and saw Velaria standing before the window, reaching for her clothes.

'You're awake early,' he remarked, enjoying the view of her bare skin. He pushed aside the coverlet and came up behind her to kiss her nape. The scent of her skin aroused him instantly, and he wrapped his arms around her.

'I'm going to train this morning,' she said, reaching for a pair of men's trews. 'Will you join me?'

Ever since their arrival at Dunbough, she had returned to her fighting, as if it filled an empty place within her. Her body was still lean, but she had regained some of her muscles, and he couldn't help but slide his hand over her firm skin, admiring her. She caught his hand, and her smile turned sensual. In the past few weeks, she'd begun to trust him, and despite all the nights when he'd shared her bed, he could never get enough.

He took her in his arms and nuzzled her neck. 'I would very much like to join with you.'

Velaria's expression turned soft. 'That's not what I said.' But she dropped the trews and her hand moved down his naked body in a silent caress.

He gritted his teeth when she explored his skin with her fingertips, her blue eyes holding him captive. He did the same, finding the sensitive skin of her breasts, the dip of her waist, and the firm curve of her backside.

'I want a child of our own,' she whispered, just as her hand moved to his erection.

'So do I.'

And although they were still waiting for his audience with the king, and they had to make decisions about where to live—the thought of his wife growing round with a baby brought an ache within him. He wanted to be a father to their child in the way he'd never had a true father.

He moved his hand between her legs and dipped a finger inside her slick heat. Her fingers dug into his shoulders as he aroused her body.

'Come here,' she whispered. She fitted him to her wet entrance, and he slid home. Velaria's expression transformed with desire, and she raised her leg over his hip. He palmed her bottom and lifted her hip, striding to the wall.

Velaria squeezed him inside as he claimed her body in slow, deep thrusts. By now, he understood what she needed, and he bent to take her nipple in his mouth, suckling her as he entered and withdrew.

'Savaş,' she whispered in a husky voice.

He claimed her mouth in a hard kiss, and she began to move in counterpoint to his thrusts, her body slick with her own arousal. He seized her by the waist and took her against the wall, until he was trembling with the force of his need.

'Now,' she pleaded. And with her command, he thrust in a swift rhythm, revelling in the way she arched against him, crying out until he spilled himself within her depths. His body was still rigid, even after he'd found his release, and she trembled with aftershocks. But he couldn't move if he'd wanted to.

'We could stay here,' he suggested. 'No one would miss us for a few hours.'

She laughed softly and said, 'I wish we could.' After a slight pause, she added, 'Uncle Ewan sent word that the king's armies have arrived upon the Hook Peninsula. They're travelling north. Many of the noblemen have joined in a rebellion, and the king has come with thousands of men.'

At that, his smile faded. For even if she didn't want to admit it, the danger had now intensified. Although a messenger could ride faster than an army, it meant that the king's forces were only a day or two away if they'd travelled the same path.

He was torn between wanting to face his father—and wanting to hide Velaria away. During the past few weeks, he'd found contentment with his family. Morwenna had welcomed Velaria as a sister, and Robert had returned to the role of his older brother.

He didn't know if he wanted to confront John any more—especially after Rochelle's story of how he'd been conceived. It sounded as if the monarch was a man who only considered his own needs. But Brian needed to ensure that there was no threat to Velaria after Lord Marwood's death. And that meant an audience was unavoidable.

'What do you want to do?' he asked as he withdrew from her body and lowered her down.

Velaria drew her arms around him, and he held her close. 'I know you want to meet your father. Should we go together?'

'You should stay here, in case the king heard about Lord Marwood's death,' he said. 'It's safer.'

She didn't argue as she reached for her clothing. But as he studied his wife, he realised that his audience with the king was no longer about trying to build a future by gaining John's acknowledgement. It was about protecting his loved ones at all costs.

For now, he had something to lose.

Three days later

A small group of Robert's soldiers came to watch while Velaria sparred with Brian. Somehow, during the past few months, her aversion to fighting had shifted. Now it was no longer about herself—it was about protecting others. And she found that she was enjoying the training with her husband.

But during the fight, her thoughts drifted towards their

future. Savaş had mentioned visiting Lord Staunton and his wife after his audience with the king. She agreed with returning to England, and she wanted to live closer to her own family. Especially if one day soon they conceived a child.

Her sword struck his, and they circled one another for a moment. She studied his movements, anticipating his attack. When he raised his blade, she was ready to defend herself, and then she fell into the familiar pattern of parrying his blows and returning with her own strikes.

It was almost like a dance between them, predicting one motion, then the next. But in his eyes, she saw the challenge and warmed to it. Just as he struck again, she leapt out of the way, laughing.

But then their sparring was interrupted by the sudden sound of horses approaching. She turned and saw a group of soldiers at the gates.

Savaş kept his sword unsheathed. In a low voice, he said, 'Go inside the keep.'

Velaria started towards the stairs when the soldiers entered. She overheard Lord Dunbough speaking to the men, but she kept her back to them, trying not to draw attention to herself.

Just as she reached the top of the stairs, a voice called out, 'That's her.'

'You are mistaken,' Robert said calmly. 'If the king wishes to know my loyalty, let him come and speak with me himself. All of us are his faithful subjects.'

Velaria hesitated on the parapets, wondering whether it was better to disappear or risk a glance at her accuser. But when she dared to turn around, she saw him—the witness who had been among those who had attacked Mairead and herself. From his attire, he also appeared to be a nobleman.

A slow smile spread over his face, as if he anticipated

justice. 'I've been tracking her for weeks now. And she will answer for Baron Marwood's death.'

Fear pounded within her, but Velaria forced herself not to run. It would be an admission of guilt, so she stood and faced him.

'You are wrong,' Robert said smoothly. 'She is the granddaughter of the Earl of Ardennes and the daughter of Sir Ademar of Dolwyth. She is my sister by marriage.'

'I watched her kill him,' the witness said. 'And she will face the king's justice.'

A coldness seemed to encircle her, and Velaria felt frozen inside at the thought of what was to come. She didn't know whether it was better to run or stay and pretend they were wrong.

Savaş was already on the stairs, his sword drawn to defend her. 'You will leave my wife alone.'

'We have orders to bring her into custody,' another soldier said. 'She will stand trial before the king.'

Robert motioned for his own soldiers to come forward. 'She is going nowhere with you.'

'If you defy the king's orders, then His Excellency will know that you are traitors to the Crown. Your lands and title will be forfeit.'

At that, Velaria realised there was no longer a choice. If she dared to run now, the consequences would fall upon Robert and Morwenna. But if she gave herself up, there was a chance she could seek her own escape later.

Velaria slowly raised her hands in surrender and turned around. When Savaş tried to intervene, she shook her head. 'I will go with them. I won't risk anyone else's lives or Robert and Morwenna's lands until this is sorted out.' To her husband she said, 'Go and speak with the king. Tell him what happened, and he may show mercy.'

'I'm not letting them take you.'

He reached out to hold her, and she insisted, 'Then follow them.' She was trying desperately not to show fear, but her mind was racing.

The men bound her hands in front of her and led her over to a horse. Velaria tried to remain brave and calm while they helped her mount, though she could see the fierce emotions on her husband's face. It was clear that Savaş wanted nothing more than to charge forward and attack. But if he did, his own life would be forfeit before he'd ever had the chance to speak to his father.

She tried to shield herself from the fear, but she worried that the others would be harmed.

'Where is His Grace now?' Savaş dared to ask.

'A few days south of here,' the soldier answered.

Robert's face had gone grave. 'Then we will join your men and speak directly to the king.'

One of the soldiers shrugged. 'Come if you wish, but we won't be waiting for you.' With that, they turned and rode out of the gates. Velaria turned back to look at her husband, and Savaş was already giving orders for horses.

Although she was terrified of what would happen now, one matter was clear. He would not stop until he had brought her back home again.

They rode for hours without stopping. Brian was grateful for Robert's presence, and they had agreed that they would do nothing to endanger Velaria. He had told him the truth about the attack and how his wife had defended herself.

Yet, he didn't know if it would be enough to save her from the king's anger. Nor did he know whether John would even care who he was. For months now, he'd considered what to say to his father, hoping the man would acknowledge him as his son. And now, all he wanted was to protect his wife. She mattered more than all else.

They made camp nearby, and though he wanted to move closer to the soldiers who had taken Velaria, Robert warned him to stay back. 'Don't give them an excuse to kill you.'

He knew the man was right, but neither did he want to leave her unprotected. 'Velaria only defended herself. She shouldn't be in custody at all.'

'And with any luck, the king will agree,' Robert said.

Brian didn't like the idea of his wife's fate resting upon a king's whims. Not when they could so easily change. He fully intended to rescue Velaria, even if it meant disappearing with her.

'You need to consider what we can give that King John needs. Loyalty and a strong alliance,' Robert said. 'Piers is the new Lord of Penrith and Tilmain. He will be glad to grant his support if we ask it of him.'

It had been years since he'd seen Robert's half brother, Piers, but he remembered the man as a strong fighter. 'I would be glad of any help. We need to send word to Velaria's family and the MacEgans.' Sir Ademar would come, and he believed King Patrick would also send men after what she'd done to save Mairead.

Even as they continued tracking the king's men, it enraged Brian to think of his wife in their hands. His only consolation was that he had a bow and arrows. If any man dared to touch her, it would be the last move he ever made.

Then he turned to Robert and said, 'I have another plan in mind. But I'll need your help.'

His best friend's expression shifted. 'I'm listening.'

The journey to the king's encampment lasted several days, but Velaria could hardly remember how many, since the days and nights blended together. No one left her alone for a single moment, and her hands were always bound.

They'd given her a little food and water, but it was barely enough to survive. She suspected they'd done it on purpose, to weaken her and make it impossible to attempt an escape without becoming dizzy.

When they reached the encampment, tents had been hastily set up, as far as she could see. Never in her life had she seen so many soldiers—there must have been thousands. Although there were several hearths outside and wagons of food, it was clear that the king was moving swiftly north. And with so many soldiers, she didn't know if it was possible to slip away without being seen.

The men brought her to be imprisoned with several other captives. Velaria had thought about trying to steal a blade, but it was impossible with her hands bound. They tossed her within an underground pit, and as she struck the bottom, she rolled to keep from being injured. It appeared that the original house had burned, and the area below ground was now being used as a makeshift prison. The top of the pit appeared to be the height of two men.

From the small number of prisoners, she wondered how long they would stay here—or whether the king meant to have them killed quickly. She studied her surroundings and noticed that the other prisoners appeared to be Norman, not Irish. But as the only female prisoner, she didn't know if they were a threat.

It was likely better to feign helplessness than reveal her fighting skills. She lowered her shoulders, and it wasn't hard to conjure up silent tears. All she had to do was think of Savaş and the fate that awaited her.

She should have known that the king's men would hunt her after she'd defended herself from the baron. Women were supposed to be meek and subservient, never a threat. But after she'd been touched against her will in Constantinople, she'd sworn it would never happen again. Not to her and not to Mairead.

She could feel the men staring, although she didn't know if they would actually try to harm her. With her head lowered, she let her hair hide her face while she turned back to them. She saw at least four men, but only one seemed curious enough to get closer.

'What did you do to earn such a punishment, sweet girl?' He spoke in the Norman language, and she pretended not to understand him. Instead, she shrank away, drawing her knees up as he approached.

'Did the king grow tired of you? Did you refuse him?' he asked in a voice filled with false compassion.

Velaria ignored the man until he took another step forward. Then she stood and faced him down. 'Leave me alone.'

She was already considering what to do if he made another move—whether to strike him and run to the other side or whether to attempt to climb up from the enclosure. Near the top of the walls, it was only mud, so she doubted if she could get high enough to escape.

But before the man could say another word, another prisoner was shoved down into the enclosure.

He rolled away, and a familiar voice above them said, 'You'll await the king's justice for what you've done.'

In that moment, Velaria lifted her head to see who had spoken, and she recognised Robert of Dunbough standing above the pit. Her heartbeat quickened, and when she turned back to the new prisoner, there was no doubt of who he was… Savaş.

It took everything in her not to run to her husband and

embrace him hard. But at least he was here, and she was no longer alone. His very presence soothed her, and when he staggered to his feet, he didn't look at her. Instead, he spoke in the Byzantine tongue, broken words that only they could understand between them.

'I have a blade. Stay near me,' he said. 'Robert will go to the king.'

Velaria understood then, that this was his way of guarding her. She didn't speak, didn't let anyone know that she'd understood him. Instead, she huddled in the corner, as if she were utterly unable to defend herself.

This time, the tears upon her cheeks were silent tears of joy. Savaş was here, and a flood of grateful emotions poured through her—thankfulness, hope, and an intense love of this man. There was no way to know whether they would escape this enclosure or find a means of gaining the king's favour. But for now, his presence was enough.

They waited for hours until darkness descended, a clouded night where the air smelled of impending rain. Velaria's back ached, but she didn't dare move. Only the flickering light of torches illuminated the space. Savaş sat in front of her in silent defence, and it took an effort not to embrace him. She remained behind him, and only after the other prisoners fell asleep did she reach out in the darkness. She held his hand, stroking his palm with her thumb.

'I'm glad you're here,' she whispered, as softly as she dared.

'I will always come for you,' he answered, squeezing her hand. 'No matter what happens.'

And she inwardly vowed that somehow, they would find a way to free themselves.

Chapter Twelve

It was late morning when Robert arrived. The man's expression appeared grim, but the soldiers brought both of them up from the pit. Though Brian wanted to ask whether Robert had gained an audience for them, something made him hold his silence. Tension radiated from his friend, and he feared the worst.

Velaria did her best to tame her hair and smooth her gown. Even so, he could see the terror in her eyes as they walked together.

Robert led them towards the king's tent while soldiers flanked them on all sides. Along the way, Brian considered what he could say to his father. He wished he had a ring or a token that would prove without a doubt that he was John's son. But he had nothing except Lady Rochelle's word. There was no way to know whether the king would accept him.

And he needed that status, beyond all else, to protect Velaria from harm.

She gripped his hand as they walked together, and he murmured, 'It will be all right. I promise you.' He would do everything in his power to guard her. Already, they had sent word to the MacEgans, hoping that King Patrick could intervene in some way.

They walked alongside hundreds of tents, past men who

were sharpening their weapons while others stood beside outdoor hearths. It was clear that the king had come not only to subdue any Norman rebellions, but also to display a show of force among the Irish kings.

After several minutes of walking, they finally reached the king's tent and were forced to wait outside for their audience. Velaria's face paled, and she admitted, 'I'm afraid, Savaş.'

So was he, but he tried not to show it. Instead, he raised their joined hands to his mouth and kissed her knuckles in silent reassurance.

When at last they were allowed entrance into the king's tent, they both bowed before him. King John stood on the far end of the tent, with a golden goblet in one hand. He motioned for them to come forward, and at last, Brian had his first look at the man who was his father. He recognised his own nose in the king's features, along with his eyes. For a moment, he felt the sudden yearning for recognition in the hope that his father would see him as a man of worth.

But for now, the king's attention was fixed upon Robert.

'Dunbough claims that you are both loyal subjects of the crown and that you have come to beg our mercy,' the king began. 'We will hear what he has to say.'

Brian released her hand and straightened. 'My liege, I—'

'You were not given permission to speak,' the king interrupted. 'Only Robert of Dunbough.' The swift dismissal made it clear that the monarch had no interest in him. And a part of him faltered.

Robert stepped forward then and bowed. 'Your Excellency, I would like to introduce Brian of Penrith to you.' His tone remained careful as he continued, 'I believe you once knew his mother, Lady Rochelle of Banmouth. And his sister is my wife, Morwenna.'

The king's expression narrowed, but in his eyes, Brian only saw irritation and a trace of boredom. 'You are implying that this man is our son, is that it?'

'He is,' Robert answered. 'And he has come to pledge his loyalty to Your Grace.'

Brian dropped to one knee, his head lowered. But even as he humbled himself before the monarch, his own frustration deepened. He had made no demands of the king except to offer his loyalty.

King John continued, 'You hope that if we acknowledge you as our son, we will forgive your wife's crimes, is that it?'

Brian stepped forward but kept his head lowered, realising that John truly didn't care that he was his bastard son. The invisible blow clenched within him, though he should have expected this.

A quiet voice inside him seemed to say, *You were born a serf. And you'll die a serf.*

He had been too hopeful that King John would be glad to have another son. Instead, it seemed that his life held no meaning for the man, just as he'd feared. For a moment, Brian considered the implications of the king's dismissal. For so long, he'd dreamed of finding his father and filling that emptiness inside him. He'd wanted to believe that the king would help him protect Velaria.

Now he saw the truth of it. King John didn't care. Another bastard son meant nothing to him at all. And Brian knew it was better if he relied upon his own skills to save his wife. He would pay any price to keep her safe.

With his head lowered, he chose his words carefully. 'Your Grace, my wife was attacked, along with the King of Laochre's daughter, Mairead. Velaria only defended them, as was her right.'

'Do you expect me to believe that a mere woman killed Lord Marwood?' the king snapped.

Brian ignored the question and continued, 'Her grandfather, the Earl of Ardennes, was also loyal to Your Grace. As is her father, Sir Ademar of Dolwyth.'

The king's expression turned shrewd. 'Then what do you suggest should be her punishment for their deaths?'

Brian moved beside Velaria and took her hand in his. He sensed that the king's fury would not be appeased, but there was one way he could plead for her life. And if it ended badly, at least she would be safe.

'As her husband, I will shoulder the blame for what happened in the past. Let your judgement fall upon me.'

'No.' Velaria turned to the king. 'Please, Your Grace. I never intended to harm anyone.'

'Four of our men died at your hands.' King John's voice turned rigid. 'It was no accident, Velaria of Ardennes. And the punishment for murder is death.'

The words seemed to drift within the air, and Brian could hardly grasp what he was hearing. The king had no intention of showing mercy—he intended to make an example of Velaria. And Brian didn't know if there was anything he could do to gain the monarch's favour.

A thin smile spread over John's face as he regarded him. 'Do you still wish to take her punishment?'

Velaria saw the look of resolution upon her husband's face, and she could already read his intentions. But she would not let him take her death sentence. Not without a fight of her own.

'Your Grace, I beg for your mercy,' she began. 'My family has ties to the MacEgan tribe. The King of Laochre is a powerful ally of yours. He has but one daughter, and—'

'My alliance with Patrick of Laochre will not forgive the lives you took.' The King shook his head. 'We have seven thousand soldiers here. No petty king would dare oppose me.' He stared at both of them, and Velaria understood then, that there would be no mercy.

Her heart pounded with fear, but she faced the king. 'I will face the blame for my own deeds.'

'That is not your decision to make.' Her husband's words startled her. Never had he treated her as anything but an equal, but she saw the resolve in Savaş's face.

He knelt before the king. 'If you take Velaria's life, you will only anger noblemen and allies that you need, my liege.' He paused a moment and added, 'But I have no one.'

In his voice, she heard the bleakness that the king had refused to recognise him as a bastard son. Savaş didn't believe anyone would care if he lost his life. But it wasn't true at all.

Without him, her life would be empty. If he died, she simply could not endure breathing. She loved him, and she would fight for this man with all that she had.

Before she could speak, Savaş said, 'I ask for a trial by combat, Your Grace. Let me fight for her sake and let God decide how justice should be served.'

Her breath released slowly as she realised what he was doing. At least a trial by combat gave them a chance.

The king seemed to consider it, but Robert intervened with another offer. 'Or if it pleases Your Excellency, I would be willing to pay a fine for the lives of the men who died. In gold.'

The king seemed not to hear. 'The baron's son is here now, among my men. We will ask him if he agrees. Since it was his father's death, I grant him the right to make that decision.'

A rise of nausea caught in her gut. In a low voice, Velaria said, 'Savaş, there's something you need to know about Lord Marwood.'

'It doesn't matter,' he told her. 'I will do everything in my power to save your life, Velaria.'

She reached out to embrace him, and she whispered in his ear. 'His son is Sir Drogan. The man I ran away with when I was fifteen years old.'

His expression held none of the uncertainty or frustration she'd expected. Instead, his face darkened with fury. Against her ear, he murmured, 'Good. Then I can kill him for what he did to you.'

Her emotions seemed to knot within her stomach. She never wanted to see the knight again or remember the humiliation she'd endured. And the thought of watching the men fight each other was more than she could bear.

They waited for some time before Drogan arrived. Velaria turned her face away, not knowing whether he would recognise her. He wore chainmail armour, and at a glimpse, he appeared the same as he had years ago. There was an air of confidence about him, as if he had claimed his father's title with no remorse at all.

He bowed before the king. 'You sent for me, Your Excellency?'

The king's expression turned satisfied. 'Indeed. We have brought your father's murderer to justice. Her husband has agreed to take her punishment as his own, and he has asked for a trial by combat.'

For a moment, Drogan seemed not to recognise her, and she held her breath. Then his gaze narrowed. 'Velaria?'

'Sir Drogan.' She deliberately used his title to emphasise the distance between them.

'Baron Marwood,' he corrected. Then he continued, 'Is

this true? Were you the one who killed my father?' The utter lack of emotion in his face startled her, for he didn't seem at all unhappy about the baron's death.

'I never intended to kill anyone,' she answered. 'But I fought to defend myself and the King of Laochre's daughter.' Though she tried to keep her voice even, the edge of fear sliced through her.

Savaş came to her side and took her hand in his in a silent show of defence. It brought her comfort to have him standing beside her.

As she compared the two men, she realised that what she'd once felt for Drogan was nothing compared with the feelings she held towards her husband. Savaş had already proven, time and again, that he was steadfast and loyal—whereas Drogan had only ever cared about himself.

Drogan studied her husband with interest. 'And you are asking for a trial by combat, to avoid a death sentence for Velaria?'

Savaş met his gaze. 'I am, yes.' His expression turned intent. 'I will fight you. Or any man of your choosing, should you wish it.'

Drogan turned back to the king, but Velaria didn't like the look of satisfaction on his face. He held the expression of a man well pleased by the turn of events. When he turned back to the king, he said, 'With respect, Your Excellency, I do not wish to allow a trial by combat. There is evidence enough of her guilt, for she has admitted to killing my father. I defer to your judgement.'

The blood seemed to drain from her body, and she couldn't stop the tremor of fear that overtook her. She had never expected him to refuse.

'Let Velaria of Ardennes suffer the justice you have

chosen,' the knight said. And with a bow, he retreated towards the back of the tent, awaiting permission to depart.

'So be it,' King John said. 'Velaria of Ardennes, because you have confessed that you killed Lord Marwood, I hereby sentence you to die at dawn.'

Before Brian could react, Robert gripped him with all his strength. Tears streamed down Velaria's face as the soldiers took her away. 'I am sorry, Savaş.'

He wanted nothing more than to lunge at the soldiers and seize his wife. And yet, Robert was right to restrain him. His mind and temper were battling for control, and he had only hours to save her.

Although he believed the MacEgans would send help, there was no time left. He was dimly aware of Robert asking permission for them to leave and the king lifting his hand in dismissal.

'Keep silent,' Robert warned, as he took him outside the tent. 'Say nothing until we are alone.'

Brian walked alongside him, their steps swift, even as he wanted to go after Velaria and rescue her. But Robert was right—they had to make their plans carefully and find a way to save her.

His mind was spinning, but Robert caught his arm. Brian stared back, but he managed to suppress the anger and fear, replacing it with icy resolution. He would find a way to free his wife, no matter the cost.

He loved Velaria—her courage was far beyond that of anyone else he had ever known. She meant everything to him, and he could not stand aside and let the king's judgement stand.

Only when they were alone did Robert finally speak. 'What do you want to do?'

'I won't let her die,' he insisted.

'But if you defy the king—'

'I will speak to Drogan first,' he answered. 'And then the king, if he will listen.'

'John may not grant you another audience,' Robert warned. 'It would be better if you allowed others to speak on your behalf.' He reached out and touched Brian's shoulder. 'I will offer more gold and men for your sake.'

'I can't let you do that,' he started to say, but Robert shook his head.

'You have always been my brother, even before I wed Morwenna. And we won't hesitate to help you.' He paused a moment and his hand tightened. 'I know what you're thinking. Don't do it.'

He met Robert's gaze, the bleakness filling him up inside. 'I would sacrifice everything to save Velaria. And since the king did not recognise me as his son, my life is worth nothing compared to hers. If I offer myself again in her place—'

'No.' Robert's voice went rigid. 'We will find another way.' He released his grip and regarded him. 'What can I do to help you?'

He thought about Robert's words and considered his choices. Already he had come to his father, humbling himself in the hopes of gaining the king's approval. But perhaps it was time to change his approach. Humility had brought him nothing.

It wasn't the man he'd been in Constantinople. There, he had relied on his wits and his strength to defeat his opponents. He had won because he had refused to consider any alternative—and because he'd wanted to return to Velaria each night.

'You're right,' he said to Robert. He considered his

choices, and another approach was needed. 'If you're willing, could you speak to the new Lord Marwood?' He lowered his voice and explained what he needed. It was a grave risk, but he was counting on the baron's vanity and sense of standing.

Robert gave a curt nod. 'You have my word. What about you? What will you do?'

Brian straightened and met his brother's eyes. 'I'm going to save my wife.'

Velaria had wept when they'd tossed her back into the pit, first out of fear…but then her emotions turned to rage. She didn't deserve to die for defending herself and the daughter of a king. And she had no intention of blindly submitting to a judgement she didn't deserve.

She and Savaş had saved themselves from the fighting pits, working together to escape their enemies. This was no different at all.

After they cast her back into the pit, she'd continued to feign tears to avoid notice. But she was studying her prison, searching for its weaknesses and a way out. She already knew that Savaş was trying to save her. But she was no meek lady who would submit to an execution without a fight. She was a warrior, just as he was. And if she fought her way out, they could disappear to other lands across the seas, where no one would ever find them.

The pit was nothing more than the remains of an underground chamber where food had once been stored. The walls were formed of mud and earth, and the depth was more than twice her height. Outside, it was growing dark, and a cold rain began to fall. Most of the men were gathering inside one of the tunnels to gain shelter.

But she had no intention of joining them. The rain was

a blessing, for the soldiers left their posts and took turns going inside a nearby tent. Velaria walked the entire distance of the pit three times, searching for stones or sticks. When she spied a fallen bone, she reached down and picked it up. It would have to do.

She walked to one of the walls and huddled low. But she used the bone to carve out a foothold for herself in the mud. It was slick and dangerous, but if she could somehow get part of her foot inside, she might be able to climb her way out. Not until nightfall, though. She couldn't risk being seen by the other prisoners.

Instead, she waited until no one was looking and began carving out handholds for herself. She would have to climb high enough to reach more of the mud. It was an impossible task, and she well knew that failure was likely. Yet, she had to try.

Velaria tied her skirts around her ankles, but the weight of the wool only made it worse. The first time she stepped within the first crevice, she managed to reach high enough to the handhold, but the slick mud and rain caused her to lose her balance, and she fell back down. She needed to remain close to the wall to keep her weight there. And she needed more than mud to hold on to.

She wanted to emit a cry of frustration, but she silenced herself.

Think, she warned herself.

What she needed was something of a stronger material to help her climb out. Steel was best, but wood could suffice. But where could she get it? All around her, there was nothing, save earth. And even if she did manage to climb out, she could be caught within moments if even one soldier happened to see her.

Her mind turned over the problem, and as she searched

for a solution, she focused her thoughts upon Savaş. He would find a way to her—of that, she had no doubt. No matter the years they'd spent in darkness, he had been her shield and a man who had fought for her. He would never leave her here to die.

A wave of grief threatened to overcome her, and she shoved it back as she dug her fingers deeper into the mud. Because of him, she'd found the lost part of herself, the young woman who had believed in dreams of a future. And when she reached for the next crevice, she imagined she was reaching for him.

Until she saw the glint of chainmail and a soldier staring down at her.

Chapter Thirteen

Never would he forget the sight of Velaria's face when Brian reached down to her, disguised as a guard. He'd lowered a rope and had lifted her up from the pit.

'You came for me,' she breathed, embracing him tightly.

'I swore I would always come for you. And I keep my vows.'

His wife was covered in mud and soaked, but he brought her into the nearby tent, knowing the other guards had gone to sleep elsewhere after he'd bribed them. With the heavy rainstorm, they'd readily agreed to let him keep watch over the prisoners.

'Savaş, what are we—?'

He cut off her words and kissed her, pulling her body against his. 'Trust me.'

'With my life,' she answered.

'Then take off your clothes.'

She eyed him with confusion. 'Savaş, I don't know if this is the best time…' But regardless, she started to unlace her gown.

It was then that he showed her the chainmail armour with the cowl to hide her hair. It was the best disguise he could come up with, for in an encampment with seven thousand men, she could walk freely among them.

A smile caught her. 'For a moment, I thought you were wanting something else.'

'I always desire you, Velaria.' Already, he was entirely too distracted with his wife stripping off her clothing. To prove his point, when she reached for her shift, he pushed her hands aside. He caught her mouth in a deep kiss as he lifted the sodden garment slowly. His hands caressed her hips, moving slowly over her stomach to the softness of her breasts. He took his time removing the shift, stroking her nipples and pulling her body close to his as he took it off.

'If we had another hour,' he murmured against her lips. With reluctance, he let her go, gritting his teeth when he saw her bend over to put on trews and a light shirt beneath the armour.

But soon enough, she had covered her hair beneath the cowl. When she reached for the helm, she now looked like just another soldier.

'Can you bear the weight of the armour?' he asked. Although she was slim and strong, she would have to walk among the others without slouching.

'I can.' She accepted the sword he gave her and looked back into his eyes. 'Now tell me the rest of your plan.'

It was now time to enact the second part of their strategy. In the darkness before dawn, Brian borrowed clothing from Robert and dressed himself as a nobleman. It was armour of a different sort, and he was prepared to fight the next battle. Once again, he walked towards the king's tent to speak on her behalf.

But when he arrived, the hum of disorganised activity was evident. Good. After Velaria had gone missing, there would be no execution. He'd left her on the opposite side of the encampment amid other soldiers while he walked with

Robert towards the king's tent. But before they arrived, he saw the new Baron Marwood.

Robert sent him a sidelong glance, but Brian kept his emotions restrained. Velaria was safe, and that was all that mattered for now. What he needed to do was ensure the king's pardon—and that meant facing the baron.

'I've been wanting to speak with you, Lord Marwood,' Brian began. 'About my wife.'

The new baron straightened, but there was no remorse upon his face. 'Justice must be served for what she did.'

Robert stepped in. 'But you're not at all displeased about your father's death, are you?' He studied the baron and added, 'As the heir to the Marwood estates, you finally have the title you've always wanted. And from what I've heard, your father's lands have yielded a poor harvest during the past few years. You're also in need of an heiress to help you pay the king's taxes.'

A thin sneer spread over the man's face. 'I *had* intended to wed Velaria of Ardennes.' With a gloating look, he added, 'I convinced her to run away with me.' He turned back to Brian. 'But you already know this, don't you?'

The taunt was a vicious reminder of how he'd hurt Velaria, and the need for vengeance burned within Brian.

He tightened his grip over his temper and answered, 'Velaria's father refused to grant his permission or a dowry,' he said. 'It seems he was right to do so.'

'She was worth nothing to me without a dowry.' The baron glanced at Brian. 'But even so, I still had her first. She willingly gave me her innocence.'

Without thinking, Brian struck the man across the face, damning the consequences. 'You will never speak of her in that way again.'

Blood ran from the baron's nose, and his eyes blazed

with fury as he unsheathed his sword. 'I'll speak of her however I choose.'

Fury flooded through his veins, and Brian circled Drogan. He would not step aside or ignore this fight. This nobleman believed his bloodline made him the better man, but he'd abused and abandoned Velaria. She deserved retribution for what he'd done to her.

'You will only speak of her with respect, as she deserves,' Brian said softly.

'I'm going to make you bleed,' the baron spat. 'And when you're dead, I will take your wife.'

The words were another weapon, but Brian refused to rise to the bait. The very air seemed to still, and the heat of the afternoon sun reminded him of Constantinople. The only difference was the weight of his armour and the knowledge that he would never again be any man's slave. He was a man of honour, a king's son and a husband. Perhaps one day, he would become a father.

Drogan was a well-trained knight, and he wore the armour like a second skin. His golden hair glinted in the sun, and his brown eyes held hatred.

When the baron swung his sword towards Brian's head, he blocked the blow and stared back at the man. 'You will never lay a hand upon Velaria again.'

'And *you* will never again try to give orders to an overlord,' Drogan said. 'I'm going to kill you.'

'You can try,' he said. 'But I have faced hundreds of opponents far more skilled than you.'

Drogan's movements became erratic as he went on the offensive, striking swiftly and with brutal strength. With each one, Brian met the blow and deflected it. For now, he intended to measure his enemy's skills.

But when Drogan struck his sword towards Brian's

scarred shoulder, he had to move his body to parry the blow. Although it was slightly better, the old injury prevented him from fully turning his blade.

He tried to avoid a second strike, but Drogan noticed the weakness. He continued the swift slices, forcing Brian to move backwards.

Several soldiers encircled them, but none made any move to stop the fight. Brian defended himself, and before the baron could land another strike with his blade, he reminded himself that he had survived death, day after day in the fighting pits. He had fought for his life like a gladiator from the stories of old—and now he had the chance to avenge Velaria's honour.

The blade came towards him, and he struck the ground, letting Drogan believe that he'd found his weakness.

'Men more skilled than me?' the baron taunted. 'I don't think you've ever fought a trained knight before.'

Brian held his position, waiting for the right moment… almost there…

Abruptly, he rolled back to his feet and threw a clump of mud at Drogan's face. Instinctively, the man flinched, and Brian used the advantage to go on the offensive, his blade moving towards his enemy's as if it were sliding through water. He used the fighting techniques of the East, using Drogan's movements against him until the baron appeared clumsy.

Over and over, he moved his sword until at last, Drogan's attention flickered, and Brian disarmed him. He held his blade to the baron's throat.

'You are going to ask the king for an audience and tell him that you've decided to grant Velaria mercy,' he said evenly.

'If you think I'll intervene for her sake, you're mistaken,' the baron spat.

Brian gripped the man by his throat and kept the sword pointed at the soft flesh. 'Oh, you will indeed. Or no heiress will ever wed you. You've inherited an estate of debts and poverty, Lord Marwood. And we will ensure that everyone knows it.'

'You have no power or influence in England,' the man scoffed.

'But I do,' came the voice of Sir Ademar. A breath of relief filled Brian as he saw Velaria's father step forward. He didn't know where the knight had come from, but he was grateful for the man's presence. Before Brian could greet him, another familiar voice joined in.

'And so do we.'

Brian turned and saw Piers Grevershire, the Earl of Penrith and Tilmain, standing alongside his wife, Gwendoline. Robert grinned, embracing his half brother. 'How did you ever arrive in time?'

'Because I told my husband I wanted to visit Morwenna and our new niece.' Gwendoline stepped forward and from her swollen figure, she was clearly with child. 'We arrived only a day after you left Dunbough. Morwenna told us what happened, and I told Piers we should intervene for your sake.'

A surge of thankfulness filled Brian as his new family surrounded him. When he turned back to Lord Marwood, he said, 'It would be wise if you would reconsider speaking to the king.' To emphasise his words, he pressed his blade against the man's throat until a thin line of blood welled upon his skin.

'If you do not, I will p-personally use my influence to

ruin you,' Sir Ademar vowed. 'This is your only chance at redemption f-for what you did to my daughter.'

Drogan's face was purple with anger. 'Do you think I will let a knight or a king's bastard tell me what to do? I am not your serf to command. I am an English lord, and I do not take your commands.'

Brian turned to face the baron with his own blade. 'You also lost this fight. I suggest that you obey our orders before you lose your future.' He wished he could kill the man for what Drogan had done, but they needed his cooperation right now.

The other men flanked him as Brian gripped the man's arm and marched him towards the king's tent. Drogan's nose was still bleeding, and he stared forward with defiance. There was still a grave risk that the man would not speak on Velaria's behalf—but their time had run out.

They were granted permission to enter the king's tent a few moments later. King John glared at Brian and turned the full force of his rage on him. 'How do you *dare* defy us? My soldiers said that your wife escaped last night.'

Brian met the king's fury evenly. 'She did not leave, Your Excellency. Last night, she was moved away from the other prisoners for her own protection.' The lie slipped easily from him, for he had no intention of Velaria becoming a captive again. With any luck, she was concealed among hundreds of other soldiers. But his words did little to appease the king's anger.

'We will not tolerate such disobedience,' John snapped.

Drogan stepped forward then, though it seemed he'd been shoved by one of the men. He stiffened as Piers came up behind him. 'My liege, I…ask you to reconsider the lady's execution.' His words were gritted out, as if he didn't want to speak at all. Brian glimpsed the flash of a hidden blade in Piers's hand.

'Under the laws of Ireland, we have offered the baron *corp dire* for his father's death,' Robert said smoothly. 'He has decided to accept the body price.'

The king's expression tightened as he regarded Lord Marwood. 'Only yestereve, I sentenced her to die, and you gave your support.'

The man's expression grew uncomfortable. 'I believe it…will serve both of us better if we show mercy, my liege.'

'You are hoping to profit from this,' the king said, eyeing Sir Ademar, Robert, and Piers. 'But your father owed us a great deal in taxes.' Then he added, 'I suppose the *corp dire* will allow you to repay his debts.'

Brian stepped forward and bowed. 'Lord Penrith, Lord Dunbough, and I have also come to pledge our loyalty, Your Grace.' A moment later, he continued. 'I know you have come to unite the Irish people, as well as Normans, under your reign,' Brian answered. 'If you grant my wife mercy and the opportunity to make reparations, we would be grateful.'

Before the king could speak, Brian got down on one knee before his father. 'We are united in blood and marriage, my liege.'

'Over the life of one woman?' the king mused.

'We are family,' Brian said softly. 'And since your blood flows in my veins, that loyalty runs true. Give us the opportunity to prove our worth.'

Velaria continued walking among a group of soldiers, careful not to reveal herself in any way. Savaş had cautioned her to find her way south, to the edge of the tents. She was about to break away from the men, when their commander stopped in front of her. 'I don't know your face. Who are you, and where is Aelfrid?'

She dropped her voice as low as she could. 'I took his place.'

'By whose orders?'

Her heartbeat stuttered as she fumbled for an answer. 'By his.' She pointed to a mounted knight, even knowing it was unlikely the commander would believe her.

His eyes narrowed. 'I don't tolerate lies. Where is he?' He strode towards her, and Velaria slipped past the men and began running. It was better if she fled now and tried to blend in with another crowd than risk being caught.

The weight of the heavy chainmail slowed her down, but she hurried past one tent, then another. When she escaped their view, she joined behind another group of soldiers, standing amid them before she moved again.

There were horses near the edge of the encampment, some already saddled. If she could reach even one of them, she could try to ride away. Her lungs burned from exertion, but she darted around one tent, then another. Behind her, she could hear commands for someone to stop her, but she wore the same armour as every other soldier. Her only hope was to blend in among them to escape. Stealing a horse would have to be a last resort.

But when she finally reached the last row of tents, another group of soldiers was waiting for her. Their swords were unsheathed, their shields held in readiness.

Her heart sank as she regarded them. They expected her to surrender, but her hand rested upon her own weapon as she considered her choices.

Their leader was mounted on horseback. 'You know the punishment for desertion.'

And so, she decided to remove some of her armour to

make it easier to run. She removed her helm with the other hand and tore off the heavy mail cowl. Her hair flowed freely about her shoulders as she faced them. Her only hope was that they would hesitate if they knew she was a woman.

'Our missing prisoner,' the commander remarked. 'Take her.'

Velaria waited as the men approached. She had only one chance to win her freedom, and she intended to fight for it.

When the first two men charged at her, she seized the commander's reins and pulled hard on the horse. He started to lose his balance, and she shoved him back with her shield, knocking him down. Within a moment, she swung up on the animal and slashed downward with her blade, pushing back the soldiers who were trying to take her. She struck another man's sword and sliced a gash in his forearm when he wasn't fast enough with his shield.

The horse reared when one tried to take the reins, but she held her seat and urged it away. She leaned low in the saddle as the animal obeyed and started galloping away from the encampment.

But then suddenly, all along the horizon, she saw an army of Irish forces lined up. The morning sunlight gleamed upon their armour, and she recognised the colours of the MacEgan tribe. She could not count the number of men advancing, but six men led their armies, and she saw King Patrick surrounded by his brothers and his son Liam.

Velaria sheathed her sword and increased her speed, riding as fast as she could towards the men. It was a risk that the soldiers might pursue her, or worse, try to shoot her with an arrow. She was careful to change her horse's direction as she rode, hoping to avoid being captured. But thankfully, the soldiers did not follow—instead, they created a line of defence on the edge of the encampment. They kept their weapons drawn, their shields side by side.

Velaria reached Patrick, who wore a golden circlet upon his head to proclaim his rank as an Irish king. He motioned for her to go behind them, and she joined her aunt Honora among the female fighters.

'Why did they come?' she asked. She couldn't imagine so many MacEgan fighters travelling here for her sake.

'We are here to remind the king of our strength and the advantages of our alliance,' Honora answered. 'And for Mairead.'

'Mairead? Is she all right?' Concern rose within her for her cousin's sake. She hadn't seen the young woman since the day she'd been found at Ennisleigh.

Honora's expression turned serious. 'All I can say is that her father will not let anyone harm her. And King John will lose Éireann if he does not honour the ties among us.'

Patrick continued riding towards the English soldiers, flanked by his brothers and his son. Velaria noticed a chest that several men carried beside them. In a loud voice, the Irish king proclaimed, 'We have come to remind King John of our alliance and to bring tribute to His Grace. Let us pass.'

The soldiers hesitated, but one of the commanders ordered the men to allow them entrance. He ordered their formation to shift until two lines of soldiers guarded against Patrick and his brothers. Within moments, they created a pathway for the king and his men.

Behind them, Velaria saw her father and Brian riding in front, along with Robert and another man. Even as the MacEgans continued their way forward, Velaria only had eyes for her husband.

Savaş continued riding until he reached her side. With both hands, he framed her face and caught her mouth in a fierce kiss. 'The king has accepted the *corp dire* for your life,' he said, 'and has granted his mercy.'

Velaria caught him in her embrace, feeling the surge of relief. 'Thank God.'

She embraced him hard, but he flinched slightly, as if his shoulder pained him. When she drew back, she noticed that he had a nick upon his face, as if he'd been fighting. 'What happened?' She touched the spot of blood to emphasise her question.

'Drogan of Marwood made the mistake of challenging me to a fight. He won't bother you again.'

'You didn't—'

He shook his head. 'He's alive but deeply indebted to the king with taxes his father didn't pay. Ademar, Robert, and King Patrick have paid the body price on your behalf, and King John was more than willing to accept.' He stroked her hair, and his touch brought her a comfort she couldn't name. 'If Drogan dares threaten you again, he will die. I swear it.'

His vow of protection twined within her, and she couldn't stop the words from coming forth. 'I love you, Savaş,' she murmured, touching her forehead to his.

'I would fight any man for your sake,' he answered. 'I wanted to protect you from the first moment I saw you. And I want us to spend the rest of our lives together.' He kissed her again softly. 'I love you, Velaria. And when we're alone again, I intend to show you how much.'

She breathed in the scent of this man, savouring his arms around her. Her other questions were silenced when her husband leaned in against her ear and whispered all the things he intended to do to her later that night.

They had travelled north alongside the king's men during the past few days, only turning west when the king stopped at Carrickfergus. The MacEgans were already returning south, but Velaria suspected Mairead was with them now since there was no haste in their journey.

She had met Piers, a stoic man who had been like a brother to her husband. His wife, Lady Gwendoline, brought her horse up beside hers, but Velaria noticed that the woman's face appeared pained. She also appeared to be pregnant.

'Are you all right?' Velaria asked. 'Do you need to stop?'

'It's all right. This is our third child, and we'll be stopping soon enough,' Gwendoline replied. 'I left our twins with Morwenna in Dunbough.' She rubbed her swollen abdomen. 'I imagine they are terrorising her, even now.'

'I'm surprised your husband allowed you to travel.'

Gwendoline sent her a secret smile. 'Piers doesn't "allow" me to do anything. Oh, he argues with me, that's for certain. But I have my own ways of convincing him. And I know he missed his brother Robert and Morwenna, so I told him we would come visit.' She eyed Velaria and said, 'Will you be living at Dunbough with them? Or would you prefer to return to England?'

'I don't know where Savaş wants us to go,' she admitted. 'We intend to visit Staunton, and my father has also invited us to dwell at Ardennes.' But she would follow her husband anywhere in the world.

'Why do you call him Savaş?' Gwen asked. Curiosity shone on her face.

'He earned that name in the arenas of Constantinople. He was the greatest fighter within the city. I want him to remember that, even when others try to treat him as a serf.'

A warm smile came over the woman's face. 'Savaş. It's a warrior's name, isn't it?'

Velaria nodded. 'It is.' She'd heard about her husband's fight with Drogan from Robert, and she wished she could have witnessed it for herself. But it warmed her to know that he'd done what he could to avenge her honour.

Soon enough, Savaş drew his horse beside hers. After murmuring a greeting to Gwen, he said, 'We're going to stop for the night, near that stream. We should reach Dunbough in the morning.'

Gwen wisely moved her horse back towards Piers and winked at Velaria as she rode to her husband's side. Savaş took the reins and led her a slight distance away from the others.

'Where are we going?' she asked.

'Away from everyone else,' he muttered. 'It's been too long since I've held you. And I don't want our tent anywhere near the others.'

Velaria rode alongside him towards a nearby forest, and his urgency made her smile. The moment they reached the trees, he pulled her off the horse and crushed her into his embrace. His mouth claimed hers in a storm of wild demand. She kissed him back, and he pulled her so close, she could feel the heat of his desire.

A rush of sensation slid beneath her skin, making her yearn for him. For a moment, he continued kissing her as if he couldn't get enough. When he pulled back at last, he said, 'I was never going to let you die, Velaria. I would have done anything to save your life—even take your place.'

She reached up to touch his face. 'I'm glad you didn't.' But the thought of him sacrificing himself for her sake was unthinkable. 'We survived, just as we did in Constantinople. But now, we're going to *live*, Savaş.'

He caught her hand in his and covered it. 'Aye, we will.' Then he moved both his hands over her shoulders and down to her waist, where they lingered. He bent to kiss her throat, and shivers erupted over her skin. 'Wherever you want to go.'

She took him by the hand and led him deeper into the shadows of the oak grove. 'I have a place in mind. At least, for now.'

In his eyes, she saw the fierce need, and in the shadows, she began unlacing her gown. He caught her hands and brushed them aside. 'Let me.'

Within moments, she was naked, and he stripped off his own clothing, lowering her upon his cloak. The scent of pine and leaves surrounded them, and she welcomed her husband into her arms. With his lips and his hands, he worshipped her body, causing her to arch with her softness against his strength.

And when he filled her body with his own, she moved against him, loving this man. His mouth covered her erect nipple, and the echo of sensation ached between her legs. He moved within her, slowly and deeply, until she felt the tremors rising from within her.

She reached up to touch his shoulder, and as he thrust and withdrew, she arched to meet him. He sheathed himself fully and held still as he stroked her hooded flesh. Her breathing grew ragged as he circled her, pressing gently until the delicious sensation rose hotter and she squeezed his length deep inside.

Then he began to move again, and she inhaled with a shuttered cry as he penetrated deeper. He quickened his pace, thrusting inside until the wave of release broke through, and she sobbed with the intensity of her pleasure. He followed her a moment later, panting hard as he spilled himself within her. Then he lay down, covering her body with his own.

Velaria's heartbeat thundered as she wrapped her legs around his waist. 'I don't care where we go, Savaş. As long as we're together.'

He kissed her gently. 'I would walk across the world for you.'

And as he rested against her, their bodies tangled together, she made a promise of her own—to love this man with everything in her.

Epilogue

Four years later

'Find your balance,' Brian said, adjusting his three-year-old daughter's stance as she held out a wooden sword. Elisa beamed, holding her weapon out.

'Not like that,' he corrected, glaring at her. 'Be fierce.'

She growled and pointed her wooden sword at him. It was an effort to hold back his smile, but he nodded in approval. 'No one will ever bother you, little one.'

'They would have to go through us first,' Lord Staunton remarked. He held out his arms, and Elisa dropped the sword, scurrying towards the man who doted upon her as the grandchild he'd never had.

'They will indeed.' Brian watched as Alexander swept the child into his arms, while Elisa chattered to him about swords and a puppy that she wanted.

A few years ago, Brian and Velaria had first come to Staunton to visit, out of thanks for their lives. Lord and Lady Staunton had welcomed them into their home, but every time they meant to leave, the baron and his wife had begged them to stay longer.

Yet over the years, their true home had become Tilmain.

As the heiress to both Penrith and Tilmain, Lady Gwendoline had asked them to care for the estate as their own. She and Piers preferred to remain at Penrith with their children, and Brian was grateful that the people of Tilmain had accepted him and Velaria to rule on their Lady's behalf. It no longer mattered that he lacked a title or the birthright of a king's son. He had a home, a wife he loved, and a daughter who filled their home with joy.

Lord Staunton's face softened with contentment while Elisa continued to sit in his lap. A moment later, his wife, Clare, came up behind him and reached for Elisa. 'It's my turn to hold her now.' Lord and Lady Staunton adored the little girl, since they had never borne children of their own.

'Alexander and I have been talking,' Clare began, dropping a kiss upon Elisa's head. 'There's something we'd like to discuss with you both.'

At that moment, Velaria joined them, and Brian drew his arm around her waist. His wife sent him a silent look of amusement that Clare had appointed herself as another grandmother, despite Katherine and Rochelle.

'And what is it you'd like to discuss?' Brian prompted.

'It's about Elisa,' Clare continued. She exchanged a look with Alexander, and the man continued.

'You and Velaria are like the children we were unable to have. Were it in my power to grant you Staunton, I would make you my heir and give all of this to you.' The warmth in the man's voice was genuine, and it filled Brian with a sense of thanks.

'I wish you had been my father,' Brian said honestly. After leaving King John's encampment, he had not heard from the monarch again. There had been a time when it would have sharpened the sadness of not being acknowledged. But Alexander of Staunton had filled that emptiness, welcoming them back for many visits with open arms.

'My younger brother, Marcus, is my heir by law,' Alexander continued. 'But I have spoken to him, and he is willing to consider a betrothal between Elisa and one of his sons. She may choose a husband from among them if she wishes. And then, one day, she would become part of my family in name.'

Velaria came forward and embraced Lord and Lady Staunton, with Elisa between them. 'Your offer is very generous, Lord Staunton.'

'It is,' Brian agreed. 'But it is a decision Elisa should make when she is older. She deserves the freedom to choose the husband she wants.' He would not consider making a formal betrothal before she came of age, though it was sometimes arranged.

'So she will.' Lord Staunton inclined his head. 'Our offer stands.' Then he joined his wife, holding her hand as they returned to the castle together, with Elisa between them.

After they were out of earshot, Velaria said softly, 'They have been married twenty years. And he still looks at her as if she means the world to him.'

'I know how he feels.' He took both of her hands in his. 'Even forty years would never be enough time with you.'

She leaned in and kissed him. Against his mouth, she murmured, 'Sometimes, when I think back on our captivity, I remember how you were my strength in the darkness. Whenever I needed you, you were there.'

'Just as you were for me,' he answered. 'And I thank God every day for it.'

The sun rose high above the horizon while the land bathed in a sea of light. Brian held her hand, and Velaria leaned her head against his shoulder. 'I love you.'

The words sank into him, taking root with the happiness he felt whenever he was in her presence. 'I love you, too.'

And as they stared out together at the land before them, Brian could not imagine any greater blessing than spending the rest of his life with her hand in his.

* * * * *

If you enjoyed this story, make sure you're
caught up on the first two installments
in The Legendary Warriors miniseries

The Iron Warrior Returns
The Untamed Warrior's Bride

While you're waiting for the next book,
why not read Michelle Willingham's
Untamed Highlanders duology?

The Highlander and the Governess
The Highlander and the Wallflower

HARLEQUIN
Reader Service

Enjoyed your book?

Try the perfect subscription for Romance readers and get more great books like this delivered right to your door.

See why over 10+ million readers have tried Harlequin Reader Service.

Start with a Free Welcome Collection with free books and a gift—valued over $20.

Choose any series in print or ebook. See website for details and order today:

TryReaderService.com/subscriptions